WHILE WE'RE HERE

A NOVEL

HENRY GRAY
HG
PUBLISHING

Granada Hills, CA
"Select books for selective readers"

For information, contact: henrygraypub2022@gmail.com

Publisher's Cataloging-in-Publication Data:

Names: Manchester, T.A.
Title: While we're here/ T.A. Manchester.
Description: Granada Hills, CA : Henry Gray Publishing, 2025. | Identifiers: LCCN 2025904387 | ISBN: 9781960415462 (hardcover) | ISBN: 9781960415479 (pbk.) | ISBN: 9781960415486 (EPUB)
Subjects: LCSH: Coming of age – Fiction. | Football – Fiction. | First loves – Fiction. | Families – Fiction. | Grief – Fiction. | Bereavement – Fiction. | BISAC – YOUNG ADULT FICTION / Coming of Age. | YOUNG ADULT FICTION / Sports & Recreation / Football. | YOUNG ADULT FICTION / Family / General.
Classification: LCC PS3613.A53 W55 2025 | DDC 813 M--dc22
LC record available at https://lccn.loc.gov/2025904387

Made in the United States of America.
Published by Henry Gray Publishing, P.O. Box 33832,
Granada Hills, California, 91394.

For more information or to join our mailing list, visit
HenryGrayPublishing.com

WHILE WE'RE HERE

A NOVEL

T.A. MANCHESTER

1

1

The worst days arrive disguised as ordinary ones–eggs over easy, crisp bacon, and a family of four at County Line Café. When the Browdys slide into their familiar corner booth, the vinyl seats creak beneath them. Ten-year-old Murph races a small Matchbox car across the table's grimy surface, its tiny wheels leaving trails in the crumbs. The sight draws a laugh from his mother, Ailea, her eyes crinkling at the corners and filling with warmth.

"Our speed demon right here," she comments, messing up Murph's unruly hair. The texture reminds her of dandelion fluff, soft and wild. Across the table, her husband Wilke's leg brushes against hers as he scans the menu. A half-smirk works its way across his five o'clock shadow.

Their server, Jessie, appears, snapping her gum with a pop. "Let's get some grub for the early birds," she says. Her voice carries the rasp of too many late-night shifts. "The usual for everyone?"

"Figure that'll do it," Wilke confirms, his deep voice rumbling with contentment. "Two pecan waffles, extra syrup. And Junior here will have his dippy eggs and bacon. Right, buddy?"

Murph, absorbed with racing his toy, doesn't respond. Ailea recalls when Murph was a baby and how quickly he would become occupied by the simplest things as his tongue pokes out in concentration. She steps in. "Let's scramble those soft for him. White toast cut small, please." There's a hint of protectiveness in her tone, born from years of having to step in and be the boy's voice.

Jessie turns to sixteen-year-old Morgan, who's gazing out the rain-streaked window. The patter of raindrops forms a quaint backdrop to the diner's hustle and bustle. "And for our quiet one?"

Morgan turns, pulled from his daydream. The cool glass against his forehead had lulled him into a trance. "Oh, uh...just chocolate chip pancakes, I guess. Thanks."

His attention drifts back to the window as they wait for their food. He spots Emma, a girl from school, leaving the corner store across the street. The sight of her sends a flutter through his stomach. She catches him leering through the window and gives a slight wave.

Moments later, she appears at their table, greeting the family. Her strawberry shampoo wafts over, stirring something in the teen boy's heart.

"Spying on my secret hangouts?" she teases, sliding in beside Morgan. Their knees touch under the table, sending a jolt through him that causes his throat to catch.

The bell above the diner door chimes, and a few of Emma's friends enter, waving her over.

"Shoot, I gotta go, we're gonna be late," she groans, jumping up faster than she swooped in. "But I'll see you at the game," she calls, her voice carrying the hint of a promise that causes hormones to fire uncontrolled in Morgan's gut.

As the door swings shut behind her, Morgan realizes the sudden silence at their table. He risks a glance up, only to find Wilke and Ailea exchanging loaded looks. A sly grin tugs at the corner of Wilke's mouth as he cocks his eyebrow. Ailea's eyes dance with contained amusement, her lips pressed together as if holding back an obvious secret.

Heat creeps up Morgan's neck, flooding his cheeks. He hunches his shoulders, wishing he could disappear. His fingers fidget with the paper wrapper from his straw, shredding it into tiny pieces as he avoids meeting their eyes.

"So," Wilke drawls, breaking the calm. "She seems nice."

Morgan groans, sinking lower in his seat. He'd give anything for the floor to open up and swallow him whole. The knowing looks and poorly concealed smiles are all too much. He mumbles something unintelligible in response, his ears burning as red as the ketchup bottle on the table.

Ailea reaches across, patting his hand with affection. "Okay, we'll drop it," she chides, but her eyes sparkle with motherly interest. "We remember what it was like to be young and sweet on someone."

The mood shifts when Ailea notices Morgan's expression change to something dark. "What's eating you?" she asks, her intuition prickling. "You've been quiet all morning."

Morgan shrugs, his shoulders heavy. "Coach said I'd be off JV by now, but here I am at another Saturday game." The words taste bitter in his mouth.

"With A.J. out, doesn't that mean there's an opening?" Ailea probes, trying to find a silver lining.

"Yeah," Morgan replies. "And I'm still riding the bench." The frustration in his voice is palpable.

Wilke's jaw tightens. "Morgan, we've talked about this. If you don't step up, maybe you should quit." His words cut like a knife.

"That's not it, I–" Morgan starts, but Wilke cuts him off, his patience wearing thin from a discussion that's graced the table several times.

"Nobody's going to hand it to you."

Murph, oblivious to the undercurrents, pipes up. "Hooky, he's a hooky!" His childish voice breaks through like a ray of sunshine.

Wilke's eyes narrow, his gaze sharpening. "You've been skipping practice?"

Morgan tries to explain, but he's been outed. An uncomfortable quiet descends on the table, broken by the clink of cutlery and the distant sizzle of the griddle.

Wilke sighs. "Listen, I know you've got a lot on your plate. But you've got to have faith that if you keep putting in the work, your moment will come." His words are tinged with the wisdom of experience.

"Yeah, great pep talk from the Pancake Provider," Morgan retorts, half regretting the sharpness of his words. "Not like you know what it's like."

"No, I'd have no idea what it's like to be an angry teen–" his father laughs, dropping his hand on Morgan's head and giving him a playful shove. "Eat up before you disappear."

2

The crisp autumn breeze bends the tall grass outside the hulking football stadium, its massive concrete walls looming over the deserted parking lot like ancient monoliths. The Browdy family walks across the asphalt expanse under a slate-gray September sky, their footsteps echoing in the vast emptiness as they head toward a weathered Ford pickup after the game.

Ailea walks, shoulders hunched against the biting cold, her breath forming white clouds. The wind whips strands of her hair across her face, and she can taste the metallic hint of approaching winter. Wilke lumbers beside her, his face flushed crimson from the chill, the creases around his eyes deepening as he squints against the wind. Morgan trudges along, gaze fixed on his phone, thumbs flying across the screen.

Murph skips beside his mom. His sneakers squeak on the damp asphalt with each bouncing step. He looks up, messy brown hair falling into his eyes–those bright green orbs that seem to absorb every detail of the world around him, good or bad, with the same fascination he shows when playing with his beloved cars at home. In unfamiliar settings, he's rather quiet. But here, surrounded by family, he chatters about the intricacies of a V8 versus a Supercharged Turbo.

Wilke presents Murph with a vibrant team pennant, its colors a defiant splash against the monochrome day. "Stay close to your mom," he says as he guides the boy towards Ailea. Morgan trails behind, his football gear slung under one arm, the pads clanking with each step.

Ailea turns to her older son, trying to catch his eye. "Maybe you'll get to play next week," she says, injecting hope into her voice even as she sees the disappointment on the set of his shoulders. Morgan doesn't look up, just smirks at his phone and mutters, "Yeah, right..." His voice carries a bitterness that makes Ailea's heart ache.

She nudges Murph, desperate to lighten the mood. "Bet they'll put you in, won't they, brother?" Murph's face lights up, his grin wide and infectious. "Right, brother!" he shouts, his voice carrying across the empty lot as he skips along, the pennant fluttering like a bright ensign in the cold, stormy wind.

3

Wilke's calloused hand envelops Ailea's, the rough texture a familiar comfort against her skin. He pulls her close, a small smile playing at the corners of his mouth, his eyes crinkling with affection and desire.

"Been thinking 'bout tonight," he murmurs, his voice low and husky, sending a shiver down Ailea's spine despite the chill in the air. His aftershave causes a flutter in her stomach, a mix of anticipation and nervousness. "Not in front of them," she whispers, pulling her hand away. Her cheeks flush, and not just from the cold.

Wilke, undeterred, persists with a playful glint in his eye. "No one's watching," he says, his arm snaking around her waist. Ailea squirms away, her fingers combing her wind-tousled hair.

"Let's see who can spot the truck first!" she calls out to the boys. She taps Murph on the shoulder, and he takes off like a shot, the pennant streaming behind him like a banner of joy.

"Not too far!" She calls after him, her voice tinged with worry.

"Morgan!" Wilke barks, his voice sharp enough to cut through the wind. "Go with your brother. Get him to the truck."

Morgan stops, his shoulders sagging with teenage annoyance. He drops his gear on the grimy asphalt with a dull thud. "Fine..." he huffs, trudging after his brother with the enthusiasm of a prisoner on a chain gang.

"Stay with him!" Ailea adds.

He responds with a vague wave, his eyes never leaving the glowing screen of his phone.

Wilke's frustrated shout of "Hey!" registers a reply.

"I know, I know," Morgan mutters, more to himself than anyone else. His distracted compliance is automatic, ingrained from years of half-listening to parental instructions. He follows his brother's path, but his mind is miles away, engrossed in the drama unfolding in his text messages.

4

With the bright pennant in his hand fluttering like a beacon, Murph races on, skipping around parked trucks and SUVs. The family's old, rusty truck looms into view at the far end of the lot.

"Get in the truck," Morgan mutters, his voice flat. He gives Murph a push, his eyes never leaving his handheld.

"Dad said, Dad said–" Murph's singsong voice carries on the wind, a melody of innocence and excitement. His words bounce off the nearby cars.

"Just get in!" Morgan snaps, his irritation palpable.

Murph, caught up in his own world, ignores his brother's command. "Look!" He waves the pennant side-to-side, nearly hitting Morgan in the face.

Morgan swats it away, his patience wearing thin. "Stop, you're so annoying!"

"Am not!" Murph retorts, sticking out his tongue. He dances away, waving the pennant even more dramatically.

"I said stop!" Morgan lunges for the pennant, but Murph dodges, laughing.

Frustration boils over, and Morgan snaps. He shoves Murph hard, intending to push him toward the truck. "Just get in–"

The push is harder than Morgan intended. Murph stumbles backward, losing his grip on the pennant. Wind gusts, awakening the world. It tugs at the pennant, now free from Murph's grasp, scooting it further into the lane.

Murph cries out, his words punctuated by hiccupping sobs. Without warning, he lurches forward, arms outstretched towards the escaping pennant, his focus solely on retrieving the bright object that had moments ago been a source of comfort and fascination. Morgan's eyes widen in horror as he realizes what's happening.

"Murph, stop!"

At that moment, a sedan comes tearing by, its engine roaring with abandon. The screech of tires on asphalt cuts through like a knife. There's a horn blast, followed by the shriek of brakes.

5

Wilke takes Ailea's hand as they make their way toward the car. His lips find the soft curve of her neck. Her perfume mingles with the crisp autumn air. This time, Ailea doesn't pull away; instead, she leans into his touch, her body relaxing against his without the fear of getting caught by their children.

"Where's this sweet talk been all this time?" she laughs. Her voice carries a note of surprise and pleasure as if rediscovering a part of herself long forgotten. The warmth of Wilke's body against hers feels like coming home after a long, cold journey.

A terrified yell shatters their moment of intimacy. Wilke's body goes rigid, every muscle tensing as if preparing for a fight. The faint, desperate cry of "Mom!" reaches their ears, carried on the wind from across the way.

Ailea's eyes dart across the parking lot, her maternal instincts kicking into overdrive as she tries to make sense of the unfolding chaos. Without hesitation, she takes off, weaving between parked cars, her heart racing from a primal fear that claws at her insides.

Wilke follows, his face a mask of terror as he struggles to keep up with Ailea's frantic pace. His breath comes in ragged gasps, years of sedentary life catching up with him in this crisis.

The world around them seems to blur; the once-peaceful parking lot transformed into a nightmarish landscape of obstacles and shadows. Each passing second seems like an eternity as they hurry towards the origin of that heartrending cry, their minds imagining worst-case scenarios with every stride.

6

A single, horrifying dent mars the sedan's polished chrome fender and cherry paint—a gaping wound the size and shape of sweet Murph's body. This grotesque mark stands as a testament to the tragedy that unfolded in seconds.

Ailea stands frozen before Murph's bright pennant, now lying dirty and abandoned. Her world seems to tilt on its axis as she struggles to comprehend the limp body of her baby boy lying broken on the cold asphalt. The ashen-faced driver of the sedan sits slumped against his vehicle, eyes glazed and distant.

Minutes pass like an eternity. The distant wail of sirens grows louder until the slamming of ambulance doors and walkie-talkie chatter replaces them. Two police officers question the driver while the EMT crew gets to work.

Morgan's eyes stay locked on a black body bag, which rests on the pavement, awaiting its grim purpose. Soft rain patters against the plastic surface. Nature's quiet tears for a life cut short.

Just beyond this nightmarish tableau, Murph's once vibrant pennant lies face down. Its vivid colors are fading, as if surrendering to the tragedy that has come for its young owner.

The family stands frozen, each person lost in their own bubble of shock as the total weight of this moment settles upon them.

7

Two weeks after Murph's tragic accident, a pall of grief shrouds their home. Each room is haunted by memories of laughter that won't be heard again. A half-finished coloring book gathers dust on the coffee table, and tiny fingerprints remain frozen on the windowpane. In the hallway, growth marks on the wall abruptly end, while a backpack hangs forgotten on its hook, waiting for a day of school that will never come.

Ailea drifts like a specter, her hair now a tangled mess, her face gaunt from tears and sleepless nights. The vacant look in her eyes shows a pain too deep for words.

The kitchen counter, once a place of family meals and homework sessions, now groans under the weight of unpaid bills and untouched casseroles from neighbors. The stench of these spoiling dishes mingles with the musty scent of a house in mourning.

"Mom, just eat a little," Morgan pleads one afternoon, his voice desperate as he stands outside her closed door. His fingers trace the worn wood grain, longing for the barrier between them to dissolve. Though they are only a room apart, his mother's silence is deafening.

10

Wilke's grief manifests in bursts of anger that shatter the heavy stillness. The crash of a plate against the wall, the bark of a curse word, the slam of the door as he rushes outside–these violent outbursts punctuate their days. But it's the muffled sobs that Morgan hears through the thin walls at night that break his heart. In those moments, he squeezes his eyes shut and prays to turn back time.

As days stretch into weeks, the world outside continues its march. Bills marked 'URGENT' pile up. Raw nerves fray, leading to tearful arguments that leave everyone hollowed out and spent. Ailea's refusal to attend therapy hangs between her and Wilke like an unspoken accusation.

One night, drawn by raised voices, Morgan finds himself at his parents' bedroom door. Through the crack, he sees clothes strewn across the bed, his mother folding and refolding as if she could tuck away her grief along with the laundry.

"This won't last forever, Lea..." Wilke's words are heavy with hope. "We can get through this if we stick together–you, me, Morgan..."

But Ailea seems beyond reach, lost in the pain. Often, she cries over the boxes of baby photos. Each image reminds her of the future they've lost and of the milestones Murph will never reach.

It's not just Murph who's gone, but the family they once were. The realization dawns on Morgan, unsure if they'll reunite in this sorrowful haze.

8

The last golden rays of the setting autumn sun filter into the classroom, bathing everything in a warm glow. Dust motes dance in the light as the American flag and school pennant hang on the wall, their shadows stretching across the room.

Students hunch over their desks, pencils scratching as they write answers on paper. The sound of their scribbles mingles with voices from the hallway.

Morgan sits by the window, his pencil untouched. He stares at the orange sunset, his mind wandering from the classroom.

Students rush between classes, exchanging books and chattering at the gray lockers lining the hall. Laughter echoes around, but Morgan remains oblivious. The smile he once wore has vanished, replaced by a mask of indifference.

The bell jolts him back to reality. He blinks, then shuffles into the stream of students heading to their next classes. Voices hush, and eyes dart away as he passes.

When he rounds the corner, he finds his locker adorned with notes from happier days. He rips them down in one motion, scattering the crumpled remnants across the scuffed tiles.

Near to him, Corey Ellison, struggling with his math textbook, casts furtive glances towards Morgan. The air between them holds the remnants of a friendship that was once vibrant with shared experiences–Little League games, Fourth of July fireworks–now tangled in the awkwardness of repeated condolences...you can only say "I'm sorry for your loss" so many times.

As Corey's textbook escapes his grasp and clatters to the floor, he retreats, the latest in a list of old friends unsure of how to act around him.

9

Morgan navigates the congested hallway, fragments of gossip permeating the surrounding air. He finds Emma by the stairwell, a beacon of familiarity in his world of upheaval. Her wave elicits a surge of relief, a glimmer of normalcy.

"Emma, hey," he calls out, his voice tinged with gratitude.

As he draws near, the scene before him shatters his sense of comfort. Emma pivots, laying a kiss on Adrian from his math class. Morgan halts, the hallway seeming to distort around him, reality fragmenting like a fractured mirror.

"Uh...Morgan, hi," Emma stammers as she and Adrian disengage, a flush coloring her cheeks. Her arm remains draped around Adrian's waist, proclaiming their intimacy.

Morgan stands unmoving, his books threatening to slip from nerveless fingers. His gaze darts between the pair. Adrian fidgets, avoiding eye contact.

"Look, I'm...I'm sorry about your brother..." Emma ventures, attempting to bridge the chasm of awkwardness, but the bell cuts short her condolences.

Morgan struggles against the constriction in his throat, words eluding him. Their closeness now seems a cruel farce, the memory of her hand in his a taunting reminder of unfulfilled potential–the text exchanges, once treasured, now meaningless.

10

Body spray and shampoo saturate the locker room after the conditioning class. Morgan removes his sweat-soaked shirt amid the chatter of his classmates. He reaches for his deodorant, a defense against the assault of scents surrounding him. Looking upwards, the absence of his clothes surprises him...a prank.

Three sophomores engage in antics by the sinks, pouring shampoo onto their heads and sculpting mohawks. Their laughter echoes off the tiles as they shove each other, foam dripping down their faces. A whispered exchange follows when they catch Morgan's leering gaze, and their eyes, tinged with mockery, look away.

Dejected, Morgan sits on the aged wooden bench. Generations of students wore its surface smooth. His fingers trace their initials carved into the wood–a record of emotions and connections carved in this space. As he sits there, the reality of his transience settles in. He, too, will fade, he thinks, becoming another forgotten echo in this place.

11

The school has been empty for hours, but Morgan walks the dark halls of the sixth-grade wing. His sneakers squeak on the shiny floors, reflecting the dim overhead lights. Empty classrooms with open doors line the hallway. Old decorations hang on bulletin boards, like memories of happier times.

Morgan stops at a plain locker with a handmade label that reads 'Murph Browdy'. It's remained untouched since That Day. He runs his thumb over his brother's name, wishing he could see Murph's smiling face, talking about cars or cartoons. Even his annoying habit of tugging on his sleeve or asking for piggyback rides would bring comfort now, like medicine for a wound that won't heal.

On his first day of the year, he recalls bringing Murph to this locker...

"Come on, this way!" Morgan had called, weaving through the crowded hall. Murph followed, looking around wide-eyed at the middle school kingdom.

"Six-one-six–" Murph shouted, holding up six fingers. "Locker number six-one-six." He grinned at Morgan, wanting praise for remembering.

Murph's pride moved him. "That's awesome, bud," he said, messing up Murph's hair as the boy flapped his hands.

At locker 616, Murph hung up his old Avengers backpack from the donation center. He seemed proud to have his own space in this confusing world, except for the large, metallic gash along the front.

Seeing Murph upset about the scratched locker, Morgan offered a solution. "Want to put your name here?" he asked. Murph nodded.

Now, only emptiness answers when Morgan speaks. The cheerful sixth grader who once bounced down these halls is gone.

12

The phone's ringing shatters the hush enshrouding the living room. Wilke snatches the noisemaker off its cradle, fumbling it onto the carpet. Dark circles like bruises ring his bloodshot eyes, hinting at the sleepless nights since the world collapsed.

"Mel, I told ya twice; we already talked to them," he says, anxiety creeping into his hoarse tone despite efforts to stay calm. "Yes, the funeral home..." He scrubs a hand down his unshaven face as he paces the same path for minutes. "Yes, they got our paperwork... payments and such..."

The threadbare carpet holds witness to countless worried footsteps stamped out by a distressed father over years of battling layoffs and foreclosure threats. Now, it looms to unravel under his trajectory from the kitchen to the front bay window and back.

On the lumpy thrift store couch pushed against peeling floral wallpaper, Ailea sits curled amidst rumpled throw pillows. The television plays unwatched before her empty stare, its flickering light casting shadows across features grown gaunt and pale from grief and emotional exhaustion. A solar system of wadded tissues and discarded meals orbits around her, on stained TV trays bought in happier times for family movie nights. Unwashed, blonde hair hangs over her hunched shoulders, obscuring a face that Morgan realizes he has not seen smile since The Day.

In the cramped corner armchair buried under a mountain of half-folded and abandoned laundry, Morgan picks at a loose thread on his shirt sleeve to distract himself from waves of bad thoughts. He watches his parents move around the dim room like lost souls. So far from their normal loving selves, he wonders if they'll ever be the same.

The old clock ticks on top of the TV, its cracked screen glowing. Like always, the porch light comes on at 6:32 p.m., lighting up the messy front yard. The giant oak tree that used to shade the grass is bare now, its branches reaching up to the gray sky that won't even rain to wash away their pain.

13

Inside the JV locker room office, sunlight filters through the narrow window on the concrete block wall. Coach Nichols looks at Morgan, slumped in the doorway.

Looking into the boy's downcast eyes, shiny with tears, the coach can't find words to comfort him. He watches as Morgan picks at his hands, pale from being clenched to hold back his grief.

When Coach tries to penetrate the heavy air, his voice sounds strange. He speaks of choices that should not burden any family. Suggestions shift from taking time off this season to intense counseling with Mrs. Lawrence to heal. But Morgan stays locked in his pain, biting his nails to the quick.

Coach squeezes the boy's shoulder like a father. But no comfort reaches him. Alone, the locker room door slams shut with a clang, a song for the abandoned boy.

14

Abanner proclaiming "MAKE IT A GREAT DAY TO BE A BULLDOG!" in bold letters hangs on the wall behind Morgan.

He stares at the slogan, his face an emotionless mask. Then, in a burst of rage, he rips the banner from the wall. He hurls his books down the hallway where they crash against the linoleum, pages scattering across the floor.

With an anguished scream, Morgan lets out the pent-up fury and grief that has been brewing within him for months. He kicks over garbage cans, sending trash scattering into classrooms and causing students to rush out in unison.

Coach Nichols emerges from the locker room into the chaos, freezing at the scene before him as Morgan tears posters from walls in absolute torment. The big man grabs Morgan by the shoulders, attempting to stop the tantrum. "Son, breathe," he urges in a low tone. "Just breathe."

Morgan is beyond reason, consumed by months of repressed rage. With a snarl, he slams the coach against the lockers, knuckles to the man's lip.

"Dammit, son!" Nichols barks, wiping away a trickle of blood from his mouth.

The hallway falls silent as students gape in shock at the altercation...Morgan punched a teacher.

Coach Nichols pants, pointing a finger toward the exit. "You get your shit and get out," he orders. "Now."

Morgan turns and stumbles away without looking back, rage spent. He stops before Murph's faded locker. With trembling fingers, he peels the name badge away. Clutching it like a lifeline, he shuffles from the school for the last time, past the stares of faculty and students, including Emma.

15

The midnight hour looms. Sleep is an elusive ghost as Morgan lies in bed. The house groans around him, a chorus echoing the broken hearts. As the clock ticks past twelve, voices seep through the walls–Wilke's tired rumble cracking under Ailea's sharp words.

"We can't keep avoiding this," Wilke pleads, his voice muffled but raw. "Putting it off won't change anything."

Ailea's reply cuts like a knife, too low for Morgan to catch.

"The morgue needs answers. Cremation or burial...costs to figure out." Wilke's voice wavers. "Ailea, please, don't shut me out."

Dread coils in Morgan's gut. He eases out of bed, wincing at every creak of the springs. Tiptoeing past his parents' door, he drifts down the hall, a shadow in a house that resembles a tomb with each passing day.

In the kitchen, bathed in moonlight, he finds a pack of birthday candles Ailea bought before everything shattered. With shaky hands, he places a candle in a stale cake on the counter.

His fingers trace the faded frosting that reads 'Happy B-day Murph, The Big 1-1!'–before he snuffs out the flame with one breath. The darkness swallows him, and he realizes nothing will ever be 'happy' in these walls again without his little brother's light.

"Make a wish?" Ailea's voice, brittle as an old woman's, startles him. Morgan turns to find his mother's haunted eyes staring at him from the hall. He searches for some connection, some unbroken thread between them, but Ailea's gaze slides away, her shoulders curling inward. Morgan sees the permanence of loss written in every line of her body and knows they're all adrift now, unmoored in a sea of sorrow.

Seventeen years old today, he thinks. *What a happy birthday this is,* bitterness coating his world like ash.

16

The burial day is beautiful, which only seems to highlight their sorrow. The sky shines a deep blue, and everything stands out in sharp detail as they walk to the grave. A woodpecker's tapping of a nearby oak belies the fact no one pays attention to the birds singing among the headstones.

Like Ailea's heart, empty from loss, the open ground can't keep her steady against the wind that threatens to push her. Strong arms grab her drooping shoulders, bringing her back to the moment. She leans against Wilke out of habit—his musky scent still familiar. But the man holding her up feels like a stranger now, closed off behind walls he's built to protect himself.

Forgotten, Morgan stands alone, unable to look away from the hole swallowing the pale coffin. Through the closed lid, he pictures how they dressed Murph in his favorite yellow shirt and jeans. He'd wear it when pretending to be Christopher Robin from Winnie-the-Pooh. In his head, he hears Murph's cheerful laugh turn into cries when the coffin hits the hard ground.

As the first clump of dirt hits the coffin, Ailea breaks down. Wilke raises his drink in a useless toast to their bad luck, and Morgan realizes he'd give anything to be the one sent into the ground instead.

2

1

The car's engine hasn't even cooled when Ailea storms into the house, a tempest of grief and fury. She tears into the bedroom, ripping open drawers and flinging clothes onto the bed. The closet door groans as she yanks it open, dragging out a suitcase straining at the seams.

Wilke lingers in the doorway, deflated, his eyes puffy from nights of prayer. His voice scrapes raw. "Lea, please...what are you doing?"

"What's it look like?" Ailea snarls, cramming clothes into the suitcase. "Everything here is killing me."

Wilke stumbles forward, reaching for her. "Baby..." His fingers brush her shirt before she whirls, eyes blazing.

"Don't touch me," she hisses, knocking his hand away. Wilke recoils, unrecognizing the venom twisting her features.

"I lost him too, Lea!" Wilke chokes out, desperation bleeding into his words. "We'll get through this–"

Ailea's laugh is sharp. "Our family died with Murph in that parking lot. Whatever this was, it's over now."

"But I love you..." Wilke's confession falls on deaf ears as Ailea elbows past him.

"I'm staying with Ruthie," she says.

"You're leaving me for your sister?" Wilke's voice cracks. "What am I supposed to do, Lea?"

In the hall, Morgan's eyes burn with tears, realizing any hope of comfort in these ruins has gone up in smoke.

"Where are we gonna go?" Wilke asks.

Ailea folds sweaters with precision. "You've got your own family," she remarks. "Why not try your long-lost father?"

Before Wilke can defend, the bedroom door shudders open. Morgan stands there, pale as a ghost.

"I...I thought you said Pa was dead," he rasps, shock numbing his senses.

Ailea freezes, face turned away, while Wilke gapes. He sags onto the bed, once a cradle of their love, now catafalque to its end.

Lingering words suffocate, mirroring Morgan's agony. The revelation of his supposedly deceased grandfather overwhelms him like a crashing wave. Morgan's eyes dart between his parents, searching for an explanation.

Wilke replies in a whisper. "Son, we...I never meant for you to find out like this."

The words do nothing to ease the betrayal.

For the first time since Murph's death, Ailea looks at Morgan. "I'm sorry," she says, the words shallow. "We thought...I thought we were protecting you."

Morgan's hands clench into fists. "Protecting me?" he spits out. "By lying to me my whole life?"

The accusation hangs, unanswerable. Wilke makes a sound but offers no defense.

The ground beneath Morgan's feet feels like quicksand. As he turns to flee, Ailea's voice follows him. "Morgan, wait—"

But he's gone. His footsteps echo through the house like a fading heartbeat, punctuated by his slamming door.

2

Days slip by in a haze of wordlessness, and the house grows cold and lifeless, like the family within it.

Wilke jerks awake, sweat chilling his skin. The living room is a maze of boxes, each stuffed with fragments of their shattered lives. He fumbles for the lamp, its light revealing the vacant spaces where Ailea's belongings once stood. Her discarded wedding ring remains, a reminder of vows broken.

Morgan hasn't slept. He sits in Murph's doorway, eyes roving over toy-lined shelves and walls papered with rockets and spaceships. A photo on the nightstand captures two grinning boys frozen in happier times. Dust has already settled on the relics of his brother's childhood.

His fingers close around a red Matchbox car, its dented fender a mirror to the cold reality.

"What did I tell you?" Wilke's voice makes Morgan start. His father looms in the doorway, flicking on the light. "This stuff stays."

The moment stretches, taut like a wire, before Wilke stalks away. Morgan pockets the car, a secret talisman, and abandons the half-packed box of toys.

Outside, he loads the luggage into their rust-eaten truck which groans with the burden of their possessions. Wilke climbs in without a glance at the house that was their sanctuary.

As they pull away, Murph's bedroom light remains, a beacon in the gloom. A FOR SALE sign juts from the earth like a headstone in the neglected, weed-choked front yard.

Carrying what's left of their family towards an uncertain future, the truck creaks down the street, leaving behind the ghosts of all they've lost.

3

With its headlights piercing the gloom, the pickup rattles down the winding road. Croplands and marshes blur past, their surfaces shimmering as the sun ascends.

They pull into a gas station. Wilke leans against the old pump, watching numbers tick upward as the tank fills. Morgan emerges from the store, plastic bag in hand, and passes his father a fistful of jingling change before getting in.

Through the windshield, Morgan's gaze snags on a sign, paint peeling like scabs:

THANK YOU FOR VISITING THE TOWN OF BLESSING

The irony isn't lost on him.

Wilke climbs in and slams his door, his eyes fixed on the seemingly never-ending road that lays before them.

"Anything else you want to tell me?" Morgan's words cut.

The engine sputters to life under Wilke's hand.

"Like...do I have a twin?" Morgan presses, acid in his tone.

Wilke's jaw clenches, but his gaze remains locked.

"Are you even my real dad?" The question hangs unanswered.

Frustration boiling over, Morgan hurls a chip bag at a trash can. It misses, landing in the dirt.

Without a word, Wilke grabs a bottle and lobs it out Morgan's window. It lands in the can with a direct thunk.

"Has anyone identifying themselves as your grandfather come to our door?" Wilke asks, finally eyeing Morgan. "Buckle up."

4

The sun bleeds across the cracked asphalt as the truck slows to a halt. Exhaustion etches lines on Wilke's face as he grips the steering wheel, avoiding his son's gaze. The void between them is a living thing since they left town.

A 'Vacancy' sign stands out in the twilight, its glow a beacon. Their footsteps crunch on cement as they approach the office, its lights casting shadows.

Inside, a clerk looks up from his magazine. Wilke clears his throat, rough with unease. His hand trembles as he counts their funds. The clerk's indifference is tangible as he exchanges cash for keys. No warmth, only acceptance of their presence here.

As they reach their door, the key scrapes in the lock–neither can help but think how far they've fallen from the home they knew. The room offers little comfort, merely a refuge in an un-welcoming world.

5

The motel room's gloom deepens as night settles, broken by the neon filtering through flimsy curtains. Wilke perches on the edge of the creaking mattress.

He clutches the receiver of the room phone, voice strained as he pleads with his former boss. "No, I told y'all I was leav-ing about three days ago," he says, anxiety bleeding through his forced calm. "Yes, I know it ain't proper two weeks' notice, but dire circumstances and all..."

Morgan emerges from the bathroom, cup in hand, leaning against the door frame while watching his father's negotiation.

Wilke's shoulders slump as he hangs up, defeated. Morgan's question–"So what's for dinner then?"–hangs like an accusation.

"I ain't got a stomach for food right now," Wilke grunts, not meeting his son's eyes.

"Well, I'm starving, so..." Morgan pushes, temper flaring.

"We need the rest of the money for gas to get there," Wilke snaps, fear masquerading as anger.

Pain and defiance war on Morgan's face. He spins, spitting "Whatever" as he moves to leave.

"Where are you going?" Wilke asks.

"Outside," Morgan bites back.

As Wilke's phone buzzes, he warns, "I don't like the idea of you wandering around; it's dangerous—"

"How do you know it's dangerous?" Morgan challenges.

"Because it's cheap..."

The ringing phone underscores their unease.

"Well, I can take care of myself," Morgan starts.

Wilke cuts him off, words sharp as knives. "If you could do that, we'd still be in our home."

Morgan's face darkens. He grabs a handful of bills and storms out, the slamming door an exclamation point to their fractured relationship.

6

The motel parking lot bleeds sunset colors, matching the bruises on Morgan's heart. He sits on the truck's tailgate, an island in a sea of cracked asphalt. Cold fries chase each other around a greasy box on his knees, distracting from the memories of Ailea's words before she left them.

Across the lot, local teens laugh and roughhouse, their skateboards clatter over broken pavement. Morgan watches them with longing, aching to trade his grief for their recklessness, if only for an hour.

But the mirage dissolves, leaving him adrift. He grinds spent cigarette butts under his heel, watching as darkness devours the traces of sunlight.

In this space between day and night, Morgan feels untethered. The laughter of the departed teens resounds, a reminder of the everyday life that's slipped beyond his reach. He stares into the empty motel lot, searching for answers in a world indifferent to his pain.

7

The truck groans down Main Street, a holdover in a town time forgot. Faded banners flutter overhead, their colors bleached by seasons. Boarded-up storefronts line the sidewalks like missing teeth, the few locals shuffling along with a weariness that permeates the air.

NEW LIBERTY HIGH SCHOOL looms ahead, its brick facade a mockery of its sign. Dark windows stare out like cavernous eyes, and grass and weeds reclaim the grounds. Although the fence can't contain the aura of abandonment that seeps from its cracks, students still filter from their cars toward the front doors at the bell.

Kicking up dust clouds that obscure the fields stretching to the horizon, the truck lurches onto a dirt road. With a sputter and clank, the engine's gears grind in protest. Wilke stomps the gas pedal as their speed bleeds away.

He turns to Morgan. "Good thing you got those large fries."

The truck shudders to a halt, ticking in the dust. Ahead, the road stretches on a ribbon through barren land. Wilke lets out a sigh.

8

Father and son push, Morgan guiding the wheel from outside the driver's seat. The truck fights to a halt atop the slope, where

Wilke and Morgan's efforts leave them breathless in the dust. Before them, a portrait of rural decay unfolds.

A farmhouse slouches against the horizon, its porch sagging like a tired limb. A fence encircles the property, dotted with rusting car carcasses. Under an oak, a tire swing hangs by a thread. A flag bearing the word 'Tigers' flutters, its spirit as faded as the house itself.

Black smoke billows from the fields, where a burn rages in organized mayhem. JD Browdy, grizzled and commanding, directs workers wielding swatters in their fiery dance. His Labrador stands sentinel, eyes scanning the inferno.

The dog's bark pierces the air as a shed erupts in flames. JD pivots, his shouts cut through the blaze, but efforts to save the structure prove futile. The men watch as it collapses into ash and the fire's march continues.

JD pauses, wiping sweat from his brow, disappointment and failure permeating his features. His gaze drifts to the figures of Wilke and Morgan, standing by their vehicle atop the nearby hill.

Past and present, stranger and kin, seem to converge in the smoke. Morgan can't help but wonder about the man in the hellscape, directing fire's mercy.

9

The bulb above the kitchen table casts light over the wood surface. JD washes his hands in the sink, rinsing away soot and grime before taking a chair and clomping a boot on his nearby footstool. Across from him, Morgan devours the food on his plate: a thin leftover steak and some potatoes.

Wilke stares at the faucet. It drips repeatedly.

"You ever feed this boy?" JD asks with a grin. "Hell, if I'd known you were coming, I would've saved the other half of Flutie's dinner."

The black lab in the corner looks up at his name but turns back to licking his paws. A hush falls, broken by Morgan's fork on the plate.

"You should fix that faucet," Wilke says.

JD glances at the leak, then back to his son. "By the looks of your truck, I guess this isn't just a short visit?"

Morgan stops eating, picking up on the tension.

"Speaking of, why don't you go check on our things," Wilke orders the boy. Morgan's chair scrapes as he stands and heads outside, Flutie following.

JD rubs his nose, leaving a smudge of soot. "That boy looks at me like I'm a ghost–"

Wilke stares at the table, jaw tight. "That's not my fault," he says.

The drips from the sink continue under JD's laugh containing no humor. "Do you want to get into this now?"

Wilke's expression doesn't change. "Murph is dead, Dad."

JD pauses. He finally stands, ending the drip by turning off the faucet.

"There was an accident..." Wilke continues.

JD looks out the window and sees Morgan struggling by the truck, silhouetted against the growing night sky.

10

The twilight air is strangely humid as the last light fades across the sky. Morgan strains to lift the boxes, each one filled with memories he'd rather forget.

JD's boots scrape a rhythm on the porch, his approach cautious as a stray dog. "Need a hand?" The words tumble out, rough-edged and uncertain.

"I'm fine," Morgan grunts, refusing to acknowledge the man he does not know.

A box teeters, then falls. JD's hands dart out, catching it. In a fleeting moment, they connect through cardboard and the ghostly could-have-been.

Morgan drags the box across the porch boards, each scrape an accusation against the emptiness. JD retrieves a football from one bin, its leather worn smooth. "You play?" he asks, hope disguised as interest.

The boy's muteness is answer enough. JD tosses the ball, a peace offering sailing through the air. Morgan catches it, muscle memory betraying his resolve. Their quick back and forth of fragile pitch and catch crumbles when Morgan sets the ball down.

"Think I'm gonna call it a night," he says, weariness seeping into every syllable.

"Yeah, of course. Should get some sleep," JD replies, his gruffness a veil over disappointment.

Morgan pauses at the threshold, words forming like storm clouds. "I was surprised when Dad said we was coming here."

JD shifts, and the porch creaks like his joints. "Why's that?"

"He spoke about you like you was dead." The screen door slams, a period at the end of a sentence JD never wanted to hear.

The porch light flickers, casting shadows of regret and missed chances.

11

Dawn breaks across the sky, its pink shimmer penetrating. Inside the shed's skeleton, JD's silhouette looms, a cutout against the ashen backdrop. Flutie's presence comforts JD as he plunges the shovel into the ruins, each thrust stirring up clouds of soot.

Upstairs, the farmhouse creaks as if protesting the intrusion of new life. Morgan sorts through the detritus of his existence, laying clothes on the mattress like pieces of a puzzle that no longer fit. A rap at the door precedes Wilke's entrance, charging the air with a palpable weight.

"There's breakfast downstairs," Wilke grunts, words falling flat.

Morgan's lack of reply is a wall between them, his jaw set in defiance.

"Don't get comfortable," Wilke warns, his voice frustrated. "Don't know how long we're stayin'."

The boy whirls, anger flashing like lightning. "Then why'd we even come here?"

Wilke's hand scrapes across his chin, a sound like sandpaper on wood. "Could you stop arguin' with me?" The words snap out.

Morgan stands his ground, arms crossed like a shield. "If you can tell me what happened between you two, then yeah, maybe."

The groan of floorboards, each step an admission of defeat, marks Wilke's retreat. "Breakfast is downstairs," he repeats as he flees the battlefield of questions and truths.

With his father gone, Morgan is alone, weighed down by family secrets, surrounded by boxes in a room that feels like a prison.

12

The charred doorway of the burnt shed frames Morgan like a portal to a past, his sneakers whispering to the ashes beneath. The air is thick with the scent of burnt memories, making his nostrils flare. JD's shoveling punctuates the morning stillness.

"What is all this?" Morgan's question hangs as heavy as the smoke that once filled this space.

JD's response comes out rough, like words scraped over gravel. "It's twenty years of nothing I knew what to do with. Notes, reports. Some junk collectibles."

Morgan's eyes roam. Twisted metal cabinets emerge from the rubble like shipwrecks, their contents spilled and charred. A statistics sheet, its numbers dancing in faded ink, catches his eye. Nearby, a younger JD stares out from a team photo, frozen in a moment of promise.

"Did you coach or something?" The question is tentative, a bridge built of curiosity.

JD's nod toward the shelf is an invitation to explore. "Few good men I knew went on to win some big games." Trophies on a small bookshelf stand defiant against the destruction, tarnished sentinels of glory days past.

Morgan's fingers trace the smudged engraving, connecting it with a history he never knew existed. "I wanted to ask you something," he starts, the words catching.

JD's attention settles on the boy. But Morgan falters, courage evaporating in the heat of the moment. "Never mind," he mumbles, retreating.

"Hold up." JD's voice halts Morgan's escape. He gestures to a bag of seeds, clean amidst the ruin. "Could use some help plantin' the cover crop." A moment of hesitation passes.

Morgan hefts the bag. Without a word, he follows JD out into the fields. The morning sun beats down as they walk, two figures moving across the open land.

13

JD and Morgan slump in exhaustion, sweat glistening. The man's back cracks while stretching, eyes focused ahead on the landscape.

"Ya know, every time I try to leave this place, it's views like that which keep me here," he says.

He arcs a canteen through the air. Morgan catches it, drinking. JD settles into seed bags with a grunt, Flutie bounding over, finally getting his previously neglected attention.

"Why do you call him Flutie?" Morgan asks, returning the water.

"Named after an old football buddy," JD replies, lost in memory. His hand strokes Flutie's fur as his eyes cloud with something Morgan can't read. "A man who made the impossible look easy."

Quietude stretches between them, filled by Flutie's panting. JD's gaze sharpens on Morgan, curiosity glinting. "What do you do?"

The boy shakes his head.

"You play anything?"

Morgan shifts his weight, kicking at a clump of dirt. "Special teams," he admits. "Always wanted to play quarterback, though." The words are heavy with longing.

Crickets start their chorus as JD considers this. His eyes narrow, assessing. "Well, apparently, you're gonna be going to school here. New school...could be a new start."

"What's the school like here?" Morgan asks, interest piqued. He tries to keep his voice neutral, but hope creeps in.

JD's eyes drift, seeing ghosts of glory days past. "Used to be the best in the state. Scouted three All-Americans that went on to the Big Ten, several more after 'em. Above average." Pride flickers, then fades. "But–that was a long time ago..."

Morgan watches JD's face, searching for answers. "Is that why you retired?"

The old man's jaw tightens as he opens the canteen. The metal cap scrapes in the quiet evening. "No." The word is final, a door slamming shut.

The boy hesitates, weighing his next move. Something in JD's tone, in the posture, speaks of buried hurt. The lure of possibility is irresistible. Morgan squares his shoulders, decision made. "Think I got a shot?"

For a moment, JD says nothing; he just studies the boy standing before him. Then, a gruff smile forms on his weathered face. "How's about tomorrow we go find out?"

14

The crackle of the radio fills the kitchen. JD, Wilke, and Morgan huddle around the table, dinner plates shoved aside like unwanted memories. Each drop from the faucet echoes.

JD's spoon clatters against his mug of coffee, the sound piercing the quiet. "If the boy needs anything for school, just say the word."

Wilke's stare remains on his plate, pushing peas around as if they hold the answers he seeks. "Passed a store on the way in," he mutters, words clipped. "Gotta pick up some things tomorrow morning."

"I'll drive you," JD offers, leaning back in his chair. The wood groans in protest, mirroring the tension between father and son.

"I can manage," Wilke bites out, each word sharp enough to draw blood.

JD's face deepens with impatience. "Your truck's running on fumes," he growls, stating the obvious like a challenge.

"Thought I'd borrow one of your lawn ornaments," Wilke retorts, sarcasm dripping from every syllable.

"Good luck getting 'em started–"

Wilke's plate skids across the table with a screech. "Guess I'll hoof it, then."

JD's upheld hand silences the brewing storm. "Just shut up and let me take you," he commands, his tone leaving no room for argument.

A muscle jumps in Wilke's jaw as he swallows his retort. The radio's melody continues, oblivious to the silent room.

15

The car sputters to a halt on the fractured asphalt just outside the high school, gray clouds racing across the autumn sky. The Browdy men step into the wind, the morning air filling their lungs with chill.

JD's eyes lock with Wilke's gaze over the car's roof. "We'll meet you here," he rasps, his breath a fog. Wilke responds with a nod before striding off towards the shops, his shoulders hunched against the gusts.

Morgan and JD make their way to the practice field, weeds scraping against the chain-link fence as the wind whips across the grass. Coach Tully stands, arms crossed, observing his team's drills. His whistle is a precursor to endless critiques.

Tully, a stocky man with creased cheeks from squinting at the sun, wears his cap low, shading sunglasses that guard eyes so dark they're black. Those eyes catalog every weakness of his struggling team. A scowl seems hardlined into his face, his mouth a grimace of disapproval.

As JD approaches, Tully turns, squaring his torso in a show of dominance. Surprise flashes across his face. JD meets the look, not one to be cowed by his former protégé.

"Sonofabitch, you're still kicking," Tully remarks, eyeing JD.

"A surprise to me, too. My wife had other ideas," JD returns. He nods toward the players. "How's it going, Tully?"

The coach's face twists as if tasting something bitter. "0 and 4. Half injured, the rest can't decide if they want to throw the ball or suck the air out of it," he gripes.

"Tough season…" JD commiserates.

Tully's gaze rakes over JD, then flicks to Morgan. "Who's the pup?" he asks.

JD's hand settles on Morgan's shoulder. "He plays ball. And…it looks like you could use the help."

After a long look, Tully grunts, "What's he play?"

"Quarterback," JD states.

Tully laughs, jabbing a finger toward Nash Wheeler, who fumbles on the field. "Got one of those already," he snarls.

JD's eyes narrow, zeroing in on Wheeler. Despite being shorter than Morgan, Wheeler carries himself with a swagger, his lips frozen in a sneer. The old man immediately notes the stutter in his drop-back.

"He's a split second late in his drop, and his release is slower than molasses," JD assesses. "If you want a real quarterback running this offense, you know where to find me."

As they turn to leave, Tully speaks up. "It's in his blood then?"

JD meets Tully's stare, hands balling into fists. "The hell's that got to do with anything?"

"Does he remind you of anyone?"

JD glances at Morgan and sees the set of his shoulders and the determination on his face. He looks back at Tully, his expression a mask. "Kid can throw. That's all that matters."

After a beat, Tully lifts his whistle to his mouth. "Bring him by next week then. We'll see what he's got."

The challenge slices through. JD nods, then guides Morgan off the field, unspoken history hanging between them.

16

The last vestiges of daylight fall from the sky as the Pontiac GTO growls down the rutted driveway. It comes to rest with a protest, tires sinking into the grass beside the porch. In the car, a pause lingers, interrupted only by breath clouds.

Wilke shatters the quiet, shoving his door open with a shriek of metal. Without a word or glance, he storms inside, the screen door slamming behind him like a gunshot.

JD watches his son vanish. He turns to face Morgan, hidden in the backseat shadows. When JD speaks, his voice is gentle. "You still set on this? Playing ball again?"

Morgan swallows, then nods with resolve. "Yeah. Yeah, I am," he declares, his words ringing with conviction in the car's confines.

JD's expression remains guarded, but a hint of something–satisfaction, perhaps, or something more profound–ignites in his eyes.

"Practice is every day after school. You're here drilling with me whenever you're not on that ball field. Sunup to sundown on weekends. Think you can handle that?" The words carry an edge of concern beneath the challenge.

Morgan meets his stare through the mirror. "Yeah, I can take it."

JD searches the boy's face a moment longer, then nods before opening his door.

Morgan watches the old man's silhouette fade into the house, then drops his gaze to the football in his lap. His fingers trace the Big East logo stenciled into the leather, lost in thought as the night deepens around him.

17

The weak yellow light from a solitary lamp illuminates the cramped, cluttered bedroom. A bare mattress sags on the frame and fresh tools in plastic shopping bags rest atop a faded quilt.

An envelope and blank paper sit on the scarred desk, its drawer ajar. Wilke hunches on a rickety chair, his gaze beholden to the empty parchment, as if staring hard enough would somehow produce words.

A burst of restlessness propels him to the closet. He yanks open the warped door, revealing dust-coated boxes long forgotten. He pulls one from the bottom, flipping back its flaps.

Inside, old Polaroids and photographs show a young boy grinning in oversized football gear. Wilke lets out a breath he didn't even know he was holding. His fingers dig through until they find soft fabric: a football jersey, its colors dulled by time.

He strokes the material, raw emotion blossoming on his face. Footsteps in the hall snap him back. He shoves the box into the closet's shadows. As he wrestles with the swollen door, the final hinge snaps off, detaching from the frame. "Well shit," he mutters.

18

Morgan lies awake, leering up at the ceiling as the old house moans around him. Muffled thumps filter through the thin wall from Wilke's room, followed by a loud crash.

He rolls over with a tired sigh, spotting Murph's tiny Matchbox car on the nightstand. His fingers find the metal toy in the dark, clinging to it like an anchor in this strange sea with no beacon to guide him home—his real home is now just a painful memory.

An image of his little brother surfaces. Coming home from grueling football practices, he often remembers finding both Wilke and Murph playing together. Peering into a perfect world he couldn't access, he was an outsider.

His mind lands on one vivid memory...

When the bedroom door creaked open, he saw a scene straight out of a happy childhood memory. In the middle of the room, Murph was sitting on the rug with his legs crossed, surrounded by his army of toy cars and action figures.

Each toy had a story, and Murph was eager to share. Sitting at the side of the bed, Wilke watched over Murph, his smile beaming as he took in the joy and excitement his youngest son found.

Just outside the doorway, almost blending into the shadows, stood Morgan. His clean uniform served as a reminder of another day spent mostly on the sidelines.

Watching the scene inside stirred up feelings of jealousy in Morgan, feelings becoming all too familiar.

Murph must have felt Morgan's eyes on him, because he suddenly looked up. Their eyes met for a second, and Morgan felt compelled to speak up.

"Coach kept me on the bench again," he said, trying to sound casual even though he was disappointed.

The room was silent, only the Cat-Clock ticking on the wall.

Morgan had an idea. "If I could practice here sometimes, I think I'd maybe even start next season," he suggested, hopeful.

Wilke sighed, his tired face revealing a long day. "I'm busy with your brother right now..." he replied, sounding as tired as he looked.

The alarm sounded, signaling the end of playtime. "Time's up!" Wilke announced, getting up from the bed. "C'mon, sport, time for pajamas."

As Murph started picking up his toys, Morgan lingered in the doorway, watching.

"Why do you still play with those stupid things?" he sneered before he turned and walked away, leaving behind the happy scene that he just couldn't seem to be part of.

Alone in the tattered bed, he's back in the empty shell of a home, just as emotionally vacant as the one he left.

19

A veil of mist shrouds the field as dawn light filters through the fog around the farmhouse. Morgan and JD meet in the yard, the old man cradling a football in his hands. Flutie lies nearby, ears pricked.

Morgan yawns. JD fixes him with a stern look. "Time to focus," he grunts. He raises his hands. "Toss it here. Let's see what you got."

Morgan attempts the quarterback stance, feet planted awkwardly. His hips remain stiff, weight off balance. JD catches the inaccurate throw with ease.

"Three things you need to learn," he lectures. "Accuracy, footwork, mentality." He holds up three fingers, breath steaming in the cold air. "You can have the strongest arm in the league, but chuckin' it far don't make you the best. It's about precision–putting that ball where it needs to be every time." His eyes assess Morgan. "Show me your stance."

The boy shuffles his feet wider. JD steps in, adjusting Morgan's body with impatient hands. "There now. Shoulder-width...relax them arms..." Morgan looks more balanced. "Good," JD approves.

He presses the ball into Morgan's grip. "When I snap this ball, four things need to happen," he instructs.

"One: Bring that ball up tight to your chest, grip it with both hands." Morgan complies. JD positions the kid's torso. "Two: Get that non-throwing shoulder aligned on your target."

Morgan pivots, left shoulder aimed at a gnarled tree downfield.

"Now lift, get that ball up to ear-level." JD watches as Morgan adjusts his hold. "Bend those knees...dig that foot in–" Morgan sinks, dominant foot anchoring into the damp earth.

"Three: Weak hand off the ball. Cock that throwing arm back, twist that ball." Morgan's left hand drops as he coils his throwing arm. "Four..." JD holds up four fingers, his championship ring catching the light. "Unleash that built up energy. Snap that ball forward on my signal."

He demonstrates, then steps back, snapping his fingers. "Again. One." Morgan winds up. "Two." Rotates his torso. "Three." Transfers weight. "Four!"

The ball rockets–mist sprays as it hurtles toward the tree, slicing through the center of the old tire swing. JD stands tall, satisfaction in his sly grin. He whistles sharply. Flutie bursts up from the grass, streaking toward Morgan at a sprint, tongue out, eyes bright.

Startled, Morgan stumbles back, tripping over his feet and landing flat on his back. Flutie pounces, paws on the boy's chest, licking his face. JD's laugh booms.

"Alright, alright," he chuckles, pulling Flutie off by the collar. He offers a hand to Morgan, who takes it sheepishly. JD pulls him up, brushing grass from his shirt.

"Tomorrow, you'll learn how to stay on those feet," he says with a wink. Morgan attempts to hide an exhilarated grin.

Inside the farmhouse, curtains shift. Wilke watches his father and son walk toward the back pasture, JD's arm over Morgan's shoulders. Something forlorn flickers in Wilke's eyes before the curtains fall closed.

3

1

Dusk's golden light fades over the rural landscape as shadows-stretch and meld together. A lone figure pounds down the dusty dirt road–Morgan, running full tilt with a football tucked tight against his ribs. His arms pump, and his breath seeps in and out of his lungs as he hurdles onward. The sun sinks below the distant tree line, painting the sky in fading hues of orange and pink.

Behind him, a plume of ocher dust churns from his racing footsteps. Flutie emerges from the haze, his black fur rippling as he gains ground on the boy. Morgan glances back to see the lab bounding after him, tongue lolling at this new game.

He feints left and right, trying to trip up his canine companion. Morgan fakes, juking as if to dodge a make-believe defender, kicking up dirt clods as he pivots.

The road stretches ahead, a ribbon of pale dust cutting through fields of tall grass. Crickets begin their evening chorus, their songs rising and falling with each of Morgan's pounding strides. Sweat trickles down his temples, soaking into the collar of his worn t-shirt.

Flutie barks, nipping at Morgan's heels. The boy laughs, his legs burning with exertion. He pushes himself harder, imagining the roar of a crowd, the clash of helmets and pads. At this moment, the empty road becomes a football field, and Morgan sees himself racing toward an unseen end-zone.

As they round the bend, the old farmhouse comes into view, a silhouette against the deepening twilight. Morgan slows his pace, chest heaving as he gulps in the cool evening air. Flutie prances around him, tail wagging, still eager to play.

Morgan drops to his knees in the soft grass by the roadside, cradling the football in his lap. He scratches Flutie behind the ears, grinning as the dog's rough tongue laps at his sweaty face. He sits there, catching his breath, savoring the quiet satisfaction. For now, he allows himself one more minute in this perfect, solitary world where it's just him, the dog, and the endless promise of the opportunity before him.

2

Wilke yanks open the fridge, snagging a beer. A water drop plunks into the sink, its steady rhythm marking time in the stillness. Through the smudged window, he watches JD erect supports for a new wall by the charred shed, his work-worn arms securing a beam.

Four beers in, the pair gather in the living room. JD polishes rescued trophies, his touch gentle as he wipes away ash from the tarnished figures. He sets them on the coffee table near a vase of wilting wildflowers.

Wilke kicks off his boots, sinking into the sofa before grabbing the remote, flicking on the old TV. Cold light flashes across his brooding face as he opens beer number five.

"Saw y'all tossing the ball earlier," he remarks, eyes vacant in the TV's glow. "Boy seems to have some talent," he adds.

JD studies him, thumb tracing an engraved name on a trophy. "Could be something special in him," he muses, a spark lighting his gaze.

Wilke snorts, shaking his head. "Don't go getting attached. We know how that plays out."

The words linger while the TV drones on, filling the room with its meaningless chatter. Wilke drains his drink, staring unseeing at the screen, shoulders tense beneath memories he can't outrun.

JD continues his polishing, with each careful stroke serving as an attempt to restore what he has lost.

3

Outside, Morgan bounds onto the porch, his cheeks flushed from his run. He falters as fragments of JD and Wilke's conversation seep through the cracked window into the heavy twilight air.

"Met a guy today who wants to hire me," he says. "Construction gig. All goes well, we'll be outta your hair soon."

The newscast's drone mingles with the crickets' evening song.

"Gonna uproot Morgan again? He ain't even settled in yet–"

Wilke cuts JD off, cranking up the TV's volume. Wordlessly, the old man gathers the trophies and stands to leave.

Morgan leans closer to the window, his breath caught in his throat. The porch boards creak beneath his shifting weight, a stark counterpoint to the muffled voices inside. His fingers linger on the doorknob, uncertain whether to enter or leave, back to the freedom of the dirt road.

As JD moves toward the door, Morgan stumbles back, his cleats scuffing against the worn wood. He descends the porch steps, retreating into the yard where Flutie waits, tail wagging in oblivious joy.

JD passes by without words. He moves for the barn, seeking refuge among its familiar shadows, leaving the burden of his past in the estranged house.

4

Morgan enters the house, the door clapping shut. He feels Wilke's stare from the other room. The TV clicks off, leaving only a ringing void.

The sound transports Morgan back to practices before their lives unraveled, back to Murph watching him play ball.

He sees Murph's face, alight with pride, cheering from the sidelines. The memory is so vivid he can almost hear his brother's voice cutting through the stillness of the present.

In the dark hallway, he stands still, caught between his old life and the unknown future ahead.

"Go to bed," Wilke's voice calls from the living room. "Unless you're fixing to run off again tonight," he chides.

Morgan recalls a humid afternoon on the worn practice field. Players grunted through drills while he sat alone on the sideline bench, rubbing the laces of a football in his hands.

At the sagging fence stood Murph with Wilke and Ailea. Young Murph bounced as he watched the scrimmage, echoing Coach Nichols' shouts.

"Run it again!" Nichols bellowed.

Murph parroted at the top of his lungs, "Run it again! Run it again!"

Morgan shifted on the bench, shoulders hunching. Murph increased his volume. "Run it again!" The repetition made Morgan wince.

Nichols glared at the boy while players chuckled and glanced toward the fence. Humiliation burned across Morgan's neck and ears.

Wilke patted Murph's head. "Yeah, run it again, buddy, that's right," he encouraged with a grin.

Murph beamed up at his father, then resumed pumping tiny fists. "Run it again! Morgan, run it again!"

Morgan launched up and stormed over to the fence, hisfootsteps thudding on the grass. Wilke lifted a hand, but it was too late. Morgan grabbed his little brother's arm and flung him to the ground.

Murph landed on his rear, mouth forming a stunned "O." His face screwed up, and he began wailing. Wilke's angry rebuke followed. "Dammit, Morgan!"

Wilke and Ailea hoisted Murph up, brushing grass from his clothes. The boy watched his brother with confused eyes, shimmered with tears.

"He didn't mean it, baby," Ailea soothed, smoothing back Murph's hair.

Murph swiped at the wet tracks down his cheeks. Ailea fixed Morgan with a scolding look before turning to Murph.

"He would never hurt you," she assured the child.

Morgan felt his hackles lower under his mother's gaze. Fury receded, his actions sat like a stone in his gut. *What did I just do?*

Murph stuck his thumb in his mouth with gap-toothed uncertainty as he studied his brother's stormy expression. Morgan opened his mouth, but no words formed, shame rendering him mute.

"No," Morgan replies to his father from the threshold of the dining room. "I'm done for the night."

5

Inside the charred shed, JD wipes an old trunk, revealing metal beneath. The hasp screams as he opens it, searching through notebooks, photos, and a clock. He grasps his prize–a bag of worn footballs, their leather still supple.

He drags the bag outside into the hazy morning light. The tire swing creaks in the breeze, hanging from ropes on a thick oak branch. Gray clouds race across the pale sky.

JD hurls a ball at Morgan. "Let's go, warm up," he growls. The boy catches it just in time, the ball smacking into his grip.

Morgan tries to set his stance.

"Three-step drop on my mark," JD orders. Morgan's eyes lock on the tire target.

"Hut!" JD's voice cracks like a whip. Morgan drops back, stumbling before his drop ends. The ball sails wide, hitting the rope with a thwap.

Morgan frowns, rubbing his furrowed forehead.

"Again!" JD slaps another ball into Morgan's grip. "Settle those feet..."

Morgan plants his feet, arm cocked. JD's hawk-like gaze takes him in. "Hold it–" He nudges Morgan's shoes. "Pigeon-toe. Angle out."

Morgan shifts. JD grunts approval and steps back. "Precision now. Hut!"

The next drop flows better, but Morgan's throw clips the tire's edge. "Shit!" he spits.

"Language—" JD snaps. "And you took an extra step. I said three steps only."

"I didn't—" Morgan retorts. "I did three steps..."

JD shakes his head, disappointment clear. He shoves another ball against Morgan's chest. "Again. Do it right this time."

Morgan exhales hard before lining up. At JD's "Hut!" he drops clean but hitches forward. The ball caroms off the tire with a bong.

"Here. Now." JD growls, pointing at his feet. Morgan trudges over, arms crossed.

"Three-step drop. Can you count, boy?"

Morgan glares. JD grabs his chin, forcing eye contact. "I asked if you can count. Yes or no?"

"Yes..." Morgan grits out.

"Then prove it!" JD releases him and steps back, challenge on his face.

Morgan bites, "One. Two. Three," each number clipped.

JD's eyes glitter. "One, two, three, what? One, two, three, throw. There. Was that so hard?"

"I did—" Morgan starts before JD cuts him off.

"Do I need to hold your hand, boy?" He grabs Morgan's wrist and pulls him back. "We'll walk through it slow so you can keep up."

He counts. "One..." Morgan joins in. "Two...Three." They stop, Morgan poised to throw.

"Now you let it rip," JD instructs, tossing a ball to Morgan, who scowls before lining up.

"One, two, three, throw!" JD calls, clapping. But Morgan drops back early, impatient.

"Hey!" JD snaps. "I said on my mark."

Morgan realigns and waits for the cue. At JD's whistle, he drops back and fires. The ball sails through the tire with a swick.

"Better!" JD praises. "Again."

They repeat the drill until shadows stretch across the field. Morgan hits the target, JD's whistle mixing with the cicadas' drone.

Morgan's arm hangs limp, sweat glistening on his brow.

JD tosses him a water bottle. "Sit," he commands, gesturing to the tire swing.

Morgan collapses onto it, ropes creaking. JD lowers to the ground, back against the oak's gnarled trunk. The air thickens, interrupted by Morgan's labored breathing.

"You're improving," JD offers, his gruff voice softened by encroaching darkness.

Morgan takes a long pull from the bottle. "Doesn't feel like it," he mutters.

JD snorts. "Feel's got nothing to do with it. Your form's tighter. The release is quicker."

Morgan fidgets with the bottle cap, twisting it. "That trunk in the shed," he starts, curiosity overriding his fatigue. "It's not just old footballs in there, is it?"

JD's eyes narrow. "What's it to you?"

Morgan shrugs, aiming for nonchalance. "Saw some old photos. Notebooks, too."

JD's gaze fixes on some distant point. "Memories," he says. "Some worth keeping, some not."

Morgan leans forward. "Of your playing days?"

JD's laugh is sharp, tinged with something darker. "Among other things."

"You ever miss it?" Morgan presses. "Being on the field?"

A flicker...pain, nostalgia, regret...pass through his downcast eyes. "Every damn day, kid."

The crickets begin their chirp as darkness settles. JD pushes himself up with a grunt. "That's enough reminiscing. Same time tomorrow," he says, brooking no argument.

Morgan rises, muscles protesting. As JD turns he calls out, "Think you'll ever show me those photos?"

JD pauses, his back to Morgan. A beat passes before he speaks, voice rough. "Maybe. If you earn it."

He strides off, leaving Morgan alone with the creaking swing and thoughts of a past he's only beginning to glimpse.

6

Wilke sits alone in the cramped bedroom, back against flat pillows. The TV's glow paints his face in blue light. A beer dangles from his fingers, dripping onto the quilt.

On the desk, blank paper and a pen sit beside a photo of Ailea. Her smile mocks from behind cracked glass. Wilke stares at her picture, throat tight. She was beautiful that day under the oak, laughing as he chased her. He remembers her minty hair as he pulled her close.

"Let me get one of just you," Ailea said, fixing her wind-messed hair. "My ball player's all handsome."

Wilke posed as she fiddled with the new Polaroid camera.

"You gonna keep me forever?" he joked, squinting.

Ailea smiled. "Long as you'll let me, Wild Man."

He turned the camera to catch them both. The shutter clicked. She waved the developing film, their future still bright.

Now he sits alone, that future shattered.

Wilke wipes his eyes, heart heavy. He lurches from the bed, almost knocking over the empty bottles. He drops into the desk chair and sets his beer down. The lamp clicks on. He takes a swig of courage before writing to the woman he still desires, despite her inability to confront him. Where to start...

7

Later, Wilke lies sprawled on the quilt, fully dressed. The room is dark, the TV is off. Empty beer cans crowd the end table next to full ashtrays, reeking of stale smoke.

A sealed envelope waits on the desk. Ailea's name is scribbled on the front in Wilke's rough handwriting. The smooth flap hides a storm of emotion inside. His pen lies nearby, spent. Crumpled drafts litter the floor, failed attempts at explanation. Turned away from his struggle, the photo of Ailea faces down.

In his uneasy sleep, the man's fingers twitch. Positioned as a fragile bridge across their distance, the letter stands ready to mend or break what remains between them.

8

In front of the old farmhouse, the morning light filters through the oak, illuminating several new tire swings at different heights.

JD pauses as he climbs down, looking proud at what he's built before stepping to the ground.

Morgan stands nearby, wearing oversized shoulder pads and an old helmet that's too big for him. JD tightens a strap and taps the plastic shell. "Need to learn to throw with these on," he says firmly.

Morgan shifts, seeking comfort in the armor as he takes position behind a pretend offensive line.

JD retreats, gaze drilling into his student. "Three-step drop–I call the target, you throw on my signal," he commands. "Hut! Tire one."

Morgan drops back, the ball explodes from his grip. It pierces the leftmost tire with a sharp crack.

"Again!" JD assesses, hurling another ball.

Morgan readies himself, muscles easing into the cadence. "Hut! Three." He launches–a precise missile, threading the third tire.

"Practice that route until it's instinct." JD loads two more balls for consecutive throws. Morgan nods, resolve in his stance.

Morgan's spikes sink into the soft ground as he drops back. His eyes lock onto the swaying tires, muscles coiling. The ball leaves his fingertips in a tight spiral, whistling toward impact. A thwack rings out as it threads the center tire.

"Again!" JD demands.

Morgan repeats the motion fluid and practiced. This time, the ball veers wide, slamming into the barn's weathered boards. A flock of sparrows erupts from the eaves in a flurry of indignant chirps.

Sweat trickles down Morgan's face, stinging his eyes. The padding chafes against his skin with each movement. His chest rises and drops, but his grip remains steady. Another perfect throw slices through a tire, bringing a trace of a smile to his lips.

JD's steely gaze never wavers. "Faster now."

Flutie's tail swishes back and forth in the tall grass like a metronome. His head swivels, following each ball's arc. As one thuds to the ground, he bolts. His nose skims the earth, zeroing in on the leather smells. Gentle jaws close around the ball. He trots tail-high back, depositing his prize at JD's feet before resuming his watch.

The sun climbs higher, burning away the last wisps of morning fog. Morgan's world narrows to a series of targets. Nothing exists beyond the next throw, the following command. His arm aches, but each successful pass fuels him. Each spiral now, a step toward greatness.

9

Hours of relentless drills leave Morgan's arm leaden. He freezes mid-throw, a grimace twisting his features as he inspects his palm. Angry welts dot his fingers, skin raw and blistered. His eyes flick to JD, pain written in the tight press of his lips.

The old man's keen gaze catches the hitch in Morgan's motion. His rough hands snatch Morgan's, probing the torn flesh with calloused fingers. Morgan's sharp intake of breath betrays his discomfort.

"Stings, don't it?" JD's voice grates low. He squeezes, drawing a flinch from the boy. "Price of dedication." His eyes bore into Morgan's. "This pain builds discipline. Teaches when to push and when to ease off. You hear me?"

Morgan nods, mute. JD releases his hand with a pat. "Toughen up. Take a run with the dog. Back by supper. School starts tomorrow."

Morgan trudges across the field, Flutie bounding at his heels. His feet drag through the tall grass, each step heavy with exhaustion while his shoulders slump forward under the practice gear he still wears.

JD retreats to his shed, emerging with sandpaper to smooth the football's worn leather.

The house door slams. Wilke emerges, cigarette smoke curling into the twilight. Fireflies blink through the gathering dusk as he takes a long drag. He crushes his cigarette under his heel. "He idolizes you," he grates, words heavy with resentment.

JD's reply cuts sharp. "Been ages since I felt that." He doesn't look up from his task, the rasp of sandpaper punctuating his words.

Cricket songs fill the charged air between them.

"Yeah..." Wilke's mouth works, but whatever thoughts still linger go unspoken. He returns to the house, pausing with his hand on the doorknob. For a moment, it seems he might say more. Instead, he disappears inside, leaving JD alone.

10

New Liberty High School towers before Morgan, its cinder block walls a dull testament to years of neglect. He steps inside, sneakers squeaking against worn tiles. His eyes dart between his crumpled schedule and the faded locker numbers.

Above, a "TIGER PRIDE" banner sags, its colors muted by time. Dented lockers line the halls, their teal paint flaking away to show rusted metal beneath. Somewhere in the building, the cafeteria preps for lunch and the smell of fries and square pizza wafts down the hallway.

A cluster of students eye Morgan as he navigates the unfamiliar terrain. Their gaze lingers until boredom takes hold, and they push through smudged doors into nearby classrooms.

Morgan wrestles with a stubborn combo, wrenching his locker open. A few notebooks clatter onto the gritty shelf, their thud echoing in the barren space. The meager contents underscore his outsider status.

The classroom welcomes him with stale air and an empty greeting. A tired tiger pennant droops beside a dusty flag, overlooking a chalkboard faded with years of use. Scattered students hunch over desks, faces hidden behind textbooks.

Morgan claims a back-row seat. His chair scrapes, drawing brief, disinterested glances. His leg bounces as his focus drifts to the world beyond grimy windows.

Beside him, a girl with wild chestnut curls frowns at her arm in concentration. Her pen moves about her wrist, bringing a lion to life on her pale skin.

The strange spectacle of this girl illustrating her skin captures Morgan's wandering gaze. She pauses, sensing it. He looks to the front of the class, but she's caught him staring. He wishes she would turn away and release him from this unexpected scrutiny. But she doesn't.

11

The class ends, a dull lesson on ionic bonds fading into memory. Morgan shuffles out, his head bowed. A student rushes past, knocking into him and almost dislodging the books under his arm.

"Pretty brave moving here mid-year."

He stops, his heart racing as he looks back. The girl with the lion drawn on her arm stares at him, her gaze direct and judgmental.

Morgan swallows hard, his throat dry. He shifts his weight from one foot to the other, unsure whether to stay or flee. "Not brave," he mutters, eyes dropping to the scuffed linoleum. "Didn't have a choice." His fingers tighten around his books, knuckles whitening.

"Do you party?" No trace of flirtation in her words. "I don't know where you moved from," she says. "But the parties here are pretty legendary."

One corner of her mouth lifts as if asking, 'can you hang?' She grabs his wrist without warning. Morgan lets her turn his palm up, too surprised to resist.

"Gross," she says, eyeing his busted blisters. "Put lotion on those."

Her fingers grip a pen, scrawling an address across his palm in bold strokes. "Last big party of the semester is tonight," she tells him, her eyes meeting his.

Morgan's tongue touches his dry lips as words fail him.

The tardy bell pierces the air. The girl gives him a knowing look and brushes past, leaving the promise of something forbidden tingling in his hand.

"Your arm..." he manages.

She turns, walking backward. "What about it?"

"Why the lion?"

"I have a birthmark. It's ugly, so I'm getting a tattoo." She waves at him. "Fix those hands, new-boy."

12

The last bell's echo fades in the locker room as Morgan sits on a rickety bench in the central aisle. Shouts and laughter from lingering players bounce off dingy cinder block walls. The pale green paint, faded by decades of sweat and dreams, absorbs the harsh glow of overhead fluorescent lights. Morgan surveys the rows of battered lockers, slouching after bearing generations of youth. He looks at the tiger-orange and royal blue jersey beside him, running a finger over the mesh.

Nearby, a group of players flick wet towels that strike like whips. Cruel laughter erupts as Tyler Hagan and his crew torment Sam Smith in the next stall. Tyler jabs a gray ham sandwich through the locker's lattice, hours old and rank. The mess lands on Sam's clean gym clothes with a wet slap.

Morgan ignores the scene. Anticipation builds in his gut as he ties his mud-crusted cleats, which are still damp from morning drills with JD. His soles hit the concrete, the thump echoing through the room.

Hands clammy, he dons the jersey. New chance or dead end? He's about to find out. He smooths the fabric over his body, his pulse marking time until this unexpected chance begins.

13

The team is all huddled up in the field, high-fiving and not giving two shits about their record as the sun sets. Coaches huddle near the sideline, pointing and checking clipboards as if seeing the turf anew.

Morgan takes in their world, unlike JD's rigid training. As he waits by the bench, grass and sweat mix with autumn's crisp chill. Across the field, Nash Wheeler and others eye him with open hostility. Two whistles slice the air. "Bring it in!" Coach Tully's voice booms, his chest straining his orange polo. The team falls silent, gathering around him. Tully stands wide, hands on hips.

"What's so funny?" he challenges the smirking players. "We've lost four straight. Henderson, keep laughing–you keep missing tackles, we'll pack your ass with cotton." The mirth dies.

"We need to win out for Divisional and change our legacy," he growls. "What kind of men will you be?" The question hangs heavy.

An assistant passes Tully a worn clipboard. Without looking up, he barks orders, splitting the team into groups.

Two whistle blasts scatter the players. Morgan maneuvers the bustling maze to catch Tully.

"Coach...Where should I go?"

Tully stops, eyeing Morgan's frame. "Who are you?"

"Morgan Browdy, sir. I'm...a quarterback." The words spark a thrill in him.

Recognition flashes. "Browdy's grandson," Tully mutters. "Come on." He waves for Morgan to follow.

Ball in hand, Morgan lines up beside Wheeler, the starter glaring from behind his mask.

The offense watches as Tully directs receivers to flank the invisible pocket by the quarterbacks. "Jimmy, five-yard-out. Lester, mirror him," he orders. He fixes Wheeler and Morgan with an expectant look. "We'll go on two. Wheeler first...let's see who wants this job."

Morgan's pulse races as he readies, Wheeler tense beside him. At Tully's signal, Wheeler drops back and throws hard but low. The ball bounces off Lester's feet.

"Reset!" Tully snaps. "Browdy, on my mark." Morgan breathes deep, centering himself. "Ready...hut!"

Morgan drops back and lofts a ball just over Jimmy's reach as he breaks the route.

"Lower that arc, Browdy!" Tully shouts. "This throw needs to hug the ground. I want heat on those out-routes."

Wheeler sets up. Tully's whistle blasts. He drops back. The throw sails high.

14

Morgan and Wheeler trade poor throws. Tully's face darkens with each miss.

"Wheeler, you're why some animals eat their young," he growls, as Nash fumbles his timing. Lester leaps to catch the errant pass.

Morgan lines up, determined to match Wheeler's last spiral. But he throws short as Jimmy bolts along the back line.

Jimmy's scoop fails. The ball hits the turf with a dull thud. Morgan avoids Tully's burning glare, fury radiating from the coach.

"How long is this travesty gonna continue, gentlemen?" Tully demands. Neither boy answers. He checks his watch with exaggeration.

"Sun's setting. We'll stay all night until one of you decides they want this job." He jabs a finger at the offense. "Lap, everyone. We run until these two decide to play football. Hope they figure it out fast–"

Amid murmurs, Wheeler and Morgan retake positions, doubt churning beneath their helmets as the tryout continues under darkening skies.

Fifteen minutes later, Lester and Jimmy gasp for air, sweat-drenched in the fading light.

Morgan's turn. His throw hits Jimmy's numbers in perfect rhythm. A triumphant "ha!" escapes his throat.

Wheeler shoulder-checks him, whispering, "Heard you're only here because your grandpa paid off the coach."

Tully claps. "Again!"

They realign.

At the whistle, Wheeler throws perfectly while Morgan's pass skips behind Jimmy.

Each miss brings a groan from the team circling the field.

Jaw clenched, pressure screwing tighter, Morgan concentrates on slowing his frenzied heartbeat. No way does this chance slip through his sweaty fingers after days of dawn-to-dusk training on the farm.

"Posts!" Tully barks, changing the pattern. The receivers angle diagonally toward center field, presenting larger downfield targets. Morgan takes his drop–one, two, three, plant–then unwinds, torquing his whole body behind the throw. The ball rockets from his grip, a heat-seeking missile homing in on Jimmy's outstretched hand–it's snared in mid-sprint without breaking stride.

They reset, and Wheeler answers with a respectable ball. But as the drill continues, his passes lose zip, accuracy fading as fatigue sets in. Morgan remains locked, repeatedly striking his mark with coiled power. Still, uncertainty gnaws his gut as Tully straightens from his hands-on-knee pose of scrutiny.

This is the moment of truth.

Tully chews his whistle, surveying both teens. He points at Wheeler. "That'll do. Join Lindsey's group with the backs."

Two sharp blasts pierce the air. The jogging team collapses, rolling onto the ground, gasping.

Morgan exhales, unaware he'd been holding his breath. Wheeler glares, ripping off his helmet as he leaves the field.

Tully's gaze fixes on Morgan. "Browdy, my office after practice."

He turns to the exhausted players. "Grab water, then line up for Gassers!"

The team lines one end-zone, poised for the dreaded drill.

Tully raises his whistle, squinting against the sunlight breaking through clouds. The tweet splits the air.

The squad sprints 100 yards. At the opposite end-zone, another blast orders them back. Barely catching breath, the whistle commands a second round-trip.

Some players crumple at the finish, lungs burning, legs failing. Others bend over, gasping, sweat pouring onto the grass.

Tully, impassive behind dark lenses, surveys the scene and blows his whistle. "What kind of day is it?" he shouts.

The team responds: "A great day...to be...alive!" Someone retches in the back.

Whistle after whistle drives them on, legs quiver, hardly supporting failing bodies. Dark clouds continue to close in, foreshadowing the grueling conclusion of the season to come.

15

Morgan edges through Tully's door, hit by stale cigar smoke. The office walls vanish behind stacks of papers and shelves crammed with playbooks, tapes, and bobbleheads. Tully's bulk nearly disappears behind his massive desk.

At Morgan's knock, Tully's face emerges, gleaming under harsh light. He eyes Morgan's damp hair and stained uniform, grunting approval.

"Good arm, kid," he admits, rubbing his chin. "Too gun-shy, though. Need you stepping up more to lead this crew."

Morgan nods, then catches himself. "Yes, sir," he says, straightening.

Tully slides a thick binder across the desk. "Your bible now," he states as Morgan's name comes into view. "Four days to know every play cold." Tully studies him, lips pursed, hopeful. "Hit the showers."

Pride rising, the new Tiger quarterback departs.

16

Steam billows as Morgan steps under the sputtering shower head. The hot water cascades over him, a welcome relief after hours in the biting fall cold. Dirt and grass rinse from his tired limbs, muscles relaxing under the warm stream. Players' laughter echoes off tile walls, voices louder in the small space as AC/DC blasts from a radio in the locker bay.

Morgan keeps his eyes forward, discomfort building with each glimpse of bare chests and swinging towels. The urge to finish and run pulls at him, a basic instinct in this testosterone-filled room.

A sharp wolf howl grabs attention. Wheeler skids across the slippery floor, now a makeshift slide of soap and sideways sprays. Huge boys slide, crashing like human bowling balls, their laughter harsh.

Morgan winces, reaching for the tap. Too late–two linemen appear, pushing him toward Wheeler's mean look. Their grip, still slick with soap, leaves no way out.

"Drink, bitch!" the ex-quarterback snarls. A stream of piss arcs through the steam, hitting the tile near Morgan's bare feet. Laughter and insults hit his ears as he backs away, the smell of shame rising with the steam.

"Look at his face, he likes it!" Wheeler yells. The team roars with laughter, except for a few caught in the crossfire.

Anger boils in Morgan's gut, ready to burst out. But self-preservation wins, a cold choice in this heated moment. Jaw clenched tight, he spins away toward the doorway hidden in steam. Their mocking yells follow his exposed back, a last attack as he leaves.

A loud rumble from the GTO engine as the old muscle car comes up the ramp into the school lot.

Morgan wipes his eyes, leaning against the brick building. He rubs his face as the car stops in front of him.

As Morgan gets in, exhaust fumes swirl in the cold air, sitting stiff. Without a word, JD turns the heater on high, hot air fogging the windows.

"How'd it go?" he asks, warm air hissing from the vents in the small space. "They give you a good chance out there?"

Morgan nods, his jaw muscles twitching. He looks away, staring at the dark maze of fences by the practice field.

JD waits a bit, then asks, "Tully work you hard?"

"No harder than you," Morgan says, staring at nothing.

"How'd the team take you?" JD probes. No response.

JD tries again. "Tully say anything about your performance?" Morgan's disdain lingers.

"You hungry? We can stop." JD offers, searching for a reaction. Morgan remains stone-faced, gaze fixed on the world outside the car.

With a sigh, JD puts the old GTO in drive. The tires spin on asphalt before gripping. The ride continues, with questions unasked and unanswered hanging in the fall air.

17

Morgan pushes through the back door into the cramped farmhouse kitchen. His playbook binder lands on the chipped counter with a dull thud. He turns the tap, but erratic drips splatter from the broken faucet under the sink.

Mid-drink, the sporadic drips surge into a steady hollow splash. Morgan twists the handles until quiet blankets the room again.

Heavy steps approach. Wilke enters, gripping his battered toolbox. His bearded face tightens at the sight of the ancient plumbing's exposed guts. "I'll fix it," he mutters while lowering himself onto cracked floor tiles.

Morgan moves aside without a word as parts clatter onto the pitted floor. A taut stillness grows between them, punctuated only by the harsh sounds of repair.

At last, Morgan breaks the quiet, his throat tight. "I'm...going out tonight." He avoids Wilke's sharp gaze across the narrow room between them. His eyes drift to his hand, where faded ink marks the party address.

Wilke fights with a stubborn thread, his brief pause the only sign he heard. "Pass that smaller wrench," he orders, nodding at the red box by Morgan's feet.

The boy crouches to grab the wrench. As Wilke probes the pipes, Morgan clears his throat, seeking a response.

"I might be back late," he adds.

Wilke's hands pause again before resuming their work. "You remember our talks?" His rough voice carries an odd hint of fatherly worry.

"I got it," Morgan mumbles, eyes down.

Wilke leans back, wiping dirty hands on his shirt. "We had you young...so," he starts. "Not saying you were a mistake...but you gotta be careful–"

"Okay?" Morgan cuts in, face burning.

Wilke pushes on, gaze darting as if imparting vital wisdom. "It's like a rifle–if you're aiming it, put it on safe..."

"Ew, what? I am–" Morgan protests, halting the painful safe-sex comparison.

Awkward quiet fills the kitchen, the space now feeling too small. Neither Browdy man meets the other's eyes.

Morgan stands, muscles tight with the urge to flee. He grabs his playbook.

"Hey, wait–" Wilke's voice stops him. Morgan looks back to see his father holding out a plain envelope with his mother's name on it. "Drop this in the mailbox on your way."

Morgan takes it. Something in Wilke's closed expression softens his tone. "Sure. I'll...see you later, Dad."

Wilke nods, eyes falling humbly. Morgan escapes out the back door, lungs filling with the night air. Behind him, the kitchen's lonely drips continue their uneven rhythm through the dark.

18

Crickets strike up their evening chorus as Morgan slips away, sneakers kicking up dust on the weathered path. Fresh-cut hay and distant wood-smoke burden the surrounding air, marking the end of another day that fades into all the rest. A whippoorwill calls out in the shadows of the oak grove, its mournful song echoing across fields.

"Where you headed?" JD's rough voice calls. Morgan turns to see his grandfather shuffling from the half-built shed.

"Thought you might help with that new wall," the old man says, raking fingers through his coarse hair. "You got plans?"

Morgan shifts, the playbook pressing his side. "Yeah, meeting some people."

JD pauses, studying the boy. "It's fine, I can manage alone," he nods.

"Cool...and sorry," he adds. A tense moment passes before he steps back. "I'll see you later then."

Some unnamed feeling makes him pause. "Is one of you ever going to tell me what happened?" he asks, his forehead creasing.

JD just stares, silent, until his weathered face crinkles in a sad smile. "Your father has a knack for burning bridges, even when folks aim to help." He holds Morgan's gaze a beat longer before turning away, broad shoulders sagging under unseen weight.

Lost in thought, Morgan trudges down the rutted lane. The mailbox appears around the bend, its splintered post revealing weathered wood beneath peeling white paint. Morgan walks past, his mind crowded with unanswered questions and whispered half-truths about the past.

Overhead, stars claim the sky in a dazzling display unspoiled by artificial light. Morgan continues on his way, blind to the celestial show above. His tunnel vision leaves the mailbox shrouded in the dust cloud rising behind him.

The letter meant for his absent mother waits between pages of Iso-Formations and Wishbone plays.

4

1

A steady thrum pulses through Morgan's chest long before the raucous party comes into view. Its chaotic siren song draws him around a last bend to face the unchecked mayhem bursting from this random student's house–whose parents surely know nothing of the scene inside.

He halts under a street light to check the girl's faded script on his palm. Nerves and excitement battle in his gut. The pounding beat becomes tangible, more felt than heard, as he nears the yard. An obstacle course of empty cups and passed out teens litters the damp grass. He breathes in deeply and steps up to the porch.

Beyond the threshold, a wave of sound and frantic motion swallows Morgan whole. Massive speakers shake with bass-like depth charges aimed at flesh and bone, forcing hearts to race. The open space teems with writhing teens, fractured by strobing lights above. Someone crashes into Morgan without pause. The press of bodies and assault on eardrums carries its own drug-like pull. The initial shock stings, yet the promise of escape keeps him pushing deeper, doubts melting away like ice in warm water.

A cup appears in his hand before he can think. He drinks without hesitation, liquid fire blooming in his empty stomach. He plunges further into the churning mass of dancers like a fish fighting current. His mind reels, grasping for sense amid the barrage against eyes, ears, and equilibrium.

2

Morgan breaks into the kitchen's relative calm, an island in this sea of chaos. He sets down his playbook and the forgotten envelope, marooned among flooded ashtrays and abandoned cups.

Cruel laughter adds to the uproar. His eyes land on a group of broad-shouldered figures holding court in a shadowy corner. Despite the ghoulish face paint, Nash Wheeler's sneer stands out. The ex-QB wears a full skeleton bodysuit, hood up, black sockets gleaming between painted bones. Noticing Morgan's stare, Wheeler raises his bottle in a mock salute before slinking away.

A curtain of curls breaks his focus as the girl with the odd birthmark appears. She reaches past him for a vodka bottle, decked out in 80s gear like the others, but with more authenticity–her eye shadow is spot-on.

Their eyes lock. Her smile turns playful. "Didn't think you'd show, new-boy," she half-yells over the cacophony. Her brow arches. Challenge or appraisal, Morgan can't tell.

Over thundering bass and shrill synths, Morgan strains to be heard. Sweaty bodies crash around them, spilling drinks. Stale beer mingles with the raw energy of adolescence, a pungent reminder of youth unleashed. Bottles and cans cover every inch of graffitied counters. The music rattles Morgan's bones.

She pours generous shots for both of them. "Brave of you to come when you don't know anyone!" she shouts in his ear.

Morgan shrugs, "I know you." He downs the shot, wincing.

"Then what's my name?

Morgan freezes, realizing he never asked.

"It's Ryley," she offers, letting him off easy.

The music swells louder. Bottles dance on the counter. Morgan leans in, lips grazing Ryley's ear. "Did you grow up here?" he yells.

Ryley's face twists in confusion. Cupping her mouth, she shouts, "What?!" It's futile. The noise is unbearable.

She jabs at the speakers, shaking her head. She mouths, "I can't hear you!" and throws up her hands. Then, with a follow me gesture, she points down the hall.

3

With the shutting of the bathroom door, the party's throbbing pulse fades to a muted beat. The chaos outside makes this cramped, humid space a welcome respite.

Beneath the flickering bulb lies a scene of chipped tiles, a rust-stained sink, and a grimy clawfoot tub. A pungent smell of stale bong water and vomit fills the air.

Ryley grabs the nearly empty vodka bottle from the sink's edge, splashing more shots into their cups. Liquor spatters the floor. Without a word, they slide down the peeling wall onto cracked linoleum.

Under the harsh light, Ryley studies Morgan's down-turned face. "Your eyes are blue," she states, her gaze probing.

Morgan bites his lip, nodding. Ryley's expression softens. "Don't be scared of me, new-boy."

Morgan meets her stare. "Why'd you invite me here?" he asks.

Ryley sips before countering, "What brought you to this boring-ass town, anyway?"

Morgan shrugs, looking away.

Ryley nudges him. "Not much for talking, huh?" she prods. "C'mon, tell me something real."

"Uh, these shots really burn."

"Weak. Not what I meant," she retorts.

"Okay, what do you mean by real?"

She pokes his arm. "Something you. You're not pulling off the brooding bad-boy act."

"I don't know..." Morgan groans, stumped by the pressure of the sudden cross-examination.

"Take me, for instance." Ryley leans forward, eyes bright. "As soon as I can, I'm buying a ticket to Washington and finding a hippie colony. The idea of rotting here, judged by parking lot women and gossip-hungry waitresses–it's not for me."

"Why hippies?" Morgan asks.

"Not shaving my legs to please society...that's true feminist power."

Morgan shrugs. "Sounds like you've got it all planned–"

"No," Ryley cuts in. "But choosing who you are based on character instead of your cul-de-sac, that's real."

The boy nods.

"Your turn," she urges, gulping their cheap vodka.

Morgan's eyes drift upward, sifting through memories. "Mom used to sit and tell us stories from our childhood. We'd wash dishes, laugh away evenings..." A faint smile ghosts on his lips.

Ryley catches the pain before he drowns it with a swallow. "It was fine when I was little, but I started hating those nights as I grew up," he continues, words blurring. "Felt like there were better things to do, other people to talk to."

His gaze goes distant, past the faded wallpaper. "But I remember this story about bringing my baby brother home. They gave him this hat, which was too big and kept slipping over his eyes."

Ryley refills his cup.

"So I took it off, tried cutting eye holes with safety scissors. Wasn't good with scissors then." His smile fades. "Somehow cut the whole hat in half trying to make those holes."

He swirls the liquor at the bottom of his cup. "Knew I'd get a beating when Mom saw. So I tried taping it back together, hoping no one would notice..."

"While I'm taping, it got stuck in Murph's hair, and he wails. Mom comes running, screaming for Dad. And Dad, who had just showered, comes racing out covered in soap and slips!" Morgan realizes he's laughing at something he'll never feel again. His grin fades into a nostalgic smile. He looks up to see Ryley gazing at him.

"You and your brother were close?" she asks.

The mirth leaves Morgan's eyes. He holds up his cup as the muffled music pulses through. "This tastes like shit."

"Russian shit." Ryley says, as if the country of origin makes it taste better.

"I like this song," Morgan says, his voice sharp, cutting the conversation.

Ryley bores into him. "Should I not have asked?" Her voice drops low.

Morgan's gaze flicks to hers, then falls. "No, it's fine," he mutters, but his rigid posture screams otherwise.

In the heavy quiet, Ryley reaches for his hand on his bent knee. Her fingertips explore his wrist, then arm. Morgan lifts his eyes, hesitant.

"Fix those hands, new-boy," she echoes. She leans in, pulled by an unseen force. Morgan stays frozen, neither fleeing nor advancing. His eyelids grow heavy as the space between them shrinks. Their breaths quicken, hearts syncing with the bass pulsing through the walls. Ryley's lips part, a breath from Morgan's.

"What's your name, new-boy?" The words float in the crackling air between them.

4

The kitchen floor clings to Wheeler's Converse as he stands behind the counter littered with bottles, pouring drinks for his boisterous crew. Drunken laughter stifles the atmosphere. Wheeler's eyes land on Morgan's battered playbook, left vacant on the table. He picks it up, fingers tracing the name scrawled across its worn surface.

Wheeler flips through the pages. The white envelope falls out and lands on the dirty floor. He picks it up and finds a photo of Morgan and Murph inside. A dark grin spreads across his face as a cruel plan forms.

The music's thunderous bass cuts off mid-beat. All noise in the house dies.

"Listen up, y'all!" Wheeler's voice booms. He waves people toward the kitchen with a sinister gleam. "We got ourselves a special introduction to make tonight!"

Excited murmurs ripple through the crowd as they shuffle, drawn by Wheeler's antagonistic tone.

The bathroom door swings open. Morgan steps out, his skin crawling at the weird quiet. The usual party noise has vanished, replaced by a tense energy. Ryley follows Morgan down the dim hallway, pulled toward the growing crowd in the living room. The house feels different now–like a trap about to spring.

Wheeler's voice drips with fake friendliness. "Let's give our new friend a proper welcome, shall we?" His words wrap around Morgan like a noose. He stops dead in the doorway, Ryley a shadow behind him. The crowd splits and hungry eyes lock onto Morgan.

A cup hits his back. Cold beer soaks his shirt, but it's nothing compared to the chill in his bones. The playbook at his feet, his lifeline in this mess, calls to him. He grabs it, holding it like a shield.

Wheeler unfolds the letter, letting the envelope with Ailea's name fall to the floor. He reads, twisting the private words into daggers. Each stab tearing Morgan open for everyone to see.

The laughter that follows isn't fun–it's the sound of Morgan's world falling apart, piece by awful piece.

Wheeler's mocking voice fills the room, dripping with false sincerity as he reads:

"'Ailea, I need you here. I'm walking around the world as half a man,'" he begins, pausing for dramatic effect. The crowd snickers.

"'Every night, I lie awake wondering if you're thinking of us, too. I'm haunted by Murph. The way he'd wake us in the middle of the night...afraid of monsters.'" Wheeler's tone is sickly sweet. "'I keep telling myself you'll come back, that this is temporary. But the days keep passing, and my world feels emptier than ever.'"

The partygoers hoot and jeer, but Wheeler presses on, twisting the knife deeper.

"'I'm trying to be strong for Morgan, but failing. He needs his mother. I see the hurt in his eyes.'" Wheeler's voice cracks in fake emotion, drawing cruel laughter from his audience.

"'Please, Ailea. We can fix this. Come home. I love–'"

Unable to take anymore, Morgan charges forward and shoves Wheeler, desperately grabbing the letter. Wheeler stumbles back, his grip tightening on the paper. As Morgan yanks hard, the letter tears, leaving half in Wheeler's grasp and half in Morgan's trembling hand.

Wheeler recovers, waving his piece of the letter like a trophy. "Oops! Butterfingers!" he taunts, his eyes gleaming with cruel delight.

Fury overriding his judgment, Morgan throws a wild, sloppy punch. Wheeler dodges the emotional blow, leering.

"C'mon, sweetheart!" he sneers.

Morgan throws a quick jab. His fist finds Wheeler's cheek.

Wheeler's face twists with rage, his bony knuckles clenching into a fist. Time seems to slow as he swings, his arm plummeting with vicious intent. Morgan sees it coming, but can't move fast enough. Pain explodes as a punch lands, his head whips to the side.

For a second, everything spins. Morgan's mouth fills with the sharp tang of blood, his sight going fuzzy. Before Wheeler strikes again, Ryley intervenes. She pushes Wheeler hard, sending him into a group of enormous football players. They catch him, shock written all over their faces.

In the following mess, Ryley grabs both pieces of the ripped letter off the floor. She moves fast and sure, shoving the torn paper back into Morgan's playbook as the house fills with stunned whispers and nervous energy. Grabbing Morgan's arm, she pulls him through the party, shoving drunk teens out of their way, leading him to the front door.

Behind, Wheeler turns to the fired-up crowd, flexing his arms like he's proud. "He hits like a fairy, too!" he yells. The mob bursts into mean laughter at Morgan's shame.

5

Putting distance between himself and the party house, Morgan ups his pace. The music fades, replaced by the night's hush. His footsteps echo off silent houses, each step carrying him further from the embarrassment-hell he left behind.

"Hey, wait up!" Ryley's voice calls after.

Morgan stops but doesn't face her. "What do you want?" he asks, humiliation simmering inside like a pot about to boil over.

Ryley catches up, her breath coming in short bursts. She grabs his arm to spin him around, her touch electric. Morgan avoids her eyes, focusing on a crack in the sidewalk, a loose thread on his sleeve–anything but her face.

"I never got to tell you something about me," she says. Her words just hang there, heavy with understanding.

Morgan shakes his head. The bitter taste of rejection coats his tongue. "Don't bother telling me what you think I want to hear. I don't need your pity," he mutters, each word sharp as broken glass.

Ryley tries to catch his focus, ducking her head to meet his lowered eyes. "That's not what this is," she insists. Her voice softens, a contrast to the hard edges of his pain. "Just come with me, okay?"

She waits, the moment stretching like a rubber band about to snap. Morgan lifts his stare, surrendering to the pull between them.

6

Side-by-side, they silently walk down the block. The night air wraps around them, crisp but comforting after the party's anarchy. Their pace slows as Ryley leads them up the walkway of a small, tidy home.

She pauses at the side gate, eyes darting to the dark, quiet house. "My dad's probably asleep already, so we gotta be quiet," she whispers.

Eager to avoid the porch light, they creep across the lawn and slip through the unlocked back door into the shadowy kitchen. Ryley kicks off her Keds, and Morgan follows suit. With hushed breath and bare feet, they tiptoe into the still house and up the stairs, through the short hall to Ryley's bedroom.

A floorboard creaks. The sound is piercing in the absence of other noise. They freeze, hearts pounding. Seconds stretch like hours as they strain to hear any sign of movement from the other rooms. The house remains unmoved, now a shell encasing their shared disquiet.

Ryley's hand finds Morgan's in the dark, her fingers intertwining with his. The warmth of her palm sends a jolt through his body, more sobering than any amount of cold night air. As she pulls him towards her room, he can't help but sense the tingle of unspoken possibilities.

Ryley opens her door just enough for them to squeeze through. Closing it with a soft click, she and Morgan let out their held breath.

Moonlight from the window casts a bluish glow over Ryley's room as she turns on a small bedside lamp. Morgan lingers by the door until she waves him deeper.

The soft, amber light illuminates an impressive collection of intricate dollhouses in varying shapes and sizes. The models occupy almost every surface–shelves, desk, dresser tops.

Morgan wanders around, peering into each perfectly constructed miniature world.

"My older sister used to collect these," Ryley explains from her perch on the quilted bed, picking at her jeans. "I always thought they were kinda stupid."

"Then why do you keep them?" Morgan asks. His eyes settle on a dollhouse lying cracked open on the floor–the only one in disarray.

Ryley's face falls, her voice dropping. "She uh...she died," she murmurs. The words hover, heavy and final.

Morgan looks back at the broken dollhouse, realization hitting home. "I'm sorry," he says, his voice barely above a whisper. The apology seems inadequate, but he doesn't know what else to say.

Ryley nods. "It was a while ago," she murmurs, but the pain in her voice suggests otherwise.

Morgan moves closer, drawn by an instinct he doesn't fully understand. He sits beside her on the bed, close enough to offer comfort but not so close as to intrude. Ryley lifts her head, her eyes meeting his. In the lamplight, he sees the vulnerability she's been hiding all night behind the '80s eyeliner and blush. It mirrors his own, a connection deeper than words.

"Tell me about her." Morgan surprises himself with his ask.

"We got into this dumb fight," she starts. "I snuck into her room one night to break her favorite house, to get back at her."

She shakes her head, ashamed. "That's when we found her. She was just...gone." Her voice cracks, and she wipes sudden tears with her hand. "I don't even remember what we fought about."

Morgan considers the shattered dollhouse. Then, he removes Murph's Matchbox car from his pocket and places it in the home's cracked garage bay.

He moves back to the bed and sits close beside Ryley in wordless thought. Their eyes meet and hold for a long, weighted moment, each seeing their shared pain reflected.

She reaches a hand toward his face, fingers hovering over the fresh bruise where Wheeler's fury struck. "Does it hurt?"

Morgan shakes his head. "Numb."

"This too?" She leans in.

The space between them crackles with electricity. Morgan's breath catches, his heart pounding so loud he's sure Ryley hears it. Her face is close enough to count each lash.

Time seems to slow, stretching this moment into eternity. The room fades away until there's nothing but Ryley–the warmth of her touch, the recognition in her gaze.

Morgan's hand moves of its own accord, cupping her cheek. His thumb brushes away a tear she didn't realize had fallen. His touch is delicate, as if she could break.

"No," he whispers. "This I feel."

Ryley's eyes search his face, looking for any sign of hesitation. Finding none, she closes the final distance between them.

Their lips meet softly at first, tentative and questioning. Then, like a dam breaking, the kiss deepens. It's desperate and healing all in the same, a wordless communication of all they've been holding back. Ryley peels Morgan's jacket away. They sink onto her quilt, drawn together like magnets finding their opposite pole. Morgan's hand hovers at her waist and his mind flashes to those awkward abstinence videos from middle school–stilted teens in dated costumes on a Grease reject set.

Ryley pulls back just enough to meet his eyes, both of them breathing hard, caught in the gravity of what could be–and all the unspoken things this choice would mean. His fingers brush her cheek, and she leans into his touch, but something in her eyes holds a question neither of them is ready to answer.

As Morgan sits up, his hand brushes something under the pillow. From beneath, he pulls a frilly apron emblazoned "Sandy's Diner" in flaking gold. They break apart, the absurdity piercing their bubble. Ryley meets his startled look and crumples against his chest, laughing hysterically.

"What happened to not becoming a gossipy waitress?"

"It's for side cash," she grins, acknowledging the irony.

"The anti-establishment girl has the most basic job," he muses.

Their laughter sputters as they kiss again, erasing the world beyond her room.

7

The first pale fingers of dawn creep through the gap in Ryley's tattered curtains. Morgan lies awake, his eyes tracing the contours of Ryley's face as she sleeps. The room smells of cheap perfume and the lingering scent of their night together.

She stirs, her eyelids fluttering. Morgan watches, heart quickening, as consciousness seeps into her features. Her eyes open, unfocused at first, before they settle on him. A smile tugs at the corners of her mouth.

"Hey," she murmurs, voice thick with sleep.

Morgan's hand hovers near her cheek. "Hey," he replies, his voice both tenderness and nerves.

Ryley stretches, wincing as she bumps against the wall. The twin bed creaks beneath them, a reminder of their cramped space. Morgan's gaze drifts from the faded band posters peeling from the walls to her cluttered dresser overflowing with a jumble of makeup compacts and well-worn paperbacks. A broken skateboard leans against the vanity mirror, its shattered deck misplaced next to the array of nail polish bottles.

His eyes drift back to Ryley's, emotions swirling in their depths. "Last night was..." he trails, searching for words.

Ryley's lips curl into a soft smile. "Yeah," she breathes, glancing at the dollhouses. "Nothing kills the mood quite like a hundred tiny plastic eyes watching."

Morgan snorts, his hand finding hers. "Pretty sure that one in the corner was about to call your dad."

"The whole Victorian family would've been scandalized," Ryley adds, and they both laugh, the tension breaking.

Her gaze drops, uncertainty flickering across her face. "Was it weird that we...you know. Stopped?"

Morgan shakes his head. "Nah, we're good," he says, voice low. "Besides, I've got enough performance anxiety without Barbie's dream house as an audience."

A comfortable calm settles between them, the awkwardness of their almost-moment fading into something softer.

Dressed, Morgan stands at the dollhouse, a plastic girl figurine between his fingers.

She gets up and leans against his back, tired yet content.

"Have you thought about college?" Morgan asks, eyes on the toy family in the battered house.

"Some. Doubt I'd get in," she sighs.

Morgan considers this, then sets the figurine girl down next to a little plastic boy before turning around to face her, brushing a tangled strand of hair from her eyes.

"You better split before my dad wakes up," she yawns.

Morgan bends down to grab his rumpled hoodie off the floor and pulls it over his head. Running a hand through his own messy locks, he gives Ryley a gentle, lingering kiss before grabbing Murph's old Matchbox car from the dollhouse drive.

"See you around," he mumbles.

He creeps to her bedroom window and slides it open. The sleepy morning songs of birds filter in from outside as he straddles the sill.

"Wait..." Ryley calls.

Morgan pauses there, glancing back at her delicate silhouette bathed in the warm sunrise.

"You can't walk away after a crappy '80s one-liner like that..."

Morgan cracks a smile. "Makes up since you forgot to tell me it was an '80s Halloween party last night." He resumes his climb down.

"Stay out of trouble, new-boy," she says with a playful smile.

5

1

Morgan approaches the overgrown driveway of the farm-house, eyes red and weary. The new wooden wall on the scorched shed stands stark against the decaying structures dotting the property.

The backdoor handle turns with a quiet rattle and he slips inside, dawn light seeping into the dreary kitchen.

He sets his worn football playbook on the cluttered counter, avoiding towers of empty beer cans and dirty dishes.

On the stove, a charred meal sends wisps of acrid smoke into the air. Wilke lies slumped across the kitchen table, unconscious and snoring, an empty whiskey bottle dangling from his hand.

Morgan shuts the door with care. The faint click rouses Wilke. He lifts his head, eyes unfocused.

"Thought you'd be back last night," he slurs, accusation thick in his voice.

Morgan freezes, then answers. "Plans changed."

"Should've called—" Wilke starts, interrupted by a wet cough.

Morgan ignores him, crossing to the stove. A pan sits smoking, its contents charred beyond recognition. "Did you pass out?" he asks, tossing empty cans into the overflowing trash with a clang.

Wilke lifts his head, squinting. "Did you drop the letter?" he mumbles.

Morgan stays silent, jaw tight, trying to block Wilke's presence. The tap drips steadily, each drop resounding in the tension. He stares out the grimy window, focusing on the distant treeline instead of the man behind him.

"Answer me, boy," Wilke growls, his voice rough from drink and lack of sleep.

Morgan's shoulders tense. He turns, facing his father with an icy stare. "No," he says, controlled. "I didn't drop your letter."

Wilke struggles to sit up, swaying in his chair. "Goddamnit, Morgan. One simple thing–"

"One simple thing?" Morgan interrupts, his voice rising. "Like making dinner without burning the house down? Like staying sober for one night?"

The air grows thick. Morgan's eyes flick to the fridge. "Go on, drink up."

"I'm handling it," Wilke mutters, the whiskey bottle dropping from his grip.

Morgan snatches it and chucks it into the trash. "Yeah. You're handling it great, Dad."

He turns to the sink, running the tap over the scorched pan. The water hisses and steams, filling the kitchen with the pungent smell of burnt food and broken promises.

Wilke lurches to his feet, unsteady. "I'll finish this."

Morgan spins around, eyes afire. "I've asked you one question this whole time," he snaps. "Why do you hate him so much?" He gestures, referencing the absent JD. "That's what you do, isn't it? When it gets rough, you just erase people?"

Wilke's face hardens. "You're asking me that?" he growls. "After everything..." Their silence pulses with unfinished thoughts. "You're just a kid. You don't know what you're talking about," he growls, voice low and dangerous, trudging away.

Morgan stands his ground. "Don't I? Mom. JD. Who's next... Murph?" His voice echoes in the grim kitchen like a thunder crack.

No reply.

"That's what I thought. This is just your new normal," the boy adds coldly.

"Normal is loving each other," Wilke retorts, bitterness lacing his words. "Which I've always done for you. I didn't turn away like he did when things went bad." He points toward an old photo of JD hanging on the fridge.

Shaking his head in disapproval, Morgan's face displays his disgust. "You haven't helped me," he spits, shaking with defiance. "JD's been more of a father lately than you ever were—"

Wilke recoils. His face twists into an ugly sneer. "Watch, pray you don't disappoint him, too," he snarls. "That man, who should've stood by me, turned away and let the world tear me apart."

The sink's steam has filled the room with a cloud. The smoke alarm's piercing sound fills the kitchen, bouncing off the walls. Neither of them move a muscle.

"Whatever happened with you and Pa, you're doing a fine job repeating it with me," Morgan shouts over the noise. He spins and storms off.

Wilke scrapes out the ruined pan, slopping ashy water across the counter. He shuts off the tap, but it keeps dripping.

Morgan bursts into his room, slamming and locking the door. He slumps against it, eyes shut, willing his heart to slow. His hand finds the Matchbox car in his pocket–his lone keepsake. He turns it over, sinking into bittersweet memories.

2

He's back in the hallway of their old home, hovering outside Murph's closed bedroom door.

Morgan pushed the door open. Inside, his little brother sat on the floor, playing with his cars.

"Which one's your favorite?" Morgan asked, hesitant.

Murph retreated into his inner world, avoiding eye contact with his big brother. Then, like a switch flipped, he brightened. He shoved a red car into Morgan's open hand.

"1967 Pontiac GTO!" Murph exclaimed, his face splitting a grin.

"That right?" Morgan asked, mirroring his brother's excitement. "What about..." He selected another miniature muscle car from the sea of vehicles on the carpet. "This one? Know what this is?"

Murph snatched the car without pause, holding it high. "1972 Dodge Charger!" His voice rang through the room.

Morgan's smile grew. "No fooling you," he said, his laughter genuine. He grabbed another vehicle. "Tell me about this one..."

Spurred by his brother's interest, Murph inched closer, keen to showcase his prized collection.

Now, the car's familiar weight and color anchor Morgan in fonder memories for a short while before the present-day troubles creep back in.

A sharp knock at the door startles him from the reverie. He looks up to see Wilke, his face a mixture of discomfort and determination.

"Hey," Wilke says, his voice gruff but tinged with something softer. "Can we talk?"

Morgan turns away, staring straight ahead. "Think we just did," he mutters.

Wilke shifts uncomfortably, leaning against the door. "Look, I...I messed up back there," he begins, the words seeming to cost him. "I...it's just..." He trails off, running a hand through his hair. "We clearly have some things to talk about."

Morgan remains silent.

Wilke sighs. "I know I'm not great at this. But I want to try. How about we grab some dinner? Just you and me. We can...clear the air a bit."

Morgan's laugh is short and bitter. "Clear the air? Like that's gonna fix anything."

"Morgan, please," his voice soft. "I'm trying here."

Morgan peers up, his eyes hard. "Where was all this 'trying' before?"

The man's face falls.

After a long, tense moment, Morgan speaks, guarded. "One dinner. There's something I need to get off my chest, too."

Relief washes over, tempered with caution. "That's all I'm asking for, kid. Know a good place around here?"

3

Morgan stands at Sandy's Diner's bathroom sink, staring intently at his reflection. The noticeable bruise marks his left cheek, an angry purple stain against his skin. He touches it, wincing at the tenderness. His fingers linger on the discolored skin, tracing its outline like a map of his recent misfortunes.

The fluorescent lights cast a harsh glow, making the bruise seem even more pronounced. Morgan leans closer, tilting his head to see it from different angles. It's unavoidably visible, a badge of shame or defiance; he's unsure.

Taking a deep breath, Morgan attempts to smile. The result is brittle, cracking at the edges, and never quite reaching his eyes. "It's fine. Everything's fine," he whispers. The words sound superficial even to his ears.

He splashes cold water on his face, avoiding the bruised area as if washing away the evidence might erase its truth. The icy shock brings him back to the moment.

Morgan walks through the dining room, each step heavier than the last. He rejoins his father at their booth by the window, where Wilke nurses a coffee like it's his lifeline.

"Who gave you the shiner?" Wilke says, noticing the black and blue on Morgan's cheek.

"Dad," Morgan begins, his voice straining for a confidence he doesn't feel, "I know you don't believe me, but I'm...I'm doing really good, actually. Here. And with football, I mean."

Wilke's eyebrow arches, skepticism infiltrating. "Is that so?" he asks, his tone flat and unimpressed.

Morgan's words tumble out in a desperate rush, like a dam breaking. "Yeah. Yeah, for sure. I mean, you know, could it suddenly flip shit and get super dark? Yeah, you know. I mean, it could, but...I feel like I've found this, like, balance, where I'm happy and focused, and I'm not, like...looking to anybody else for that validation, you know?"

"The point is making the team–" Wilke begins, but Morgan cuts him off.

"Yeah. Of course, yeah. And my general well-being," he adds hastily.

"Which starts with proving yourself on the field, not in the front yard with that grandfather of yours."

"Yeah. And I've done that. I'm the starter. Officially. That's good, right?" Morgan says, his words tumbling like leaves caught in a sudden gust.

Wilke's eyes narrow. "You just said you found an amazing balance and weren't looking for validation."

Morgan stutters, caught in his own web of half-truths. "I...I did. I have. I mean, but I'm not perfect, you know, so. I'm trying, though. Harder."

"Morgan." Wilke's voice cuts, sharp as a knife. A beat passes, heavy with unspoken friction. "You haven't even played a real game. You're untested. What team is going to follow you if you lack confidence?"

A chuckle escapes Morgan's throat. "I feel like you're not listening to what I'm saying."

"Morgan, I don't think you're listening to what you're saying," Wilke retorts, his words landing like body blows.

"I feel like that's physically impossible."

Wilke's patience wears thin. "To what? Talk some bullshit?"

Morgan scoffs, the sound more pained than amused. "Huh. You know, that's what I don't understand about the world. There are tons of people who, you know, work hard and sometimes their life is good. And sometimes life's just bad, you know? It's fucking life. There's ups and downs to this shit, but, I mean, whether you believe me or not, I'm, like...I'm good."

"Yeah, yeah, you said that," Wilke dismisses.

"Yeah, it's not like I'm not trying. I'm just...I'm doing my best," Morgan insists, his voice trailing.

"My point is you haven't earned it."

A long beat passes. Morgan finally makes eye contact, his gaze a mixture of defiance and hurt. "Yeah, well, I guess a good job, son, is impossible for you, isn't it?"

Wilke takes a long sip of coffee, his hands shaking slightly. He leans back, his voice filled with something softer, maybe regret. "Okay, I'm not saying you're a bad player. We've both got our issues, and we're gonna be struggling with those issues for the rest of our lives. That's a fact. The problem is, you're looking at the wrong people for an answer."

Morgan frowns, glancing around the quiet diner. "Yeah."

A few clinks of silverware from a nearby booth. Then Morgan's voice comes again, timid this time, almost reluctant. "Dad, can I tell you something?"

"What?"

Morgan's eyes flick around the table. "Like, for real, if…if I say some dark shit, you're not gonna freak out or something?"

Wilke shifts in his seat. "Well, I'm not a therapist," he jabs.

They exchange a meaningful glance, years of misunderstandings conveyed in an instant.

Morgan doubles back, "You're a–you're a trip…forget it." His words trail off, the momentary courage fading.

Wilke presses, his curiosity piqued. "What were you going to say?"

Morgan retreats. "It doesn't matter. It's stupid."

"All right, I'm sorry," Wilke says softly. "Come on. What were you gonna say? Say it."

The boy's defense rises again. "Nah, I don't wanna."

Wilke's hardens, "Say it."

Morgan reaches for his glass of orange juice, buying time. The ice clinks as he takes a sip. The sweet-tart flavor contrasts the bitterness of the conversation.

Every word Morgan utters is a struggle, dredged up from within. "When I'm, uh, when I'm on the field, you know, when I'm present, like a part of the team, I constantly think about making them accept me. But it's darker than that." He pauses, tracing invisible patterns on the table. "And, uh, you can say that I'm looking for answers and comfort in the wrong places, but to tell you the truth, football is probably the only reason I haven't given up completely."

The confession is lead. Wilke's face shifts, surprise giving way to a grim satisfaction. "Oh," he says, the word barely more than a breath. Then, after a long exhale, "Now we're talkin'. Now you're being real. Now you're being honest. Because this whole bullshit about finding balance, that ain't true. That's a lie."

Morgan's head snaps up, defiance building. "It's not a lie."

"It's a lie, whether you know it or not, but more importantly, I don't give a fuck to hear it."

"Yeah, whatever, man."

"Whatever, *man*?" Wilke echoes, his voice dangerously low.

Morgan chuckles, frail and fragile.

Wilke's words come in a torrent, each striking like a physical blow. "Whatever, man. Listen, boy, I've been standing in your shoes since you were born. I've lived a whole fuckin' life to get to this diner to sit across from your arrogant ass, so don't you ever whatever me. You're seventeen. You don't know shit. You think you're tough? I'm tougher. You want to give up? Same fuckin' story here. You want to know why? You want to know why? I'll tell you why. 'Cause you don't know how to live life. You don't have the tools. You're too busy running around, trying to bullshit everybody into thinking you're tough and you don't give a fuck, when in reality, you give so much of a fuck, you can't even bear to be alive. So, guess what? New rule. No more wasting my fuckin' time. You wanna quit? Quit. But the least you can do is be honest. Own that shit."

The diner holds its breath. Like a chastised child, he loses his earlier bravado and is left raw and exposed. When he speaks, his voice is a whisper. "Okay."

"You feel me?"

Morgan's response is curt, barely more than a whisper. "Yep."

A few tables over an elderly couple clear their throats and shoot mean glances.

Wilke's tone shifts, becoming almost gentle. "Why are you really struggling?"

"I don't know. Can't stop my mind from racing."

"Racing about what?" Wilke presses.

"Everything," Morgan replies, his voice empty.

Wilke leans forward, his eyes intense. "Be specific."

Morgan considers the question, weighing his answer. The diner seems to fade away, leaving only this moment of raw honesty between them. Finally, he speaks, his words tinged with a profound, aching hurt. "All the things I remember about Murph and all the ways I feel like I'm failing to live up to you."

Wilke's expression softens as the words register. "Why didn't you talk to me before now?"

Morgan huffs, "Just...honestly, I didn't think you'd listen."

Wilke exhales. Long held misunderstandings sink into the formica tabletop between them. "Yeah. Man. Okay,"

Morgan's next question comes out of nowhere, raw and vulnerable. "Do you even want me on the team?"

"What kind of question is that?"

"Do you?" Morgan presses, his voice just barely audible.

Frustration colors Wilke's response. "Of course I do."

Morgan's voice is quiet and tearful, a child's pain wrapped in a teenager's body. "Then why have you never showed up?"

The question floats across the booth, unanswered. Wilke's face is a mask of conflicting emotions: regret, frustration, unspoken love. He manages a single word. "Murph–"

Just then, Ryley enters the diner, hair a mess and disheveled. She's clearly late for her shift. Morgan quickly wipes water from his eyes. A fleeting moment of vulnerability.

Wilke notices Morgan's change and raises an eyebrow, his earlier frustration forgotten. "Who's that?" he asks, his tone filled with curiosity and something harder to define.

Morgan stumbles over his words, caught off guard. "What? No, I...it's nothing."

"I'm not blind," Wilke says, knowingly.

"Dad–" Morgan starts.

"–Maybe you just think I'm stupid..."

Morgan's response is defensive. "She's just a girl from school."

"Yeah, just a girl...so was your mother..."

"There's nothing between us," Morgan insists, his cheeks flushing.

"Right...she the reason you never came home last night?"

Morgan's embarrassment turns. "What's next, another birds and the bees talk?"

"Christ, son, you're right; what do I care? Fool around or don't, but do us both a favor and quit being so goddamn coy."

They sit, staring at each other, then look away together, the moment stretched tight like a rubber band.

Just then, Ryley approaches their table with a coffee pot, her presence a sudden intrusion into their private war. "Can I top that off?" she asks in a flat voice.

"Sure thing, sweetheart," Wilke replies, his tone light.

As Ryley fills the mug, Wilke stares at Morgan with a half-grin. The moment is palpably awkward with earlier confrontation still simmering beneath the surface.

"You know what? I'm gonna go use the head," Wilke announces. He stands, wobbling slightly, and moves toward the restroom. Morgan watches him go, his face a mask of mortification.

Once Wilke disappears, Ryley takes his spot in the booth. She tucks her knees into her chest and lets out a sigh. "Don't think that coffee is doing much for him anyway," she says, her voice tinged with sympathy.

A quiet moment passes. Morgan watches her awkwardly, unsure how to navigate this sudden shift in company.

"So, what were you guys talking about?"

"Nothing really," Morgan replies, voice soft.

"Why were you crying?" Ryley prods.

Embarrassment. "What? I wasn't."

"Looked like it when I walked by."

"It's sweat," he covers.

Ryley squints. "...it's like fifty degrees here. Sandy keeps it freezing."

"I mean, just warm-blooded, I guess." A shitty cover.

Ryley's lips quirk into a half-smile. "You're weird, new-boy."

"Yeah, I guess," he admits, self-deprecation in his tone.

A pained hush stretches between them, fraught with unspoken possibilities. It's an awkward holdover from the night they shared. Ryley breaks it, her voice carrying a note of admiration. "That was badass of you to take on Wheeler at the party, by the way. Never told you that."

Morgan's hand moves unconsciously to his bruised cheek, a physical reminder of that confrontation.

Ryley chews on a thought, her eyes distant. A long moment passes. Morgan sets a wadded-up straw packet on the table, watching it un-kink.

"You know anything about iguanas?" Ryley asks.

Morgan slows. "Iguanas?"

"Yeah. They're cool as shit, you know that?" her eyes light up with enthusiasm.

With a bemused expression, Morgan shakes his head.

Ryley leans in, her voice taking on a conspiratorial tone. "They can do this thing where they hold their breath for up to four hours. Lets them stay underwater for so long. They can hide."

"Wouldn't know anything about them..." Morgan mutters, his voice trailing off.

Ryley's gaze sharpens, becoming almost unnervingly perceptive. "I think you've been holding your breath for longer than you realize." She studies him. Her eyes seem to peer into his soul.

A ding breaks the spell. Wilke exits the diner.

Morgan lets out the breath he hadn't realized he was holding. He pivots around to see his dad in the parking lot, heading toward the truck.

Quickly fishing in his pocket, Morgan drops a few random coins onto the table. "I'm sorry, I can't pay you, he..."

Ryley waves him off. "Screw it. Sandy owes me overtime for tonight, anyway."

Morgan exits the booth and heads to the door, quick and urgent.

"Hey, new-boy..." Ryley calls after him.

Morgan looks back, caught between two worlds.

Ryley's parting words are a gentle challenge and a lifeline all at once. "You should come over more."

4

An incessant pounding invades Morgan's dreams, dragging him from sleep. As consciousness returns, Murph's voice fades into the recesses of his waking mind.

A hammer's steady rhythm penetrates the thin windowpane. The boy rises from the sagging mattress, drawn by the sound.

He descends the stairs and steps into the overgrown yard, shoes half-on. JD kneels in the dirt, driving the final stake into an intricate web of ropes.

Morgan studies the odd structure, confused. "What's this?"

JD dusts the earth from his jeans. "Stable feet keep your ass upright instead of in the grass," he states. "We're doing stance and footwork for 30 minutes before school."

Morgan tosses his head. "Forget it, I have practice after–"

"You have a mandatory half hour with me first," JD says, pointing to the house. "Get a ball and come back."

Morgan catches Wilke's stern gaze from the kitchen window. "Fine. Twenty minutes," Morgan concedes. JD nods, satisfied.

His whistle pierces the morning air.

At JD's word, the boy sprints toward the rope barrier. He high-steps through the pattern, pivoting left as directed, but plants a foot wrong mid-stride and snags a tether. He crashes down hard, landing chest-first with a winded grunt.

JD blows his whistle, shaking his head. "Up, reset," he calls.

Morgan rolls over and stands, brushing his grazed palms. Without excuse, he limps back to start, pressed lips betraying frustration.

"Eyes up, focus," JD commands as Morgan readies. "Don't let a fall make you gun-shy. Again."

The dew-damp grass soaks through Morgan's sneakers as he resets his stance, leaning forward, ready to drive.

"Remember, it's all about control," JD says. "Quick steps, light feet. You're dancing, not stomping."

Morgan nods, trying to mask his irritation. He bounces on his toes, shaking out his limbs.

The faint scent of bacon drifts from the kitchen window, a reminder of the breakfast he's missing.

JD's whistle shrieks. Morgan surges forward, his feet finding a rhythm as he weaves through the first section of ropes. Left, right, crossover. His breath comes in controlled bursts.

"Good!" JD calls. "Now, change direction!"

Morgan pivots, nearly losing his balance. He recovers, pushing through the burning in his calves. Sweat beads on his forehead despite the cool morning.

As he nears the end of the course, fatigue sets in. His foot catches a rope, and he stumbles, the ground rushing to meet him. He hits with a thud that knocks the wind from his lungs.

Lying there, grass tickling his face, Morgan hears the distant call of a mourning dove. He allows himself a moment of self-pity before rolling to his back.

JD approaches, offering a calloused hand. "You're thinking too much," he says as he pulls Morgan to his feet. "Trust your instincts. Your body knows what to do."

Morgan brushes off his clothes, wincing at the sting in his palms. He glances toward the house, half-hoping to see his father, but the kitchen window stands empty now.

"Once more," JD says, moving back to his position. "This time, feel the course. Don't just see it."

Exhaling, Morgan returns to the starting point. He closes his eyes, visualizing the path ahead. As JD's whistle shrieks, Morgan launches forward, determined to conquer the challenge before him.

5

The whistle slices the twilight like a knife. Coach Tully's command lords over, and the team drops as one. Their bodies hit the turf with a collective thud, muscles straining as they push up and down. The rhythm of their movements matches the pounding of their hearts.

Two sharp blasts stop the intensity. The boys freeze, chests heaving. Coach Tully stalks before them, his eyes hard as flint. Sweat glistens on their faces, mingling with the fading light.

"Game this weekend," he barks. "What kind of day?"

Their response thunders, a battle cry born of exhaustion and determination: "A great day to be alive!"

A ghost of approval flickers across Tully's face. "Huddle up," he commands. "Time to run some plays."

The team splits, a well-oiled machine dividing into its parts. The offensive unit forms a tight knot of a huddle, pads clattering as they press close. Their breaths come in ragged, hot, damp gasps in the cooling air.

Morgan stands apart, a loose thread in the team's fabric. His uncertainty radiates off him in waves.

Coach Tully's eyes lock onto his stray player. "Browdy!" The name cracks like a whip. Morgan's feet carry him toward the sideline.

"Ever been in an offensive huddle, son?" Tully's questions.

Morgan's lack of response is answer enough. Shame colors his face, visible even in the fading light.

Tully's hand lands on his shoulder. "After every down," he starts, "You come straight back here. Wait for my call. Clear?"

The words sink into Morgan like roots, promising either growth or strangulation.

"I give you the play, you take it to the huddle and call it twice: once to the center and line, then again to the backs, got it?"

Morgan's nod is a promise, his eyes never leaving Coach's face. The responsibility settles on him like an ill-fitting uniform.

"We'll start simple," Coach decides, his voice gravel and steel. "Twins right formation. 32 dive, on one."

Morgan's feet carry him to the huddle, hope fluttering in his chest. It dies as he reaches the wall of bodies. He is not welcome here in this fortress of flesh and sweat-soaked jerseys. He forces his way in, elbows sharp, desperation sharper. The circle shifts, begrudging accommodation that seems more like rejection.

"Twins right formation. 32 dive on–"

The center breaks away, a ship cutting its mooring. Morgan's words trail off, lost in the void left behind.

He rallies, straining against the tide of indifference. "Twins right, 32 di–"

Wheeler cut him off. "We heard it the first time."

The huddle dissolves, and players drift to their positions slow and disorganized.

On the sideline, Coach Tully's face darkens like an approaching storm. "What the hell was that?" The question cracks, a whip of authority against blatant disrespect.

Morgan reaches the line of scrimmage, pulse thundering in his ears. The other players' glares pierce him, a gauntlet of scorn and disdain. Their contempt hangs thick, choking him.

He forces out the word "Down." The linemen drop into position, shoulder pads crunching like bones breaking.

His tongue is swollen, and his mouth is dry as dust. "H-hike!" The command shatters, his voice betrays him with a pubescent crack.

Before the center can move, Coach Tully's whistle cries. Morgan's head pivots toward the sound, a puppet on a string.

"Browdy!" Coach's voice carries. His finger jabs out, a sword pointing the way to Morgan's execution.

Low and cruel laughter ripples through the team. Morgan rips off his helmet, each step toward Coach an eternity of humiliation.

"Have you never called a play before this moment?"

The question hangs between them, a chasm Morgan can't bridge. The field stretches behind him, a battlefield where he's already lost. His head dips, a silent admission. Shame radiates in waves.

Coach Tully forces composure. "One warning," he growls. "Shout 'hike' again, you'll forget what a football feels like. Clear?"

Morgan nods.

Coach exhales, his breath carrying the remnants of frustration. "Green means live cadence," he continues. "Yell numbers, scream 'hut' fourteen times, I don't care. But the next 'hut' after 'Green' is the snap. Understand?"

Determination to get it right. Coach waves him off, a dismissal and a challenge. "Try again," he orders. "Make me believe you belong here."

Morgan takes his place behind center, a new presence in his stance. "Down," he calls, voice steady. "Green 18! Green 18! Hut!"

The ball slaps into his hands. He pivots, driving it into the halfback's chest. The runner explodes through the line.

Coach's whistle rings out, approval in its pitch. "There we go. Congrats gentlemen, you just graduated kindergarten!"

Wheeler jogs back to the huddle, brushing past Morgan with a forceful shoulder-check. Morgan stands firm, smoothing his jersey before calling the next play.

JD watches from the fence, his eyes gleam, a silent nod to Morgan's resilience.

6

The GTO's engine thrums, a counterpoint to Morgan's aching muscles. The brutal practice lingers in every fiber of his being, but something else takes root–a seedling of progress pushing through the soil of doubt. His jersey clings to his skin, still damp with sweat and the memory of those countless drills.

As JD drives, a nameless pull tugs at Morgan's chest. "Hey," he starts, voice neutral. "Think you could drop me somewhere? Gonna see a...friend."

JD knocks off the pretense. "This 'friend' got a pretty face?"

"Ryley," he admits, the name barely a whisper. "It's nothing."

JD watches, letting the air stretch thin. Then, "I ain't your chauffeur," he warns, a hint of amusement softening the words. "But I suppose I can drop you on the way."

Relief breaks across Morgan's face like dawn.

The car carries them through the twilight, each mile distancing them from the exhausting day. JD steers them through the gathering night. In the passenger seat, Morgan sits poised between two worlds–the familiar pain of the field behind him, the mysterious terrain of Ryley ahead.

Neon signs blur past until the welcoming glow of Sandy's Diner beams to life. The radio crackles, some old country song about missed chances fading in and out. Morgan's pulse quickens as JD slows the car.

"Here's your stop, Romeo," JD says, quirking an eyebrow.

Morgan nods, unable to speak. His hand rests on the door handle, cool metal grounding him in the moment.

"You gonna sit here all night? Go on now."

Morgan takes a deep breath, calming his nerves. "Thanks," he manages. He steps out, the car door slam echoing in the quiet street.

The GTO's engine growls as JD pulls away, leaving Morgan motionless as the taillights fade into the distance.

A memory flashes, sharp and unexpected. Years ago, slouched on the couch, flipping channels, he caught a documentary about hitchhikers in the 1970s. Grainy footage of kids with backpacks, thumbs out on dusty highways–freedom and danger wrapped up in one gesture.

One guy's story stuck with him. How he'd left everything behind on a whim. Stepped into a stranger's car and found himself. The guy's eyes, bright with remembered wildness, haunted Morgan for days.

Now, on this quiet street, Morgan feels that same electric possibility. No backpack, no highway. Hell, no comparison at all, really. Controlling the moment felt good; he can't deny that.

7

The buzz of the diner's late-night crowd sounds soft in the background as Morgan and Ryley sit on the flat roof, their legs dangling over the edge. The faint smell of grease and coffee from the vents wafts below. A bottle of cheap whiskey passes between them, its amber contents glowing in the street light.

Ryley squints at the starry sky, then points upward. "You see that cluster of stars there? Looks kind of like a spoon?"

Morgan follows her gaze, tilting his head. "Uh, maybe?"

"That's the Big Dipper," Ryley says confidently. "Or wait...maybe it's the Little Dipper. I always get them mixed up."

Morgan chuckles. "Could be a ladle for all I know."

"A cosmic ladle," Ryley muses. "Stirring up the universe's soup."

They share a laugh, the sound echoing in the empty parking lot below.

"You know," Morgan says, "I tried to make soup in the microwave once. Ended up with a small fire and a furious mom."

Ryley snorts. "Genius."

"Hey, I make a mean PB&J," he defends with a grin.

"Ah, the pinnacle of fine dining," she teases. "New game...*Would You Rather.* You go."

Morgan thinks, the whiskey warming his chest. "Okay...would you rather always speak in rhymes or always speak in questions?"

Ryley laughs. "Speak in questions? How hard could that be? Would it drive everyone crazy? Including me?" She grins. "Your turn. Would you rather be able to teleport but only to places you've been before or be able to fly but only as fast as you can run?"

"Easy, teleport. Think about it. I could revisit all my greatest hits. Like that time, I accidentally walked into the girls' locker room my freshman year. Except this time, I'd bring popcorn."

Ryley raises the bottle to salute, "to missed opportunities."

Morgan leans back on his palms, the rough texture of the roof grounding him. "Would you rather...never be able to taste food again or never be able to feel textures?"

Ryley wrinkles her nose. "That's evil." She takes a swig from the bottle. "I guess...never feel textures. Food's too important."

"Even my world-famous PB&Js?" Morgan teases.

"Especially those," Ryley laughs. Their eyes meet, and something electric passes between them. She looks away first, clearing her throat. "My turn. Would you rather know how you die or when you die?"

The question settles. Morgan's smile fades as he considers it. "When," he says, his voice low. At least then I could try to make it count, you know?"

Ryley nods. "Yeah, I get that."

Peace stretches between them, broken only by the hum of the neon sign and the occasional passing car. Morgan watches Ryley's fingers trace patterns on the roof's surface, wondering what ghosts dance in her mind.

"Would you rather," he starts, his voice softer now, "be able to read minds or be invisible?"

Ryley snorts. "Please, I already feel invisible most of the time."

The confession slips out before she can stop it. Morgan's hand finds hers, a gentle squeeze conveying more than words could.

"I see you," he whispers.

Ryley's breath catches. For a moment, they're suspended in time, two souls recognizing something in each other that the rest of the world has missed. "You ever wonder what it's all for?" she asks, her voice unassuming.

Morgan glances at her, then back out at the empty parking lot. "What what's for?"

"This," Ryley gestures at the town before them. "All of it. The whole damn circus."

Morgan lets out a humorless chuckle. "Every damn day."

Ryley pulls her knees up to her chest, hugging them close. "I used to think I had it all figured out, you know? Be the responsible one, take care of everyone else. My dad, my little sister..." She trails off, her eyes distant. "But now? I don't know. Sometimes I feel like I'm just...here. Existing."

Morgan nods, understanding more than he can express. He takes the bottle but doesn't drink. "Yeah, I get that. After Murph..." He pauses, swallowing hard. "It's like, who am I supposed to be now? What's my purpose?"

Ryley looks at him, her eyes softening. "You're not just Murph's brother, you know."

"I don't even think I was that," he says. "I failed at protecting him. I don't know what that makes me now."

Ryley reaches out, her hand finding Morgan's. "Maybe we can't save everyone," she whispers, her voice fragile. "Maybe we just focus on trying to survive ourselves." She thinks a moment longer. "Actually, screw surviving. Let's live it up while we can, you know? Make some crazy memories, do stupid stuff we'll laugh about later. If the world's going to hell anyway, might as well have some fun before it does."

Morgan's fingers intertwine with hers, "And how do we do that?"

She shrugs, a smirk playing on her lips. "No clue. I just know I don't want to spend whatever time we have left just...existing. But hey, at least we're figuring it out together, right?"

Morgan smiles back, feeling a spark of something–hope, maybe—for the first time in a long while. "Yeah, I guess we are."

Right now, being lost together is enough. "Your turn," Ryley says, her voice a little shaky.

8

Carrying a twelve-pack of beer and trash, Wilke walks down the creaking steps of the back porch towards the overflowing bin.

Reaching the barrel, he pauses and regards the unopened alcohol with conflicted eyes. But then, with a definitive grunt, he drops the entire case into the garbage atop stained paper plates and scraps of food.

As he turns to leave, a sudden breeze kicks up, freeing a torn piece of paper from the bin. He watches it flutter across the overgrown yard and sighs, following to retrieve it. But after a few steps, his progress halts.

A weathered football waits, lying in the grass just ahead. He stares at the leather oval, color leached by years. Stepping closer, he bends to pick up the ball with something approaching reverence. With rough, work-worn fingers he traces over the laces and squeezes as if testing the seams, apparent muscle memory guiding the ritual. Nearby, the empty tire swings sway back and forth with a creaking rhythm. He watches their hypnotic motion, the past calling.

With a head shake, he carries the football back to the shed, a relic from better times. But an invisible tether holds him in place a moment more.

His shoulders square. Rocking back, he launches the ball high toward one of the suspended tires with a practiced snap. It falls just short, landing in the dirt.

"You planted your feet all wrong," comes Morgan's quiet voice from behind.

Wilke whirls in surprise to see his son standing by the trash cans, half cast in shadow.

"You planted wrong, so your throw was off balance," Morgan continues. "Should never throw deep off your back foot."

He strides forward until he and Wilke stand side-by-side, facing the tire swing. Morgan shows proper foot placement, miming the throwing motion step-by-step.

"Drop back, plant firm on your left then drive forward into the pass," he explains, eyes focused ahead. "One, two, three, four."

Wilke watches, mirroring Morgan's movements for an instant. But just as quick, his face shutters, stooping to snatch up the wind-blown paper scrap instead and stalks back toward the house.

"First game's coming up, you know," Morgan calls out to Wilke's retreating backside. "Saturday's gonna be my first real game... and I'm scared that all I'm going to be thinking about is him," he admits, blinking hard against the burning in his eyes.

Wilke pauses with his hand on the screen door, listening over his shoulder as Morgan continues.

"Everywhere I go, I see him," Morgan whispers, tears welling again at the ever-present loss. "When the house gets quiet, and I can't sleep...that's when he haunts me."

Wilke turns, a shared pain carved across his rugged features. Only the muted sounds of evening insects fill the space between father and son.

Then, Wilke sighs, releasing a great weight. "I never blamed you for what happened to your brother, Morgan," he says, the absolution coming late. "Not once."

Morgan inhales as if struck by relief, a foreign feeling. He swallows hard around the tightness in his throat, searching Wilke's face for deception but finding only earnest remorse in the older man's tired eyes.

Some deep vein of anguished words, too long dammed up, now ruptures unchecked. "You told me to watch him and make sure he got to the truck safe," Morgan chokes out. "But I screwed up. I, I got mad and pushed him. It was one damn second..."

His face crumples as great heaving sobs wrack his frame at last. Wilke reaches out to brace his buckling son, guiding them to sit on the cold porch boards. He grips Morgan close, rocking the weeping boy against his chest.

"I just took it all and pissed it—" Morgan cries, voice thick with recrimination and loss. "The time I had left with him. I-I was too embarrassed having him around for who he was. And now I can't ever make that up..."

Wilke's eyes mist over as Morgan clings to him. "Listen to me—it was a terrible accident, nothing more," he asserts, as much for his own absolution. "Could've happened to anyone. We all failed."

He clutches his son close. And despite the neglect between them, a silent pact forms under the fragile porch light.

9

The whistle blast from Coach Tully sends the defense into position. Cleats crunch grass as players lower into stance, poised for the signal.

Coach pulls Morgan close on the sideline. "FB West Right, Slot 372 Y Stick," he commands. "On one."

Morgan's eyes lock with focus.

"Three-step drop," Coach stresses. "Nothing fancy."

At the nod, Morgan sprints to the huddle, shoulders straight with purpose. The plays click in his mind–building blocks of a larger vision: win the damn scrimmage.

Watching from the sidelines with crossed arms, JD notes Morgan's emerging leadership. His hat casts shadows over angular features, but approval glints in the old scout's mug.

Coach Tully cups his hands. "Execute, boys!"

The offense stands in casual circles when Morgan jogs up. They close ranks, ignoring the new quarterback.

Morgan's jaw sets. He shoves into their midst, earning hostile jabs. But he holds ground at the center.

"FB West Right, Slot 372 Y Stick, on one," Morgan announces over the grumbling. He meets each glare, refusing intimidation. Only Nolan "Rabbit" Hayes offers a supportive nod.

Rabbit, a gangly sophomore, stands five feet tall. Empathy shines behind his thick-rimmed glasses, setting him apart from hardened teammates.

As others leer at Morgan buckling his helmet, Rabbit gives an encouraging pat and gap-toothed smile. Despite limbs that tangle more than make plays, earnest goodness radiates from the player.

The team breaks apart, brushing past Morgan up to the line. They take position with defiant laziness, their message clear–the outsider remains unwelcome.

Under center, Morgan's hands quiver as he awaits the ball.

The snap comes late. The nose guard explodes through the A-gap, slamming into Morgan as he pulls away.

Tackle. Whistle screech. "Browdy, you alright?!" Coach Tully yells, scowling as the defender pushes off Morgan's flattened body with a smirk.

Gasping, Morgan rises, waving off concern. JD shakes his head at the unjust hit. Their eyes lock across the field. The lesson burns–kill your weakness or be crushed. Do better. No one will save you.

They realign. Morgan adjusts his grip, veins humming with new resolve. "Hut!"

This time, the ball hits his palm. He executes a crisp three-step drop. But the line surrenders ground. The nose guard storms through like a bat out of hell.

Sensing the danger, Morgan slides into five long strides. Side-arm, the ball zips toward Wheeler. In a calculated move, Wheeler halts, watching the ball as it careens across dirt, sabotaging a potential connection.

A blindside hit flattens Morgan.

Coach Tully's whistle screams. "Wheeler! What was that?" he bellows. "Reset!"

Morgan notices Wheeler fist bump the nose guard.

Scowling at the center, Morgan demands, "You letting him blitz through on purpose?" The lineman's eyes glitter with defiance behind his mask.

Frustrated, Morgan resumes his stance. "Ready. Hut!" he barks.

The snap hits his hands. He drops back three steps. The center sidesteps, allowing the nose guard to roar untouched. Morgan flings the ball toward Wheeler as the tackle buries him.

Howls and clashing gear fill the air. The overthrown pass glances off Wheeler's fingertips before a defensive back decks him with a sickening crack that nearly flips him off his feet.

Wheeler drags himself off the grass, helmet torn away. "The hell was that throw, Browdy?!" he shouts. Linemen part as Wheeler storms up.

"Again!" Coach Tully bellows. "Shake it off and rerun it."

Wheeler jabs Morgan's chest, forcing him back. "You trying to get me killed out there?"

"It slipped," Morgan starts. Wheeler cuts him off with a shove.

Rabbit tries to intervene. "Huddle up, guys!" His plea goes unheard.

"My six-year-old sister throws better—" The center snarls. Wheeler lunges, seizing Morgan's facemask. Metal twists as he rips the helmet off, tearing skin.

Rabbit's attempt to calm the storm evaporates under the thrill of a fight. The circle constricts, predatory. Coach Tully's whistle shrieks.

Wheeler's face contorts. "Could your dead, retard brother throw better at least?"

Time shatters. Rage explodes in Morgan's veins. A primal roar rips from his core. He rockets his helmet into Wheeler's sternum with a jarring thud.

Violence erupts. Wheeler charges, spittle flying. Fists blur. Bone mars bone. Blood sprays, painting faces and grass alike.

Coach Tully barrels in, a human battering ram. He wrenches Morgan backward, muscles straining. Morgan's feet leave the ground as he's flung. Coach pivots, ramming Wheeler with brutal force.

"What's WRONG with you animals?!" he bellows, face contorted. No response, only heads bowed in shame.

Chest heaving, he turns to Morgan. "Is this how you lead?" Coach spits. "We're not a damn gang!"

He jabs a finger at Morgan. "YOU were supposed to pull them together. What do you call THAT?"

Faces drop.

His tone shifts. "Get it together soon," he warns. He points to Wheeler's bleeding knuckles.

"Miss catches out there, the other team won't let up," he reminds Wheeler. "Their cruelty ain't your excuse." His eyes rake over the guilty faces.

"It starts and ends here," he continues. "Together."

His gaze finds Morgan on the ground. "Browdy, those gaps ain't closing soon," he says. "Stand tall, set your feet, deliver. No matter who storms through. Or I'll find someone who can."

Morgan nods, subdued. A sniffle.

Coach marches to the sideline. "Line up!"

Three sharp blasts signal a new play. Morgan rises, exchanging one last glare with Wheeler who slinks off to his cronies. The turnback reveals to Morgan how alone he is against the real enemy hiding behind false colors.

Steam rises, fogging the mirrors and clouding Morgan's vision as he stands motionless under the shower's relentless stream. The locker room's emptiness amplifies every drip, every breath.

His mind drifts further into the past, the memory sharpening with painful clarity...

Sunlight streams through Murph's bedroom window, painting golden patterns on the worn floorboards. Toy cars lie scattered like a miniature cityscape. Murph sits cross-legged at its center, his tiny hands cradling each vehicle with reverence.

"Charger! Charger!" Murph's voice rings out, pure joy in every syllable. He holds the red car aloft, a conqueror displaying his prize.

Ailea kneels beside him, her smile warm and patient. "That's right, sweetie," she says, ruffling Murph's hair. "What color is it?"

Murph's brow furrows in concentration. "Red!" he declares triumphantly after a moment's thought.

"Good job!" Ailea praises. Her eyes sparkle with pride at her youngest son's progress.

Murph's hand hovers over his collection, selecting a bulky SUV. "Durango!" he announces, beaming at Ailea for approval.

She claps, her enthusiasm genuine. "You're so smart, baby! Do you remember what color Daddy's Durango is?"

Murph's face scrunches. "Blue!" he shouts, giggling.

Morgan leans against the doorframe, watching. A pang of jealousy twists in his gut, chased by shame.

Murph's head snaps up, his smile faltering. A bruise beneath his eye stands out against his pale skin, a violent purple stain on innocence.

Ailea's demeanor changes when she sees her oldest son. Her warmth hardens to steel. "You were supposed to walk your brother home from school yesterday," she says, each word sharp and cold.

Defensive anger flares in Morgan's chest. "Well, I didn't because I had better stuff to do—" The words, like poison, spilled out before he could stop them.

Ailea rises, placing herself between Morgan and Murph. Her voice is low and controlled but trembling with fury. "You made a choice, Morgan," she says. And look what it did to your brother." Her hand gestures back towards Murph, who shrinks behind her, clutching his toy Charger to his chest.

Guilt crashes over Morgan. He stares at his feet, unable to meet his mother's scrutiny. "Yeah, well, I already said I was sorry," he mumbles.

Ailea steps forward, forcing Morgan to look at her, disappointment and anger warring. "He looks up to you, Morgan," she says, her voice fierce. "It's time you became worthy of that respect and affection."

The memory fades, leaving Morgan in the shower's unforgiving spray again. He blinks, water streaming down his face, indistinguishable from the tears he refuses to acknowledge.

11

Darkness shrouds the interior of JD's rumbling muscle car. The engine's low growl harmonizes with the hypnotic hum of tires on asphalt. Street lights flutter by, casting fleeting shadows across Morgan's bruised face. He slumps against the cool glass, eyes unfocused on the blurring landscape beyond.

"They let that guard in on purpose, you know." His fingers clench. "Pulling their blocks. Everything." The memory of betrayal twists his features.

JD's weathered hands tighten on the steering wheel. A weighty pause fills the cab before he responds. His voice carries restrained emotion. "Still didn't call for you to react like you did."

Morgan rakes his fingers through his hair, wincing as he grazes a tender spot. "They don't follow me," he fires back, anger and hurt bleeding through.

JD's following words come out a harsh whisper. "And why the hell should they?"

The car's rumble swallows his words. Silence descends once more, broken by the rhythmic click of the turn signal as JD navigates a curve. The beaming sign from a passing gas station paints Morgan's face in harsh blues and reds.

JD softens. "You gotta give 'em a reason to follow you," he says, eyes never leaving the road. The words hang with implication.

Morgan's reflection stares back at him, a ghostly overlay on the dark landscape rushing by. Each passing mile marker makes tomorrow's unfinished business feel more pressing.. The team's hostility, Wheeler's sneering face, and Coach Tully's disappointment coalesce into a knot of dread in his stomach.

The thundering exhaust fades as they pull into the driveway. Darkness shrouds the house, save for a single light burning in the kitchen window. Morgan lingers, reluctant. JD kills the engine, the sudden quiet deafening. They sit, two figures cast in shadow, the day's weight pressing down. Finally, JD speaks, his voice gruff but gentle.

"You know, respect ain't given. It's earned." He pauses, letting the words sink in. "Show 'em the leader you can be, not just the player you are."

Morgan nods, throat too tight for words. JD's hand finds his shoulder, a steady anchor. "One day at a time," he murmurs.

6

1

The night stretches long and lifeless, a vast emptiness that mirrors the ache in Morgan's chest. He sits in the car, the engine off, his fingers drumming a restless rhythm on his knees. The silence hangs thick as fog, broken only by the occasional creak of cooling metal and the muffled thump of his heart against his ribs.

A tap on the window startles him. JD's weathered face peers in, eyes shadowed with concern and something more complicated to name.

"Coming in?" JD asks, his gruff voice barely audible through the glass.

Morgan shakes his head. He can't face the emptiness of the house, not yet.

JD nods, the gesture slow and weighted. He steps back, hesitates, then turns towards the house. The door slams, silencing the world's judgments, if only briefly.

Time stretches, elastic and surreal. Morgan's eyes drift to his grandfather's bedroom window. The light glows warm amber, a beacon in the night. He counts the seconds, holding his breath. One minute. Two. The light blinks out, leaving him the sole restless spirit occupying this haunted place through the twilight hours.

Something in him snaps.

Slamming the car door, he sets off across the drive. Boots crunch on the gravel as he moves, drawn by an urge he can't name. The full moon bathes everything in ghostly silver, illuminating the neglected farmyard in stark relief–broken fences like jagged teeth, overgrown pastures whispering with unseen movement, abandoned equipment rusting into the very dirt that once gave them purpose.

A sudden flood of light makes him flinch. The utility lamp flares to life across the scrubby pasture, creating a harsh oasis around the fire-ravaged shed. Morgan stops before the painful spot marring the landscape. The old shack, once a sanctuary of his grandfather's keepsakes, now stands reduced to charred bones and ash–a mirror to the family fractured outside its walls.

Something catches his eye–a pristine stack of lumber out of place amidst the ruin. The fresh cut pine scent hits him, sharp and clean against the lingering smell of burnt memories.

Morgan's hand reaches out, unbidden, to touch the rough grain. A splinter catches his finger. He looks at the drop of blood welling up, then back at the lumber. He doesn't consciously decide. One moment, he's standing still; the next, he's hefting a plank onto his shoulder. It feels right, like penance and purpose rolled into one.

As Morgan sets the first board in place, it's almost like he can hear JD's voice in the wind, continuing to critique him. "Build it right, and it'll last a lifetime."

He works through the night. Each hammer blow is an act of defiance against the ruin surrounding him. He frames new walls against the shed's charred skeleton. Soon, his new oak beams blend with JD's earlier reconstruction efforts...progress marred in bent nails and uneven angles.

At dawn, new bones emerge from old ashes. It's far from finished, but it stands–a testament to stubborn hope that refuses to die, even in the face of overwhelming loss.

2

Morning light spills through the doorway across Morgan's sleeping face. He lies sprawled on a makeshift bed of grain sacks, one arm thrown over Flutie, the old hound snoring against his ribs. Sawdust clings to his clothes, mingling with the musty scent of fresh cut lumber that permeates the air.

JD steps inside the rebuilt wooden frame, coffee steaming in his thermos. His boots crunch on wood shavings scattered across the dirt floor. Thumbing over a protruding nail, he sets his drink aside and grabs a claw hammer from the floor.

"Rise and shine, sleeping beauty." JD drives the nail deeper with three echoing strikes, each blow reverberating through the structure.

Morgan jerks awake, heart pounding. Bleary eyes make out JD surveying his work.

"You got all this done yourself last night?" the man asks, sipping from his thermos without looking down. Steam curls around his face, softening his hard edges.

Morgan rubs grit from his eyes and sits up despite the dog's protests. Muscles ache from the night's labor as he stretches. He follows JD's stare to the bare rafters crisscrossing under the new roofline. Morning light filters through gaps in the unfinished ceiling, casting a patchwork of shadows on the floor.

JD points with coffee in hand. "I sure hate to ask the obvious, son," he remarks. "But what am I expected to do come a rainy day in this place now?"

They stare at a hole in the roof, a framed window cutout acting like a skylight. A bird perches on the edge, tilting its head at the two men below.

"Yeah, not my finest work," Morgan laughs through a yawn. He sweeps his hand over his hair, dislodging wood chips.

3

Morgan chokes down the last morsel of his pitiful breakfast, the taste barely registering as he sits alone at the pitted table. He glances up as JD strides in through the creaking door. The old wood groans under his weight, protesting the intrusion.

He pours himself a refill of black coffee before his eyes land on Morgan's battered hands resting atop the scuffed playbook.

"Got some bookwork I wanna walk through."

JD settles into the chair across from Morgan with a grunt, his coffee sloshing dangerously close to the rim. The playbook slides across the table's scarred surface as JD pulls it closer, flipping it open with practiced ease.

"Second thought, let's take this outside," he says after a moment, his eyes narrowing as he glances around the kitchen. "Too stuffy in here. Need some fresh air to think."

Under dappled sunlight, Morgan sits atop the creaking tire swing while JD paces circles in overgrown grass before him. The old scout flips through dense pages of the playbook, firing questions.

"Trips Right 387 Shift...walk me through it," JD challenges.

Morgan straightens, hands sketching players' routes in mid-air. "Before the snap, I call the shift," he explains. "That breaks the line into Trips Right: three receivers bunched on that side."

JD squints up at him. "And their routes?"

"Left guy runs a 3 route, middle an 8, right man a 7," Morgan recites, chest swelling with pride.

JD scratches his jaw. "Now say defense is showing Cover 3..."

Morgan visualizes the scenario, positions clicking through his mind like gear teeth.

"Cover 3, so three-deep zone," Morgan murmurs, concentrating. "The trips-side corner takes a quarter zone playing deep. Free safety drops to cover shallow right outside the tackle. Strong safety watches short-middle for curls and wheel routes..."

JD flips a page. "What about that backside corner?"

Morgan's gaze tracks the invisible defender. "More than likely man-coverage on his left half looking to help with short zones."

He settles deeper into analysis mode. "The strong safety would pick up any out-route from the left receiver. But..." Morgan taps his chin. "The right guy could maybe beat him deep on an 8 route."

JD nods approval. "How's he get open on that hitch 'n go?"

Morgan leans forward, arm coiling through imaginary pressure. "I look off the safety, try and get him to bite on a pump fake," he explains. "Then hit the receiver in stride over his head before the cover corner gets across."

JD smiles, shutting the book. "Starting to sound like a quarterback," he remarks.

Morgan flushes, grinning briefly. But doubt soon clouds his expression.

"What if I panic out there for real?" he worries. "The crowd, the noise, all those eyes on me...the guys barely listen. If I crack under pressure—"

"Find your rhythm," JD interjects. At Morgan's confusion, he clarifies. "Check each task off: call the play, break the huddle, read coverage, execute the throw. Stick to that pattern."

He claps four times—sharp echoes bounce off the barn. "One, two, three, four," JD counts. He pins Morgan with a hard stare. "Find your head in the storm; you'll get your team's attention, too."

Morgan swallows, but nods. They stand silent as birds chitter and the wind ripples across the grass.

JD tucks the playbook under his arm. His eyes catch on a torn envelope peeking out. Ailea's name in smudged pencil shows through the ragged edge.

4

The harsh squeal of the bell pierces the near-empty hallway, scattering the last few students toward afternoon classes. Morgan grabs one last book at his dented locker, then slams the metal door with a resounding clang.

Soft footsteps patter behind him. He glances back to see Ryley scooting to catch up, teetering under an armload of heavy textbooks. Her usual grace is off-kilter, and Morgan notices she's exchanged her contacts for black-framed reading glasses.

"So your game's tomorrow night, right?" she confirms. Her voice is bright with an eagerness that sits at odds with Morgan's mood. "Wish you luck out there, not that you'll need it."

Morgan shrugs, eyes pinned to the hallway tiles as if they hold answers to questions he can't voice. "Yeah, guess so...thanks," he mutters.

Ryley blinks, taken aback by his detachment. Her smile falters, uncertainty creeping into her expression. She's not used to seeing him so closed off, especially around her.

"Was kind of hoping I could come watch, maybe?" she ventures, her voice softening, tinged with an unfamiliar hesitance. "I won't distract or nothing, just support..."

The words hang in the air, fragile as spun glass. Morgan senses the heaviness of her gaze, the unspoken request for connection. But the demons tearing at his insides make it hard to reach back across the widening gulf between them.

The hint of vulnerability in Ryley's voice cuts through Morgan's broody abstraction. He gazes at her open, caring face and feels a pang of guilt for his indifference.

"No, you won't be any distraction," he assures her, sincerity breaking through his gloom. "They'll announce when I get crushed out there anyway, so..."

He attempts a self-effacing grin that falls flat as fresh concern crosses Ryley's face instead of laughter.

A pocket of quiet falls between them before she speaks. "Oh hey, so I applied to a college last week," she shares in a deliberately upbeat tone.

Morgan halts, his heart skipping a beat. "For real?" The words come out more sharply than he intends.

"It's just a small college," she clarifies. "But yeah...gonna see what happens."

Morgan's mind races. College. Future. Plans that might not include him. The thought of Ryley moving forward while he remains trapped in place sends a chill through him.

"Right, yeah, sure...who knows, though," he murmurs, struggling to keep his voice steady. "That's...that's great, I guess."

Morgan's eyes dart around, seeking an escape from the conversation and the fears it awakens.

"Well, hey, I should..." Ryley begins just as Morgan blurts, "I better get going..."

Their polite, empty laughs echo off the lockers. The hallway is wider than oceans between their faltering hearts.

"I'll just...see ya round then," Ryley finishes awkwardly. Morgan nods, already stepping away. "Yeah, see you..."

Ryley starts down the opposite way but stops. She turns, face twisting. "This has nothing to do with what I just said, does it? About college?"

Morgan freezes, caught between denial and the truth. "I... it's not..."

"Because if you're freaking out about me applying to school–"

"No, Ry, it's not that—"

"If I'd known thinking about my own future would be such a problem for you—"

"Ryley!" Morgan yells, drawing stares from passing students. The raw emotion in his voice surprises even him.

She seethes, hurt and confusion warring.

"That's not it, okay..." Morgan lies. "I'm happy for you. Really."

She shakes her head, unconvinced. "Changed my mind about your stupid game, by the way...just now."

The second bell shrieks through the halls. As Ryley disappears into a classroom, Morgan stands alone in the empty corridor. Echoes linger, mingling with unspoken fears of abandonment, of losing the one person who truly understands him.

5

The light bleeds from the sky, dusk settling like a shroud over the field. The harsh fluorescents beam to life one by one, casting an unforgiving glare over the ongoing scrimmage. One last chance to rehearse before the game.

Beneath their buzzing glow, a relentless offense clashes against an unyielding defense. The game's sounds—colliding bodies, strained breaths, and commands barked through face masks–mingle with the persistent drone of cicadas hidden in the overgrown grass beyond the sidelines.

Coach Tully paces the bench, arms crossed over his broad chest. Nearby, JD lingers by the chain-link fence before the bleachers, face hidden beneath the curved brim of his cap. But his eyes burn with an intensity that fails to match his casual stance.

At the heart of it all, Morgan takes his position in shotgun formation. His eyes, sharp as a hawk's, scan the threatening wall of the defensive line. Each passing second feels like an eternity, the air growing thick with tension you can cut with a knife.

"Ready..." Morgan's voice rings out, commanding the offense.

Without warning, the defensive nose guard stands upright and beckons a fierce cry that shatters the moment of anticipation. "Charger! Charger!"

The call ripples through the defense like wildfire. Linebackers move forward, hunger in their eyes, while cornerbacks retreat into deeper coverage, a coordinated shift of their initial lineup.

Recognizing the impending blitz, Morgan's center calls between his legs, eyes wide with urgency. "Audible, Browdy!" he warns, muscles tensing as he braces for impact. "Call it!"

Morgan spots the tell from his vantage point–the strong safety creeping forward like a predator sensing weakness. It confirms his teammate's frantic assessment. The defensive wave builds, a wall of muscle and determination ready to crash through the vulnerable offensive line if he doesn't adjust their play. Under the unforgiving glare of the lights, Morgan's mind goes blank, a moment of panic threatening to overwhelm.

Coach Tully's gruff voice cracks like a whip crack. "Call it, Browdy!" he commands, seeing the pocket poised to implode around his quarterback. "Change the play!"

Morgan's eyes dart across the line, desperation giving way to a spark of inspiration. He takes a sharp breath, lungs burning with the night air, and raises both hands high to call attention. "Durango! Durango!" he shouts, his voice raw and urgent. A ripple of confusion passes through both teams at the unfamiliar call from the back of the playbook. There's a heartbeat of hesitation in the face of the unknown.

Trusting the quarterback with blind faith, Rabbit explodes into motion, sprinting left with gazelle-like speed along the scrimmage line. "Durango," he echoes. "Guys, empty gun," he explains to his head-scratching teammates as he makes his way down the line.

The halfback shifts to the slot position. Morgan completes the rushed improvisation, heart thundering in his chest.

"Green 18! Hut!" The ball snaps into his waiting hands, cool leather against his palm. Instantly, the defense surges through the line with released aggression. Heart pounding, a war drum in his ears, Morgan plants his feet into the turf and throws blind as bodies converge around him, a maelstrom of motion and violence.

The pass flies low and short, a desperate prayer, just as Morgan's body slams into the ground. The impact drives the air from his lungs. Stars explode behind his eyes as his helmet bounces off the unforgiving earth.

JD and Coach Tully lean forward on the sideline as one, necks craning and eyes straining to pierce the swirling chaos. They search for any sign of the ball's fate, the outcome of Morgan's desperate gamble hanging in the balance.

The moment stretches, elastic and taut with possibility. Then, like a thunderclap, Coach Tully's face transforms. Fury darkens his features as the ball becomes visible, lying impotent and accusatory at one of the linemen's feet. He storms onto the field, a force of nature unleashed, ripping his hat from his head and throwing it down with such force it bounces.

"Intentional grounding!" he bellows, voice booming. His finger jabs toward Morgan, who struggles to his feet, face drained of color beneath his helmet. "Cost the offense ten yards." The heavy proclamation holds over like a ton of lead.

6

The team shrinks under Coach Tully's wrath, helmets bowed like penitents before an angry god. Morgan's gaze fixes on some distant point beyond the coach's twisted face, his eyes glazed as if predicting Friday's impending disaster.

As Coach Tully's tirade rages on, Morgan bends towards the discarded hat in the trampled grass. The coach's words die, re-placed by a low growl of warning.

"Don't touch that," he snarls, teeth clenched. "Eyes up here."

Morgan snaps upright, face a mask of forced calm. His hands lock behind his back, a soldier at attention before a furious commander.

"You audibled to Durango?" Coach's voice drips with sarcasm. "Refresh my memory on that one."

Morgan swallows hard. "Empty backfield, medium pass."

"So when a blitz comes howling on a mad-dog stunt, your grand strategy is to leave the pocket exposed?" Coach's anger reverberates throughout the field.

Morgan deflates but still attempts a feeble defense. "I-I thought if they overloaded the line–"

Coach Tully cuts him off, voice quick and abrupt. "No, you did NOT think!" He rounds on Rabbit. "Hayes! Blitz protocol–now."

"Check-down fast," Rabbit responds, words tumbling out. "Draw play or quick screen..." He shoots Morgan a look of pained sympathy.

Coach Tully's fingers rake across his stubbled jaw. His voice drops, each word edged with contempt. "DRAW play. Quick SCREEN," he enunciates. "Not your intermediate routes. You have two lifelines when the pressure comes. Those are...?"

The question is a guillotine poised to fall.

Morgan's face burns, but his voice remains steady. "Texas or Oklahoma, coach."

Coach offers a single curt nod. "Well. Seems you haven't forgotten everything," he concedes. "Just took embarrassing the whole team to drag it out of you."

He leaves Morgan to stew in the silent judgment of his teammates. Coach Tully stalks away, fingers clamped around his whistle. "Line up!"

The field comes alive again, players scrambling to position. But the air remains charged with Morgan's mistake and Coach's fury lingering like ozone after a lightning strike.

7

The shrill cry of the whistle slices–three sharp blasts. Like a well-oiled machine, the team drops into up-down drills at Coach Tully's command. Cleats churn the grass, tearing up divots.

"Big game tomorrow, gotta be sharp!" Coach Tully's grave reminder carries an undercurrent of lingering frustration, the sting of Morgan's mistake still fresh. "Gassers!"

Bent double, Morgan pushes himself through the punishing suicide line. He's already far ahead, legs pumping like pistons as he runs to outpace the merciless voices in his head: fool...failure...fraud...

Up-down-up-down, a relentless rhythm. The less-conditioned players soon fall behind their driven quarterback. Coach Tully's weathered face hardens as he takes note.

"Pick up the pace, boys!" The order cracks, punctuated by another piercing whistle blast. Though not aimed directly at him, Morgan feels the hostility like a physical blow.

Coach Tully's thick fingers jab toward the sweat-soaked Browdy as he jogs past. "Remind me of the check-down calls," he demands. "TEXAS or...?"

"Oklahoma!" Morgan's confirmation rings out between gasping breaths, as much to convince himself as anyone else. Coach Tully responds with a curt nod before moving down the line–still the demanding taskmaster, but the edge of his earlier fury dulled.

The field becomes a blur of motion and exertion. Shadows lengthen as twilight deepens, the glare of the field lights throwing every straining muscle into sharp relief. Morgan pushes on, each breath burning in his lungs, each step in defiance of the doubt threatening to consume him. Tomorrow's game looms large: a chance at redemption or the final nail in the coffin of his aspirations. As night falls in earnest, the team continues their grueling preparation, expectation looming.

8

Game Night. Tigers vs Laurel Ridge Vikings. Stadium lights bathe the players in uncompromising scrutiny, casting a cruel glow over the battlefield below. The home crowd seethes with violent anticipation, their hunger for blood a tangible force. New Liberty's offense huddles on the mud-slick field, their uniforms battle-scarred, reeking of sweat.

Morgan wraps his leadership around him like chain-mail. "Twins right, 88 Flood on one," he commands to grim-faced helmets. "Audible to Oklahoma on my signal–"

The center marches to the line, passing JD's side of the field–a silhouette in the stands, face hidden beneath his cap.

Nearby, the visiting coach sneers as he jabs a finger toward Morgan's mentor.

"That who I think it is?" The coach asks. His assistant's eyes go wide. "Thought the old bastard was in the ground."

Ryley sinks into her seat, each thunderous cheer from the student section hammering her resolve. "Go Tigers...T-I-G-E-R-S!" Her presence here is becoming a decision she regrets.

On the ravaged turf, Morgan rallies his troops. "Twins right, 88 Flood on one...on one!" The huddle fractures.

He strides to position. The scoreboard's red digits sear his vision. Two touchdowns behind. Time bleeds away. Their victory dreams wither with each tick.

Morgan reads the defense, cataloging threats. The safety creeps forward, just like they practiced, only now it's real.

"Down!" Morgan barks. His line drops into stance, coiled and lethal. Across the divide, Viking eyes burn with promised violence.

Morgan's tongue darts to wet his lips. He tastes copper from the cut when an errant hand punched through his mask five plays earlier.

"Hut! Hu-HUT!" War drums drown out the crowd's held breath.

Jacob Rivera, a fortress of muscle and bone, readies the snap. His hands cradle their fate. "Call it!" His voice cracks with urgency. "They're coming!"

Morgan explodes into action. "Oklahoma! Oklahoma!" he roars, hand slashing air as he retreats into shotgun formation a few yards removed from the line of scrimmage. The linemen pivot as one while the halfback joins Morgan in the backfield.

9

At the edge of the field, Coach Tully's face morphs into a fleeting grin. His meaty hands collide in approval as Morgan's gamble unfolds. "Good call, Browdy!" Pride overtakes his doubts about the gangly protégé.

The Green Call, then: "Hut!"

The snap.

Destruction looms as the defense surges forward.

The ball hits Morgan's palms but slips through his grip in the muck. "No..." The words die as a crushing sack drives him down into the earth.

Morgan lies buried beneath a twisted mass of bodies, all scrambling to get the recovery.

In the tangle of giants, unseen violence erupts. Fists hammer ribs and kidneys. Elbows crush throats. Nails rake flesh. Hidden from spectators, a savage war rages as hands claw for the ball.

"Eat shit, pretty boy!" A Viking hisses, driving his knee into Morgan's gut.

"Asshole!" Morgan wheezes back, clawing at eyes above a facemask.

Voices rise from the mire, laced with hate, as the teams curse back and forth:

"I'll break you, bitch."

"Mama's boy can't take a hit?"

"Gonna cry to daddy, rich kid?"

Blood and spit mix as insults fly. A New Liberty lineman grunts through gritted teeth: "Hick bastards."

"Faggot," comes the reply, punctuated by an elbow to his jaw.

Slurs slice deeper than cleats. Each word chosen to wound, to provoke, to destroy. At this moment, they're animals tearing at each other's throats.

A fist finds Morgan's side with cruel precision. His mind ignites with pain. A metal cleat lashes his calf, tearing skin.

As bodies rise, Morgan sees one last defender's cleat hurtling in. The kick to his temple sends electric sparks across his vision...

Spinning, the world becomes a vortex of fractured senses. His ears fill with distortion as the crowd's roar wains. He surfaces to blinding lights stabbing his eyes.

Coach Tully's face contorts, screaming words lost in the din. But his rage burns clear, even from afar. Morgan drags himself upright through sheer will, body screaming in protest.

10

All around, faces twist with primal hunger. The Viking defense circles Morgan like wolves. His team yells from the huddle, but their words mix with the crowd's roar.

The clock runs down as Morgan wobbles. His brain feels like mush. He takes a shaky step toward the blurry line, pulled by his team's shouts.

JD shoves past the coaches. He grabs the fence, his hands tight. "Son, get over here!" he yells out.

Morgan turns to the voice, a rope in the fog. He stumbles toward it like a puppet pulled by a string.

Ryley stands up, her cool mask slipping. Something new stirs in her–a caring she's kept locked away. The girl who always has a sharp comeback notices a change in her heart. Seeing Morgan knocked down breaks through her walls. In his scared eyes, she sees pain she never noticed before. His hurt wakes up feelings she's tried to ignore.

11

Morgan staggers to the bench. Coach Tully moves to give him the next play, but JD pushes past, grabbing his grandson's shoulders.

JD looks into Morgan's unfocused eyes, holding up a finger to draw his concentration. "Listen here–find your rhythm again," JD says calmly, ignoring the surrounding noise. "Focus up. C'mon now..."

Morgan lurches forward, puking on the grass.

JD holds him until it stops. "There you go, just breathe..." JD keeps his grip on the wobbly teen. "Find your flow, son. One count, two..."

Morgan croaks, "Three, four..."

"Atta boy," JD says, looking relieved.

Coach Tully barges back in, pushing his face near Morgan's. "Shake it off. 32 Blast, on one," he orders. "Keep it simple, Browdy." He shoves Morgan back onto the field.

The quarterback looks at JD, his eyes begging for help, but he has to finish strong. No weakness.

JD checks the clock. Only 30 seconds left in the game.

Not enough time to win.

12

The field pulses with hostility as Morgan barks the play. He forces it through the huddle twice, then breaks with a sharp clap. He lopes back to the line, heart racing as his teammates' eyes lock onto him. Their focus steadies his nerves.

Morgan crouches behind the center, muscles coiled. He calls for the snap and pivots, the ball finding the halfback's hands. The runner explodes through the defense, a human battering ram carving out five brutal yards as the clock bleeds dry.

Their sweat and blood stains the grass. It wasn't enough. The New Liberty Tigers taste bitter defeat.

Spent warriors from both sides form silent lines. They shuffle past each other, exchanging sterile looks of respect. Their gloved hands met in a series of ritual slaps, providing a sense of sportsmanship despite the earlier carnage.

Morgan moves through the line, eyes fixed on the ground. One by one, his teammates turn away. Their rejection hits harder than any tackle could. His fumble was a missed opportunity that could have led them to victory.

His unmet hand falls limp as he walks alone, the locker room a distant refuge from this new isolation.

13

The locker room buzzes with the usual post-game chatter. Amidst the hiss of showers and the clang of lockers, snippets of hallway gossip weave through discussions of missed plays and spectacular catches. Some share hushed accounts of sightings of the principal's toupee going askew during last week's assembly. The conversation leads to speculation about which couples will emerge from the upcoming dance, and whether the DJ will finally play something other than the same tired crap.

Morgan, pariah to it all, sits frozen on the bench, still caked in dirt and sweat. His head sinks into his hands as the room continues to spin. Vision swims, objects doubling and swaying in a nauseating dance while a dull ache throbs deep within his skull, pulsing in time with each heartbeat.

A sudden slap rocks him sideways.

"Shit, Browdy, didn't see you!" Wheeler's hyena-laugh cuts. He snaps a towel as he passes. The door slams shut, leaving Morgan in a bubble of concussed-misery.

Time stretches. The door creaks open again. Footsteps approach, but Morgan remains still until a calloused hand grips his shoulder. He looks up into JD's weathered face.

"Let's go home, kid," his grandfather says. He pulls Morgan to his feet, steadying him as they walk out. They pass the rival team's idling bus, its open doors a taunt. JD guides him across the lot to his GTO, a shadow in the night.

14

Morgan stands at the sink, wincing as he dabs blood from his swollen nose. Bruises paint his arms in violent hues beneath his grass-stained shirt. His body screams for relief after the field's punishment.

Ancient pipes rattle as the clawfoot tub fills. JD pours in Epsom salt and tests the steaming water. Too broken for shame, Morgan eases into the bath with a hiss.

JD settles onto a stool outside in the hall, his joints creaking as he leans back against the wall.

"You ever hear about the Ironman of Alcatraz?" he asks, his eyes crinkling at the corners. "Not the prison break—the swimmer. This was back in the '50s, when most folks thought swimming from Alcatraz to San Francisco was a death sentence."

With a practiced motion, JD effortlessly rolls an old coin over his knuckles. His eyes, fixed on some distant point, reflect years of similar post-game scenes.

"There was this fella, Jack LaLanne. Built like a brick house, but even he couldn't make it across on his first try. The currents were too strong, the water too cold. But Jack? He didn't quit."

The metallic clink of the coin punctuates his words as he flips it occasionally.

"He trained. Studied the tides. Learned to read the water like you read a defense. And when he tried again, he made it. But here's the kicker — he didn't just swim across. He did it with his hands and feet bound." As JD's story unfolds, he alternates between pocketing the coin and pulling it out again, a nervous habit born of years on the sidelines. He shifts on the stool, stretching out a leg stiffened by old injuries, a physical reminder of his own playing days.

He pauses, letting that sink in. "Now, I'm not saying you gotta go jumping in the bay anytime soon. But remember this: every great athlete, every person who's ever done something remarkable, they've all been where you are now. Bruised. Beaten. Wondering if it's worth it to get back up."

JD's voice grows softer. "The difference is, they chose to keep going. To learn from the pain, to let it make them stronger. That's what separates the greats from the rest. It's not about never falling– it's about always rising."

Hovering at the top of the hall steps, Wilke appears with an unusual uncertainty.

"Caught some dirty hits out there," JD says, voice neutral. "We'll have him ready next time." He rises, making his way down. "I'll leave you to it."

Morgan keeps his eyes shut against the harsh light, seeking escape from the pain. A rough hand cups the back of his head. He squints up at Wilke's blurred face.

"Hey, Moose," Wilke says, his voice low. The old nickname bridges years of distance. He smooths back Morgan's hair, avoiding visible wounds in a gesture from gentler times.

Wilke studies his son. "I'll get more ice...back soon."

Morgan hides his grimace. No lectures come for tonight's failure. Only this unspoken forgiveness passes between them, a fragile peace in the quiet bathroom.

The automatic doors part, and Wilke enters, grabbing a hand-basket. Eyes low, he weaves through aisles collecting essentials–bread, ice for Morgan, a six-pack in the corner that pulls him like a magnet. The cheap bulbs buzz and flicker, emphasizing the pallor of his skin and the dark circles under his eyes. Shit, he looks like hell.

He scans the coolers without focus, muscle memory guiding each move. His fingers brush against the cold glass, leaving ghostly imprints as he reaches for the beer.

"Wilke? Wilke Browdy?"

A shocked voice yanks him from his thoughts.

Vince, a familiar figure from bygone days, catches Wilke's attention. The man stares as if witnessing an apparition, his cart forgotten mid-aisle. "What brings you back?" Vince asks.

Wilke forces a tight smile. The muscles in his face strain with the effort. "Hey, Vince. Been a while." The words taste like ash in his mouth.

"You coaching these days?" Vince gestures, eyes gleaming with curiosity. He looks at Wilke, noticing how time and grief have transformed his former teammate.

Wilke's throat closes, halting any recap of the past, threatening to shatter his fragile present. Unspoken tragedy fills the space between them, as tangible as the chill from the coolers. His knuckles whiten around the basket handle.

"Good seeing you," Wilke mutters, turning from Vince's extended hand and probing questions. The bottles clink again as he moves, a discordant melody accompanying his retreat.

The aisles, once familiar, feel like a gauntlet. Each turn threatens to reveal faces from the past. The buzz of the overhead lights grows louder in his ears, drowning out the mundane chatter of other shoppers.

He's made it to the checkout line, totally focused on the six-pack, ice, and groceries on the belt with all those cheesy ads. Wilke's eyes dart to the rack of glossy magazines beside the register, their garish headlines screaming scandals and secrets. He half-expects to see his own face plastered across one of those trashy covers–"Local Man's Fall from Grace!" or "My Journey to Rock Bottom: The Wilke Browdy Story."

The cashier, a pimply teenager who looks barely old enough to drive, seems oblivious to the man's identity. It's a small mercy in this town where everyone used to know his name; where older residents' eyes fill with recognition and something that might be pity–or celebrity.

A young mother with a restless four-year-old joins the queue behind him. The boy laughs as she tickles his ribs, their joy striking Wilke's core. He turns, throat tightening as memories flood in–Murph at that age, pudgy legs once chasing across summer lawns, those sweet hazel eyes that crinkled with glee.

The woman glances up, sensing the man's distress in his rigid shoulders. Her bright smile fades, taking in the anguish present on his bearded face. A moment stretches between them. Wilke looks down, shifting the six-pack among the belt. He rubs a hand over his face, forcing back the familiar threat of tears. His pulse pounds, haunted by echoes of a beloved boy lost forever.

Suddenly, something in him snaps. Without warning, Wilke grabs the six-pack off the belt. He fumbles in his pocket, pulling out a crumpled wad of bills. With a shaky hand, he tosses them onto the counter, not bothering to count.

"Keep the change," he mutters.

Before the startled cashier can react, Wilke is already pushing past the other customers in line. Ignoring their protests and confused stares, he clutches the six-pack to his chest like a lifeline. His abandoned groceries sit forgotten on the belt as he strides towards the exit, shoulders hunched against the weight of unspoken judgment. The automatic doors slide open, and Wilke escapes into the night, leaving behind a wake of bewildered silence.

The air feels icy against his skin as he struggles to catch his breath beside the truck, the tightness in his chest refusing to release. He slumps, gripping the pitted door handle so hard that his wedding band cuts into his skin. A sob escapes before he can trap it.

The gravel crunches and sprays beneath his tires as Wilke races out of the parking lot, his heart pounding in sync with the revving engine. He accelerates hard, as if trying to outrun the fractures spreading through his soul–cracks too deep and numerous to ever truly mend.

16

Wilke stumbles into the house, the screen door slamming like a judge's gavel. The six-pack swings against his leg, a cold promise of temporary solace.

Like a phantom, Morgan appears from the bathroom wearing only boxers and a hoodie. Bloodied tissues sprout from his nose like gory flowers.

"Ice?" he grunts.

Wilke's mind stutters. The ice, his mission, abandoned on the distant store's grocery belt. He lifts the six-pack, a metallic peace offering. "Here," he mutters, lobbing a can.

Morgan snags it mid-air, eyes widening in surprise. He watches his father retreat, each step on the tattered rug echoing their worn-out relationship.

17

The six-pack lands with a clunk on Wilke's nightstand. The tired man leans on the dresser, head bowed like he's at a confession. A sigh, deep as buried regrets, escapes as he collapses onto protesting bedsprings. The beer can hisses open, a snake's whisper of forgetfulness. He gulps, seeking courage in liquid form.

In the next room, Morgan's cracks, creating an echo and fragile link made of aluminum and foam.

Outside, fireflies wage their nightly war against darkness. Inside, father and son fight their battles, separated by walls thinner than the silence between them.

7

1

Morgan pushes through the diner door, wincing as bruises throb beneath his jacket. The air hits him–sizzling oil, clattering dishes. He scans for Ryley's curls amidst the dinner rush. Ignoring the hostess, he eases onto a wobbly stool at the counter.

Ryley appears behind the smudged glass of the expo, pouring coffee for a raucous booth.

Morgan raises a bandaged hand in greeting.

Ryley notices him, surprise melting to guardedness before she nods, formal and restrained. As she turns back, Morgan blurts out:

"I'll take the breakfast special with extra bacon."

Ryley grabs a menu and approaches, uncertain eyes taking in his battered state. His gaze meets hers, creased with unspoken things.

"We don't serve breakfast for seven more hours." Ryley glances at the clock. "Papi fires up the grill for the 3 a.m. drunks."

Morgan nods, unconcerned about food. "Can I talk with you instead?"

Ryley tenses, wavering between icy detachment and renewed connection. Morgan forgets to breathe.

"There's an away game tomorrow. The bus leaves here at 6 p.m. In case you want to come..." The invitation hangs awkwardly between them.

Ryley sets down the coffee pot and crosses her arms. "I decided I'm not a fan of high school games. Too much meat-head energy doesn't vibe with me."

"Is that so?" Morgan quips.

She nods, puffing her lips. "Yep...went to the last one and realized it ain't my scene."

"Oh, I thought you weren't going to that game—" He retorts, half-grin widening.

"Didn't think I needed an invite to make my own big-girl decisions?" She says. "Besides, even if I was going for you, you didn't seem to notice I was there."

Morgan plays along. "I was busy getting drilled into the turf, but your screaming was hard to miss anytime your boyfriend got plowed..."

"Boyfriend?" She blinks, her teasing smirk fading. "Boyfriend–" she repeats.

Morgan winces, pulse racing. Major slip of the tongue. For weeks, he'd kept her at arm's length, and now his mouth probably just cost future intimacy with one ill-timed declaration.

Ryley glares at her boss, Sandy. "Yo, Sands, I'm taking my break," she says, untying her apron. She chucks a dishrag onto the counter.

Sandy doesn't look up from counting the change drawer.

Snatching a stale cinnamon bun, Ryley settles onto the stool beside Morgan.

"I don't recall asking some arrogant jock to be my boyfriend." Her eyes dance as Morgan's mouth dries.

Heart pounding, he attempts a shrug despite sweating palms. "Oh-uh, I didn't–listen..." he licks his lips. "I'm sorry for being distant lately. I've got a lot I'm dealing with, and I was taking it out on you..."

"You're trying to get in my pants?" she asks.

"No...I mean, yeah, but no. I actually really do like you, Ry."

Ryley worries her lip, unreadable. Then she exhales. "I'm not big on labels. Takes all the mystery out of things, you know?"

Morgan nods, tamping down rejection. Her fingers trace patterns on the counter between bites of her dessert.

"But—" She draws the word out before meeting his eyes, grin returning. "I think I can make an exception for homecoming corsages."

The knot in Morgan's chest relaxes as he registers permission to reconnect. Ryley tugs the tape binding his bruised hand.

Sandy's summons crackle on the loudspeaker, "I ain't paying you to sit."

"Keep your Spanx on, Sandy!" Ryley hollers back with mocking humor. "Let's see if you can keep up, new-boy," she whispers close. Morgan grins through goosebumps from her minty breath.

2

Apencil's incessant tap-tap-tap echoes through the room as Morgan slumps in his calculus seat. His eyes glaze over, staring at the chalkboard covered in equations. Rather than numbers and equations, his thoughts are consumed by football plays.

A snort breaks through Morgan's daze. Two rows back, he spots Rabbit. The skinny sophomore hunches over his book, enormous glasses sliding down his nose. Despite being smart enough for senior calculus, his gangly frame and mouthful of braces make him an easy target.

Morgan sinks lower as Mrs. Moss breaks the lecture for a private study session. His plan: pretend to work and sneak in a nap.

Before his head even hits the desk, Mrs. Moss swoops in. She says something to Rabbit, inaudible, then marches toward Morgan with red-lined papers in hand. "Why don't you two pair up? Nolan here can help you in derivatives before next week's test."

Morgan thumps his head on his desk.

"So this is happening," Rabbit mutters. He crunches on neon gummy bears, tapping his pencil against his braces. He holds out the candy. "Want one? Real drugs inside–sugar and fake colors. Dangerous stuff."

Morgan's hesitant smile prompts Rabbit to raise an eyebrow. "Not judging if you're failing. I crush this class. It's the proofs that sometimes trip me up, though."

Rabbit playfully tosses a gummy bear up, attempting to catch it in his mouth. It bounces off his lip at an angle and into Morgan's hood. "Looks like I miscalculated the arc of that parabola. Good thing I'm better with numbers on paper."

Morgan frowns. "What are you talking about? Look, I'm just trying to keep my C so I can stay on the team."

"I'm Rabbit, by the way–"

"I know, you're on the team," Morgan says.

"Yeah, real name's Nolan. They call me Rabbit 'cause I run so slow."

Morgan winces. "That's rough."

Rabbit shrugs. "Could be worse. They call Derek 'Boner.'"

"Why?"

"No clue."

Boredom falls.

"Should we actually study?" Rabbit taps the book.

Morgan watches him highlight a few pages in the text. Truthfully, he couldn't care less about proofs.

The ringing of the bell is like a starting gun, setting off a race as everyone quickly exits the room.

"Guess I'll see you on the field," Rabbit says, packing up.

His shy smile evaporates in a pained yelp as a random student passing by shoots out a meaty palm, delivering a cruel blow between Rabbit's legs. He crumples against the desk, dropping his books and papers.

"Shit, he got me good—" Rabbit wheezes, face pale.

Morgan crouches, helping gather the scattered, color-coded notes. "That sucks, man."

Rabbit tries to stand but stumbles. Morgan steadies him.

"You okay?" he asks with genuine concern in his voice.

Rabbit nods, forcing a weak smile. "Random idea," he says, catching his breath. "I could...help you study. If you want." "

Seriously?" Morgan asks, brow furrowed.

"You work hard on the field," Rabbit adds, his voice gaining strength. "I could help you bring those same skills to the classroom. Maybe boost your grade."

Morgan studies Rabbit's face, seeing past the thick glasses and braces to the sharp mind behind them. "Is that what you want? To be a teacher someday?"

Rabbit shrugs, a hint of vulnerability in his gesture. "Beats being alone in the library all the time. Plus, I'd be good at it."

Morgan smirks, an unexpected warmth spreading. "Look at us—brains and muscles."

"And balls," Rabbit adds, his mischievous grin returning as he delivers a light tap to Morgan's groin.

Morgan doubles over, laughing through the sting. "Jerk!"

The pair makes their way as the hallway fills with the chaos of dismissal—slamming lockers, shouting goodbyes, sneakers squeaking on linoleum. Morgan notices Wheeler and his cronies eyeing them. Their predatory grins make his stomach churn.

"Hey," Morgan says, turning to Rabbit. "You got plans this weekend?"

Rabbit blinks, surprised. "Uh, no. Why?"

Morgan hesitates, his eyes darting between Rabbit and Wheeler's approaching group. He makes a split second decision.

"My place. Saturday. Bring your gloves. We'll work on your catching and routes. Call it a trade." Morgan says.

Rabbit's eyes widen behind his thick frames. "You want to help me?"

"Yeah, I do," Morgan nods, surprising himself with how much he means it. "In return, I'll take you up on that Calc tutoring if you're up for it."

A grin spreads across Rabbit's face, brighter than any Morgan's seen from him. "I'm your guy."

3

The lanes gleam under sputtering lights at Skyway Bowling Alley. Pale flashes pulse across the worn wood, echoing the heartbeats of those gathered here. The place clings to its '70s charm like a faded memory, shag carpet lining the creaking snack bar. Yet the locals seem content, as if the decay speaks to something deeper.

Morgan tugs at his cherry-red rental shoes, nerves coiling in his gut. This outing with Ryley feels like a tightrope walk after their make-up pact. He treads, afraid to crack the new foundation.

He looks up, breath catching as he sees her. Against the seedy backdrop, her profile glows with an otherworldly light. She laughs, waving him over with a warmth that both beckons and terrifies.

As he joins her, his gaze skitters from her yoga pants to the grimy trophy case against the wall. Faded photos peer out behind dirty glass–ghosts of a town's former glory.

"Does this count as an official date?" The question hangs between them as they choose their balls.

Ryley tests the weights, undecided between the 8 or 10 pounder. "Depends...how do we measure that?"

"If it bombs, we pretend it never happened?" Morgan's smirk can't hide the vulnerability beneath.

They head to their lane. Ryley takes her stance and releases. The ball crawls toward the gutter. She turns, her smile defiant against failure. "That sounds fair."

They fall into a dance of rolls and resets. Conversation flows over the thrum of classic rock while gutter balls and stumbles on shag carpet punctuate their laughter.

4

The animated glow from the pinball machine paints Morgan's face in shifting hues. Ryley turns, sensing his raw gaze. She clears her throat. "Lots of memories here."

Pins rattle. Morgan snaps back to the present. Ryley nods toward a faded photo. "8th grade champion team."

He squints through vintage dust at the image–a wild-haired girl grinning, arms linked with teammates in bowling shoes and matching shirts.

"I was on JV cheer that year, too."

He eyes her. "Are you the mascot brave enough for that tiger costume?"

She laughs. "No! I knew the kid who wore Tigger's head, though." She gags. "Smelled like old soup inside, with one eyeball that rattled when he danced."

Morgan chuckles, imagining the scene. "Sounds like a real charmer," he jokes, his hand unconsciously finding her waist. The music shifts, a slow melody filling the air. Their laughter fades, replaced by a sudden awareness of their closeness. Morgan's breath catches as she sways slightly, whether from the punch or the moment, he's not sure.

Morgan steadies her. Heart-daring, he catches her gaze and leans his forehead to hers as the overhead music from the old juke croons Styx: *"Tonight's the night we'll make history, honey you and I..."*

As the synth fades, Ryley's eyelids flutter with an unmistakable invitation. He glimpses the same spark reflected.

"I think it's your turn," she whispers.

His hands move up her back, urgent magnetism drawing their lips closer.

"Lane Three! Pick up the pace!" bellows the manager.

They jolt apart, crashing back to the sticky carpet and garish surroundings. Morgan steps up, hoping his flushed cheeks mask the deeper flood below the surface.

He hefts the purple orb, knuckles white. Ryley slips behind him.

"Shift your weight closer." She guides, her hand resting on his hip where her embrace might line up. His body angles for a throw that will never aim truer. Her front presses flush as he releases. A dextrous twist converts desire to kinetic motion. The orb launches. One impact. A chain reaction of scattered pins.

Ryley's breath tickles his ear. "Nice shot, ace."

Morgan turns, their bodies still close. "Had a good coach."

Her eyes dance with mischief. "That all I am? A coach?"

He swallows hard. "No. You're...everything."

Ryley's fingers trace his jacket sleeve. "Careful. Saying stuff like that, a girl might get ideas."

"Maybe I want you to."

The alley fades around them. Ryley leans in and–

"Lovebirds! You're holding up the lane!" The manager's voice shatters the moment again.

Ryley steps back, a faint blush coloring her cheeks. "Rain check?"

Morgan nods, heart pounding. "Definitely."

5

From his dim corner in the alley bar, Wilke hunches over his third flat soda, a futile attempt to chase away the fog of several earlier beers. The acrid taste does little to cut through his intoxication. His bloodshot eyes scan the nearly empty room. The quiet clink of his glass against the sticky table serves as a metronome for his somber thoughts.

WHILE WE'RE HERE

From the dirty window he watches his son and Ryley prepare to leave, their hands linked beneath the sickly neon glow.

Wilke's worn face twists with pain–old wounds reopened at the sight of his son savoring young love, unblemished by harsh years. Their laughter cuts through him, sharp and jarring. It echoes a distant time when Wilke's fingers traced the soft lines of a woman who loved him before fate tore them into separate, joyless paths.

His focus drops to the fractured bar top. His calloused hands shake, clutching at foggy memories that spill over like stale beer and shattered hopes across this scarred oak shrine of his nightly vigil.

He misses the figure lingering in the alley doorway: Morgan glancing back through the hazy glass, unspoken questions brewing in his torn gaze. Wilke tosses a few bills on the counter and raises his glass to a faded photo above the taps. It shows a young man in football gear, "1982 CHAMPIONS" scrawled in silver marker.

6

Morgan lingers outside the bar, his eyes still fixed on the window where his father fishes out a couple of bills. A gentle touch on his arm breaks his trance.

"Hey," Ryley says, "you okay?"

Morgan nods, not quite trusting his voice. He allows Ryley to guide him away from the window, toward the parking lot.

Before they reach her car, Morgan stops. In a moment of vulnerability, he turns to her. Their eyes meet, and without a word, he leans in. In the warm light of the parking lot, Morgan steals a goodnight kiss, brief but tender, before she gets in and drives off.

The boy walks around the old passenger side of his dad's truck. Midway, he spots Wilke slumped against the back fender, retching.

"Why are you here?" Morgan asks. "Thought you said I needed to find my own ride tonight?"

Wilke tosses jingling keys. Morgan fumbles the catch, heart racing. "Can't drive like this," the drunk man mutters.

"I don't have a license—" Morgan protests.

But Wilke staggers to the passenger side, words thick. "Just get us back to the farm."

Morgan starts the old engine, its roar fracturing the stillness as he steers onto dark rural roads. Wilke speaks over the rattling frame.

"Can't get tied down," he mumbles, battling sleep and booze. "Only a matter of time till they break your heart."

Morgan grips the wheel tighter.

Wilke rubs bloodshot eyes. "Need you keeping clear from them all...we got just us now," he grates out. Gnarled fingers worry over his faded jacket. "Can't risk getting trapped in nowhere towns."

Morgan shifts, his eyes narrowing. "So I'm just supposed to exist in between wherever we land?" he challenges.

Regrets churning deeper than drink, Wilke sags against the window. "Want more for you, something I never..." His jaw clenches. "Ruined every chance."

Morgan glimpses genuine pain cracking through weariness and drink.

They pass dark fields before Wilke exhales, purging spirits older than booze. "Record being what it is, no woman is worth it," he rasps, biting back harsher words.

Morgan chews his lip, focused on the lonely road unfolding through high beams. "Ryley isn't trapping me if that's your point," he says defensively. "I like her, dad."

With a hoarse rasp, Wilke's voice cracks, "I know you do, Murph."

The words sting. Morgan feels as if he's been slapped, the air suddenly thick and hard to breathe. His throat tightens, a lump forming that he can't swallow past.

"Are we close yet?" Wilke asks, his words slurred and his features unsteady. His head lolls to the side, coming to rest against the passenger window with a soft thud. A deep, rumbling snore escapes him, punctuating the sudden silence in the car.

Tears well in Morgan's eyes, the road ahead smearing into a watery blur. His grip on the wheel loosens as grief threatens to overwhelm. Suddenly, a blaring horn shatters the moment. Morgan's heart leaps into his throat as the looming grille of a semi barrels toward them.

Adrenaline floods Morgan's system as he wrenches the wheel hard. Tires screech in protest, the truck roaring past with inches to spare. Their pickup fishtails, its back end sliding towards the muddy shoulder as Morgan wrestles for control. At the last moment, the tires catch, and he guides them to a jolting stop, leaving them sideways across the empty road. As their hearts pound in the sudden silence, a hawk glides over moonlit fields, indifferent to their brush with mortality.

Morgan inhales raggedly, blood thrumming in his ears. He kills the engine, now bellowing into the void. He braces against the dash in silence, breathing until panic recedes.

"Fuck!" he hisses, eyes streaming. In the rearview, he sees Murph staring back. He rubs his eyes, erasing the ghost and traitorous tears.

Wilke slumbers on, oblivious to what just happened.

Morgan settles back, biting his cracked lips to calm himself. A gnarled oak rosary hanging from the mirror stirs gently, catching his eye. He reaches out, fingers tracing the weathered beads. With a deep breath, he restarts the engine. The pickup rumbles to life, and he carefully maneuvers back onto the pavement toward home.

7

The engine sputters as Morgan jerks the truck to a halt in front of the house. His hands grip the wheel tight, fighting a slight shake. He glances at Wilke, his dad's limp figure propped against the window, snoring.

Morgan pries open the creaky door and hefts the man out of the cab. Wilke mumbles nonsense but stays limp as Morgan hauls him toward the farmhouse through the overgrown side yard. At the back steps, Morgan stops, lungs burning as he readjusts his hold. Boots scrape wood before the screen door opens, giving way to their stumbling entrance.

The kitchen light throws harsh shadows around empty bottles, standing guard over a forgotten plate of cold food. Morgan drags them towards the hallway's murky shelter, his shoulders on fire.

With a grunt, he unceremoniously drops Wilke onto the worn-out, sagging mattress before removing the man's mud-caked boots. Through the grimy window, a sliver of moon watches the sad scene–a boy bent beyond his years, cradling the worn fate of his broken guardian.

"Rough night, huh?" JD's voice breaks in.

Morgan looks up, meeting JD's weathered gaze. The dim hallway light casts long shadows across the room, illuminating the scattered bottles that litter the floor like silent witnesses.

"Why don't you get some rest?" JD suggests, his voice low. "I'll keep an eye on things here."

Morgan nods, the weight of exhaustion settling over him. He shrugs off his jacket and fumbles with his shoes before sinking into the battered armchair in the corner. As his eyes close, he feels JD drape a worn blanket over him.

In the quiet that follows, Morgan drifts off, grateful for the unspoken support and the promise of a few hours' reprieve from reality.

8

Dawn's chill seeps through crooked floorboards as Morgan drifts into the dim kitchen. His steps reverberate through the cramped farmhouse. Grit rasps under his feet, scouring away the night's lingering fragments of uneasy dreams the feeble morning light can't dispel. The corroded faucet wails when Morgan wrenches it, unleashing a flood cold enough to numb his hands. He leans against the stained porcelain, watching water snake down the tarnished drain. After gulping a glass, he slams the tap shut.

Low voices rumble from the screen porch. Morgan halts behind the faded kitchen wall, straining to listen.

"He's hanging by a thread thanks to your little show last night," JD says, his words suspended.

Boards creak as someone shifts their weight.

"Enough with the lectures," Wilke snaps.

"Morgan's stronger than you think, despite your efforts," the old man rebukes. "Why are you set on crushing his chance to believe in something?" His words, though muffled, strike true.

"Keep it down, you're gonna wake him." Wilke hisses.

JD adds, quieter now, "We failed to have something. Why steal his chance?"

A shuffle breaks the heavy pause. The screen door screeches. Morgan peers around the wall to see Wilke storming toward him. The haggard man freezes, glaring at his son's unexpected presence.

"The hell you creeping around here for?" he demands.

Before Morgan can stammer a response, JD appears in the doorway, his stance unyielding.

"Enough, Wilke," the old man warns, allowing no room for argument. He turns to Morgan. "Get ready for school. I'll drive you."

9

Tires crunch gravel as the old muscle bird throttles down in the crowded high school parking lot, exhaust fumes mingling with chatter and laughter swirling outside.

JD sets the brake and turns to Morgan, slumped against the passenger window. "Ready to saddle back up, kid?" he asks.

Morgan shrugs, his eyes following a group of laughing students across the bleak asphalt.

JD notes the boy's distant stare. "You with me? Need your head in the game for practice. Can't afford mistakes with so few games left."

Morgan blinks, as if seeing the milling students for the first time. He spots Wheeler by the front steps and sets his jaw. "Good as I'll ever be," he says.

Seeing no movement from the boy, JD presses, "Time waits for no one." He shoves open his door, the hinges groaning in agreement.

Morgan gets out. His shoes scuff the pavement as he hitches his bag higher, marching into the mundane battle awaiting inside.

Faint jeers snare his attention. The broad-shouldered seniors strut along the main walk, letter jackets gleaming. They join Wheeler at the railing.

"Look who crawled out of the junkyard again," Wheeler announces as Morgan approaches.

The group erupts into laughter. The words strip Morgan bare, exposing his outsider status once more. Fight-or-flight chemicals flood his system as the pack closes in.

"How long before the charity case is hitchhiking?" Wheeler high-fives a goon, basking in the spotlight. "Bet running from bill collectors is what made this psycho so twitchy," he speculates. The others pile on as Morgan stands facing the assault.

A sharp whistle cuts the air–JD stands by the idling car, face like thunder. "Find better ways to spend your time, boys," he calls.

Razors glint beneath surface charm as the pack moves off, Wheeler shaking his head. "See you at practice."

Morgan exhales through flared nostrils, shoulders loosening as the tormentors vanish around the corner. He senses JD's steady approach. His hand grips Morgan's shoulder, equal parts restraint and comfort until the worst passes.

"Small dogs make the most noise," JD says low. "Find a way to win his trust." But seeing only defeat in the boy's eyes, JD sighs and heads off.

The first bell rings through the chill air, urging stragglers into halls where familiar monsters wait.

10

An unusual warmth blankets the practice field. Morgan sets his stance on the turf, sweat beading as he surveys the field through his face mask. He nods once, then begins his cadence. The ball slaps into his waiting grip.

Time narrows to controlled breaths between plays. Morgan reads his receivers until a splash of auburn hair shatters his focus. Ryley sits cross-legged beyond the track, textbook open. Aware of his gaze, she glances at him with a teasing wink before placing a middle finger to her lips.

Those seconds of distraction crack the moment wide. Rabbit waves frantically, calling for the pass while Morgan admires sunlight on Ryley's frame. Reality crashes through as the ball leaves his grip off-rhythm. Morgan winces, self-directed anger swelling at another mistake exposing his friend to an incoming cornerback.

Rabbit stretches, his fingers reaching for the overthrown pass. Just as the ball grazes his fingertips, a blur of motion slams into him. The cornerback's shoulder connects with Rabbit's ribs, driving the air from his lungs.

They crash to the turf in a tangle of limbs, skidding across the grass. For a moment, Rabbit lies still, dazed and gasping.

"I'm...good!" he finally wheezes, struggling to sit up. He winces, one hand pressed to his side, the other examining his abraded palm. Despite the pain, a shaky grin spreads across his face. "I almost had it!"

Morgan spits expletives under his breath.

Wheeler chimes in, his tone mockingly impressed. "Wow. Is that what negative speed looks like?"

"Nah, he's just slowly moving backwards," one of the cronies snorts.

Wheeler's voice drops, aimed at Morgan. "This our new strategy? Bore the other team to death?"

Quiet snickers follow. Morgan's jaw clenches, the muscle in his cheek jumping.

Coach Tully's face mottles an impressive fuchsia. "Browdy, let me know next time you want to sabotage my practice with another shitty throw. Get the ball where it needs to be."

Morgan's glare softens as he watches Ryley pack up and leave.

Rabbit returns to the huddle, pulling grass from his facemask.

"Free to run routes at my place later? I could use feedback instead of these assholes making noise." Morgan nods at Wheeler's dispersing group.

"Say less," Rabbit grins, flashing braces.

11

Rabbit's old Civic sputters as they roll into the barnyard, the overworked heaters doing jack against the fall chill.

"Dude, this is straight-up villain hideout material!" Rabbit says.

Morgan snorts, a mix of amusement and defensiveness. "Yeah, well, wait'll you see our secret underground lair," he retorts, pushing open the creaky car door.

They climb out, fallen leaves crunching under their feet. The wind whispers through the bare trees, carrying the scent of wood smoke and distant harvest. Morgan leads the way, hands shoved deep in his pockets, shoulders hunched against the cold.

The pair stumble into the living room, a gust of cold air following them before Morgan shuts the door with a dull thud.

Rabbit's eyes dance around the room, taking in the eclectic mix of antiques and clutter. "Sweet place," he says, genuine appreciation in his voice. "I was thinking McMansion, but this? This has got style."

He flops into the old armchair, a cloud of dust rising around him. The chair creaks in protest, clearly unaccustomed to such enthusiastic use. Rabbit grins, running his hands over the fabric arms.

"Yeah, well," Morgan mumbles, rubbing the back of his neck, "it's home, I guess." He opens two cans of Coke from a small fridge near the TV and gives one to Rabbit.

"So what's the shit to do around here?" Don't see a gaming set-up–please tell me you're not one of those PC nerds..."

Morgan smirks. "Might blow your mind, but nope, I'm neither."

"PlayStation then...you play Warzone?"

Morgan shakes his head.

"Jeez, you're such a loser," Rabbit gawks. "What do you even do for fun?" he asks.

Morgan hesitates, the messy room feeling weird. Truth is, he hasn't done much since Murph died.

"I dunno," Morgan shrugs. "Football and school shit."

"But, like, when you wanna chill? No Call of Duty? Anime? Anything?" Rabbit presses.

Morgan shrugs.

"Bro, that's depressing," he says, but without being a dick about it. "Good thing you got me to save your sad ass from boredom."

Morgan's mouth twists. "Don't really watch TV either."

"Every loner needs a nerd upgrade, dude."

Morgan chokes back a laugh. "My own Jedi Wizard ready to culture me—how'd I get so lucky?"

"It's Jedi Master—" Rabbit starts, but heavy boots cut him off.

JD walks in, wiping grease off his arms. "Didn't expect company," he says, eyeing Rabbit.

Morgan jumps in. "Rabbit's on the team. Said he'd run routes with me."

"Kid can catch?" JD asks, looking the boy up and down.

"I'm a receiver," Rabbit shoots back.

JD smirks. "Didn't ask that. Asked if you can catch."

"Test me," Rabbit nods at a mounted football on the wall.

"No way. Not that one."

Morgan eyes the ball in its fancy case. He moves closer, checking it out. It has old school stripes on shiny leather, and the laces look game-used.

"Whatever, man," Rabbit breaks in, "I'm your only option–" He leans back dramatically in the chair, aiming for cool and casual. Instead, the ancient piece of furniture decides to exact its revenge for years of neglect. Just as Morgan turns around, Rabbit over-corrects, sending himself, the chair, and his open can of Coke into a spectacular wipeout.

Morgan clutches his sides, gasping for air between bursts of laughter. "Dude," he wheezes, "here I thought you were only clumsy on the field!"

Rabbit, rolling over, manages to shoot Morgan a mock glare. "You're supposed to be on my side–" His indignation is somewhat undermined by the fact that he's now practically horizontal, feet kicking uselessly in the air.

Even JD's stern facade cracks. A smirk tugs at the corner of his mouth, softening the lines around his eyes. He shakes his head, a low chuckle escaping despite his best efforts.

"Smooth move, hotshot," JD drawls, his voice gruff but tinged with amusement. "Clean that up before it stains."

Morgan's eyes drift back to the football on the wall. "Hey Pa," he calls, curiosity getting the better of him. "What's the story with this ball?"

"Ancient history," he says, voice gruff. "Best left in the past where it belongs."

As JD's footsteps recede, Rabbit scrambles to his feet, brushing himself off. He casts a sidelong glance at Morgan. "So...family heirlooms are a touchy subject around here, huh?"

Morgan's expression is unreadable. "Something like that." He pauses, then adds with forced lightness, "Wanna see if you can actually catch something for once?"

12

Under old school floodlights standing tall on rusted poles, Morgan focuses on tracking Rabbit racing down the yard. He raises his hand, calling for the ball. The pass leaves Morgan's grip and arcs through clouds of gnats in the night.

"Drive from your hips, keep your elbow in." JD directs from his perch on a stool by the porch. "And square those shoulders on your release. You won't throw darts all twisted up–"

Headlights crack their world open as Wilke's pickup coughs its way from the road down the drive toward them.

"Run it again now," JD hisses, firing a second ball at Morgan.

Morgan catches and digs into the damp grass to set up for another pattern as Rabbit slinks back to their makeshift line.

The truck clunks off and the door slams. Wilke's dark shape spills out, a bottle glinting in his hand.

Rabbit inches closer to Morgan. "That your dad?" he whispers.

Stopping in the middle of their game, Wilke takes a long, hard pull from the bottle before his glassy eyes settle on Rabbit. "Did Morgan introduce you to ole cock and feathers there?" He laughs, pointing at JD across the field. "Sure he told you all about me, right?"

The silence is deafening.

Wilke waves a limp arm at Morgan, ushering him over. The boy looks at JD, then Rabbit, before obeying.

As Morgan approaches, the acrid stench of stale cigarettes and cheap whiskey wafts from Wilke's direction. The smell is so strong it almost has a physical presence, clinging to clothes and making eyes water. Underneath it all is a sour, unwashed odor that speaks of nights spent passed out in the same clothes.

Wilke slings an arm around Morgan's shoulders, pulling him close. Morgan winces, trying not to breathe through his nose. "This here's my boy," Wilke slurs, his words accompanied by sour breath. "Tell 'em about that time I caught you singin' and dancin' to your mama's old records, wearing her high heels and lipstick."

Morgan's face flushes a deep crimson. He tries to pull away, but Wilke's grip is too tight. "Dad, stop," he mumbles, looking anywhere but at Rabbit.

"Boy was twirlin' around the living room, beltin' out some Dolly Parton song. Looked like a right queer with that red lipstick all over his face–" He takes another swig from his bottle, some of the liquid dribbling down his chin and adding to the potent cocktail of odors surrounding him.

"Here, drink with your old man." He shoves the bottle at Morgan, spilling it down the boy's front. The end of it jabs his bottom lip. Morgan recoils, finally managing to extricate himself from his father's grasp, stumbling back a few steps.

He dabs at his lip with a trembling hand. He glances at Rabbit, silently pleading for understanding or maybe just an escape from this mortifying situation.

JD spits, his voice full of judgment. "This what these boys need to see? Your drunk ass crawling up the porch?"

Wilke stumbles toward the house, catching himself on the rail. "He's my son, no matter how hard you try to buy his favor." His stare lands on Rabbit. "Tonight's hours don't suit schoolboys, neither. Go home."

Rabbit pushes his glasses up.

JD shepherds the boys away. He pats Rabbit on the back. "Won't have your mom worrying about our feuds. Best get home now, son."

Wilke hurls his bottle toward them. It spins, trailing amber until swallowed by darkness.

The transmission on the beat-up Civic groans as Rabbit puts it in gear. He glances at Morgan, leaning on the passenger side window.

"I can swing back later if you need," Rabbit mumbles.

"I'll be alright. You don't need to stick around."

"Just want to make sure you're good…"

Morgan nods. "Yeah. For real, though…thanks."

With a "Later" that's drowned out by the crap muffler, Morgan heads into the mess waiting for him.

He cautiously slips inside. Every creak of the floorboards makes his heart skip a beat, dreading the possibility of encountering his elusive father. There's total silence, except for a slight breeze coming through the back door.

Morgan steps out onto the weathered planks of the deck, stained by six winters' snowmelt channeled off the tin overhang.

There, Wilke stands hunches against the chipped railing, his silhouette slumped and defeated. Acrid smoke wreaths his bowed head like a tarnished halo. Morgan watches, transfixed, as sounds rattle from his father's broad form: Sob-hitched breaths. His flannelled shoulders shake uncontrollably.

It's a jarring sight—this lion of a man, broken.

"You don't think it, but I used to be something great—" he mumbles, chest-puffing around his broken heart. He clears his throat, drying his wet eyes. "I see how you look at me."

The boy watches, eyes wide and absorbing.

"You get to look up at me and think you'll never be like me. That's the privilege of teenage ignorance." He hawks bitterness into the choking air. "You think that old man out there has your best interest?"

Morgan pipes up, timid. "He's helping me get better—"

"He's using you to chase ghosts."

Wilke crushes his cigarette into a knot on the wood. "I know because I'm the one he killed."

It takes Morgan a while to form the words he wants to say. "If you'd step up and spend time with me, I wouldn't need him. Why can't you see that?"

Wilke's tone shifts like a man possessed. "He latched onto you the moment we arrived. Murph dies, and suddenly, you're his only hope. One last thing for him to control. One last grandson to mold into what he wants."

Morgan seethes through gritted teeth and tears. "Don't talk about Murph—"

"He's my son!" Wilke erupts. His face twists in rage.

Morgan can't discern who Wilke's anger targets: a mirage of JD brought on by intoxication...or him. "Dad?" escapes his cracked voice.

Wilke blinks as if breaking from a trance. He runs a hand through his greasy hair before lurching inside. The screen yawns jagged, and the door blasts back against the protesting hinge before clapping shut with a *thwap!*

Morgan grips the railing, ancient paint rough against his skin. For the first time since the separation, his mom fills his thoughts. He gazes up, stars multiplying across the night's dark canvas.

A vivid memory surfaces—Murph's innocent face, upturned one night at their bedroom window. He was too scared to sleep alone, so he nestled in Morgan's bed.

Their mom entered to carry him back. "Mommy's here to send Mr. Scary away." She made her way to Murph's side of the bed.

Murph clung to Morgan's neck, reluctant to leave.

"Want to see our special star?" Ailea whispered. Murph nodded.

She lifted him to the window. The boy was nearly her height, but she cradled him like he wasn't.

"Our Special Star always shines, watching you. Even behind clouds." Her finger pointed to a bright speck. Murph smiled, finding comfort in the idea of a star all his own.

"Can it be Morgan's, too?" She asks. "So he's brave when Mr. Scary comes?"

Morgan half-smiled.

Ailea murmured, "Enough light for my boys to hide from sadness and storms."

The weight of the memory is a bittersweet ache. Those words, once a shield against childhood fears, now seem feeble against the harsh realities of his world. Yet part of him yearns for that comfort, that unshakeable belief in a mother's power to ward off darkness.

13

Hours later, Morgan lies in his bedroom, staring up at the cracked ceiling plaster. The farmhouse groans around him. An oscillating fan stirs muggy air while a lone cricket chirps. His phone glows 11:23 for the thousandth check.

He flings aside the sweat-soaked sheet. Maybe water or a midnight lap through the house would lull his restless mind to sleep.

At the stairs' top, he pauses. His screen illuminates a text from Ryley: *u up?* As if she sensed his drifting.

Wide awake, he replies. *Wanna break me out?*

Her response makes him smile. *Be there in 20* ☺

"I wish," Morgan mumbles. His thumb hovers over the screen, heart racing. He types in a burst of rebellion: *I can come to you...* Pocketing the phone, he begins his descent into moonlit possibilities.

The first obstacle is the ancient staircase. Morgan places each foot with calculated precision, wincing at every groan of wood beneath his weight. Each step feels like a balancing act between freedom and being caught.

His eyes land on a near-empty tequila bottle in the kitchen's murky darkness. Without hesitation, he pockets it–a peace offering for his nighttime intrusion into Ryley's world.

At the warped farmhouse door, he freezes. The screen's impending squeak threatens to shatter the night's fragile calm. Heart thundering against his ribs, he eases the door with agonizing slowness. The hinges protest, each grinding whine amplified in the tomb-like quiet.

A soft *woof.* Flutie stirs from his bed on the welcome mat, lifting his head at the intruding night air and the scent of escape.

"Shhh Flutie, it's me," Morgan whispers, voice a desperate plea. He crouches, rubbing the pup's silky ears. As he scratches, he prays the dog's notorious dim-wittedness will, for once, benefit him. Flutie's tail thumps, appeased by this midnight apparition reeking of adrenaline and defiance.

Morgan steps into the yard, the night air cooling his skin. In the moonlight, the farmhouse looms behind like a dark giant. He stops at the edge of the gravel driveway. Crickets chirp in the distance, seeming to egg him on, while the old oak's shadows reach for him like grabbing hands.

A curtain moves in JD's room, spilling light onto the world outside. Morgan darts into the shadow, fumbling for his phone. He pulls up the number of his new, unlikely partner in crime.

No going back now.

The phone's harsh ring cuts the heavy quiet, making Morgan jump. He looks back to make sure no one's moving inside. On the second ring, a sleepy voice answers.

"Hello?"

"Hey man," relief at the answer. "I know it's late–"

Rustling suggests movement. Morgan holds his breath.

"S'okay. Everything alright?" Rabbit's voice, sleep-thick, carries concern.

"Yeah, totally fine now," he throttles down his tone to a whisper. "So, random ask since you're one of the few people I know with wheels."

He pauses, feeling a small bit of remorse. But he buries it. "Think I could beg for a ride? Like a just-this-once favor between friends if I super urgently needed it?"

A pause on the other end. Then, "Like right now?"

14

Morgan can hear the Civic's rumble a half mile away. It eases to the curb, bathing Morgan in harsh light. The car reeks of old takeout and a shitty dollar store air freshener...'Tall Pine' scented.

"Thanks for the jailbreak," Morgan mutters over sputtering air vents. Rabbit studies the dark road as Morgan gives directions.

"Thought your dad was trying to off you or something," Rabbit says, sounding almost disappointed. His white-knuckle grip and lead foot scream 'novice driver.' Morgan fills the trip with a recap of the night's drama, skipping family crap but stressing his need for Ryley's chill vibe.

"Ryley's folks are cool with you crashing this late?" Rabbit's eyes bug out. "Or is this a booty call thing?" His eyebrows dance, more wishful thinking than actual suspicion.

"What? No!" Morgan chokes. "Ryley gets me...knows where I'm at when things fall apart." He shrugs. "Just gotta see a face that doesn't make me wanna puke."

Rabbit's smirk sticks as they round a bend, the car's headlights sweeping across a weathered "Whispering Pines Estates" sign. The irony of the name isn't lost on either of them as they enter a neighborhood that's anything but pine-filled.

A patchwork of modest homes with patchy lawns and sagging porches line the block. Street Lights flicker intermittently, casting elongated shadows across cracked driveways. A dog barks in the distance, its echo bouncing off vinyl sidings and vinyl fences.

Morgan leans forward, squinting through the windshield. His eyes dart from house to house, searching for familiar landmarks in the dim light. A child's forgotten bicycle lies toppled on one lawn, its wheel slowly spinning in the breeze–a silent carnival ride for no one.

The truck rumbles over a speed bump, the suspension groaning in protest. A cat darts across their path, momentarily caught in the glare of the headlights before disappearing into the shadows between houses.

"This should be it," Morgan points, his finger directed at a house not unlike the others. Its porch light flickers fitfully, a moth's erratic dance punctuating the gloom. A rusted swing set stands in the side yard, creaking softly with each gust of wind.

"How you gonna 'see her face' without the whole block thinking you're some creeper?" Rabbit asks.

Morgan texts: *U still up?*

Rabbit rubs his chin. "You check if she's riding the crimson wave?"

Morgan snorts. "What are you talking about?"

His phone lights up: *WTF u srs??*

Rabbit snickers. "As your bro, I gotta say. If Aunt Flo's in town, you're shitouttaluck."

"Sure thing, Dr. Phil. I'll take notes," Morgan scoffs.

Morgan's clammy hand touches the door when Rabbit hits the lock, trapping him. "Hold up–you sure about going solo in there?" His eyes shine with worry behind smudged lenses.

"Chill, man. This ain't my first rodeo here."

Seeing Rabbit's doubt, Morgan squeezes his bony shoulder through the Batman tee. "I owe you big time. Just keep watch, yeah? If shit hits the fan, I'll give the uh...Bat signal. Caw caw."

Rabbit winces. "That's not–have you ever seen Batman?"

"You get it," Morgan says, flipping the lock.

Click! The lock drops again. Morgan sighs. "Dude, you're literally cock-blocking me."

"What if you miss practice?" Rabbit asks, dead serious.

"What do you think hooking up entails?"

Morgan shoves the door open, not waiting any longer. Rabbit's apprehension dissolves into a crooked grin. He whispers, "Godspeed!" as Morgan makes his way up the dark drive.

Heart hammering, Morgan pulls up his hood against the cold, focused on the girl waiting ahead.

15

His sneakers sink into the grass, leaving dark prints across the wet blades. He peeks at the house, then hops the gate, trying not to make noise. He stops, listening. A dog barks somewhere, and a car whooshes by, but no one yells or flips on lights.

He breathes out and creeps across the lawn, grabbing his phone, he texts: *knock knock*

As he walks across the patio, the delightful aroma of lavender wafts up from the flower beds.

His phone lights up. *Password?*

Grinning, he types *jock strap* and can almost hear Ryley laugh.

The curtains move in an upstairs window. He sees her, all sleepy and messy. His heart races as she leans out.

"Thought you'd be asleep," he whisper-shouts. "Can we talk? I brought booze." He winks like an idiot.

"That's your romantic midnight move?"

Morgan shrugs, a lopsided grin on his face.

"You know my dad will absolutely murder you if he catches you here, right? Like, actual murder. Not the cool kind." Despite her words, there's a glimmer of excitement in her eyes. "Give me two minutes. I'll meet you at the back door. And this better be some damn good booze, you idiot."

With that, she gives him a quick, conspiratorial grin before disappearing from the window.

In the Civic parked a few houses down, "Secret Agent Man" plays softly on the radio. Rabbit slouches in the driver's seat, his fingers tapping an erratic rhythm on the steering wheel.

"I was just driving by, officer," he mumbles under his breath, then shakes his head. "Nah, that's stupid. Um...I'm here to pick up my friend. What booze?"

He glances nervously in the rearview, then back to the empty street. "Goddammit, Morgan," he hisses. "Why'd you have to drag me into this? 'Just a quick stop,' he says. 'Won't take long,' he says."

He straightens up, adopting a more serious tone. "Sir, I apologize for the disturbance. We were just leaving." Then, slumping back down, "Yeah, right. That'll work."

Just then, a van turns onto the road, heading their direction. Rabbit ducks, his eyes peeking up over the side of the door as it passes by. He makes out the words 'Tanner Construction' on the side.

His heart races as the van slows down. Rabbit's mind whirls, connecting dots he'd rather leave unconnected. With shaking hands, he fumbles for his phone and dials Morgan's number.

The phone rings once, twice. Rabbit's eyes ping-pong between the approaching van and Ryley's house, his pulse quickening with every foot of pavement the vehicle covers.

"Come on, come on," he mutters.

Finally, Morgan picks up. "Dude, what–"

"Does Ryley Tanner have any connection to Tanner Construction?" Rabbit interrupts, his voice a harsh whisper.

There's a pause on the other end. "Yeah, that's her dad's company. Why?"

Rabbit's blood runs cold. In a moment of panic-induced madness, Rabbit does the only thing his frazzled brain can think of. He takes a deep breath and yells into the phone:

"CAW! CAW!"

The sound echoes in the quiet night, a bizarre bird call that's equal parts warning and complete absurdity.

"What the hell?" Morgan's confused voice comes through the receiver.

"It's Ryley's dad!" Rabbit shouts, no longer caring about subtlety. "The van! It's her dad! Run!"

With that, Rabbit throws the phone down, starts the engine, and peels away from the curb, leaving Morgan to deal with the approaching storm of parental fury.

"Shit, shit, shit," he mutters as he guns it.

"Fuck—no—shit," Morgan yelps, nearly falling on his face. He looks up to warn Ryley, but she isn't there. Gasping and trying to get his stupid legs to work, he finds the only place to hide...he plunges into the deep end of the turquoise pool. The splash echoes like a cannon shot in the quiet.

Cold water takes his breath, arctic needles pricking his skin. For a heartbeat, the smothering water extinguishes thought. Then, survival instinct awakens. He curls into a ball and pulls himself deeper into the midnight blue sanctuary, away from the danger of being discovered and stuffed by Ryley's dad like some teenage trophy for his man cave.

At 8 feet down, he looks up, trailing fingers through crystalline columns of light. All remains still, his unplanned dive unnoticed, though not for long. Suspended in the drink, Morgan watches the light filter down until familiar legs drop in. He shoots upward.

Sputtering as night air hits his face, he tries to crack a smile at Ryley sitting on the ledge.

"Nice move," she mutters, yanking Morgan to his feet. Her fingers dig into his arm as she steers him towards the back of the house. They creep along the side wall, ducking under windows.

Through the kitchen window, they catch a glimpse of the front hallway. The main door swings open and a bulky silhouette fills the door frame–Ryley's father, shoulders slumped from a long night shift.

"Give me fifteen minutes, and I'll open the back door," she says.

Morgan fights his shivering. "Fifteen minutes? I'll freeze–"

"Wanna be dead in there?" She points to the kitchen where her dad sets his lunchbox on the counter.

"He always eats, then watches replays of the game before passing out," she explains.

"Where do I go? I'm freezing–" Morgan protests.

Ryley heads to the back door. "Figure it out. You're the first boy to dive in my pool. Stay hidden."

She slips inside. Her dad mumbles something, and she replies, "Nothing, just taking out trash."

16

Morgan hugs himself, his soaked frame shaking in the night air. Through chattering teeth, he mumbles, "F-fifteen m-minutes...n-no problem..."

The wind cuts through his wet clothes, painting his shrinking skin blue and purple. He flails his stiff arms. Maybe exercise can spark warmth before it's too late?

Miserable, he squishes behind the barbecue, its brick facade a shield from the wind. He tucks his knees to his chest and prays his shaking doesn't crack teeth or chip bones. He pulls out the tequila meant for Ryley and drinks it. Almost retching at the taste, he forces another swig. He smacks his lips as the liquid blanket spreads warmth. "Okay, Morgan, that's better," he whispers.

His shivering brain conjures up a memory of a survival video he once watched. He snorts out a laugh, startling himself.

"Right," he mutters through chattering teeth, "that video...what did that guy say?"

The memory swims hazily into focus. It was one of those cheesy outdoor survival shows, hosted by a buff dude with perfect hair and blindingly white teeth. Morgan remembers how the host had dramatically ripped open his shirt to demonstrate skin-to-skin contact.

"For severe hypothermia," Morgan mimics the host's overly enthusiastic voice, "find a warm buddy and get naked!"

He glances around at the empty patio and laughs bitterly. "Fresh out of warm buddies. Guess you're stuck with me, brick wall."

The video host's voice echoes in his head: "If you're alone, do whatever it takes to generate heat! Jumping jacks! Push-ups! Dance like your life depends on it–because it does!"

Morgan attempts to stand, his legs wobbling in the cold like a newborn fawn's. He manages one pathetic jumping jack before collapsing back behind the barbecue. "Nope," he wheezes. "Not happening.

In the kitchen, Ryley's dad drones about defensive strategy and replacing point guards while slathering mustard on gray meat. "Sure thing, Pops," Ryley replies, glancing out the window between fake phone scrolling.

After endless minutes, her dad climbs upstairs. Ryley holds ten fingers to the dark patio, mouthing, "Stay down." Morgan slumps against the cold brick, clenching his jaw to keep the heat in. At last, the slider opens, and Ryley waves him inside.

17

She turns up the thermostat before tossing a towel and some of her dad's clothes. "Shower. Now. Before you set off the alarm with chills."

"Your dad's clothes?" Morgan questions.

"Yeah, so what?" She asks.

Morgan eyes the oversized boxers. "Just didn't expect mine and your father's junk to share the same threads..."

Ryley grimaces. "Gross. Too much info."

Morgan stumbles to the bathroom, peeling off cold, wet layers that slap against the tiles as they drop.

He twists on hot water and plunges into the steam. The cascade stings, and then heavenly heat seeps in, driving frost from his bones.

Morgan feels life returning. His blue skin flushes coral as blood flows. Soon, only occasional tremors ripple as warmth sinks deep.

His mind wanders. He thinks of Rabbit's crude comment about Ryley being on the rag, dismissing it. But what if it's true? That'd ruin his hopes for the night, despite denying that as motivation to himself.

A knock startles. "You alive? I made hot chocolate," Ryley calls.

"Much better. Be right out," he answers, stepping from the steam. He dries off and pulls on her father's sweats. He takes another tequila swig and gives himself a silent pep talk.

Ryley sits on her bed. "Here, liquid warmth with marshmallows," she says, handing him a mug topped with whipped cream. Their eyes meet over the rising steam. They laugh awkwardly, melting the last icy grip on his chest.

Morgan clears his throat. "So, about all this. Not my best idea, I know." He gives a shy smile. "But I thought it was time to make a romantic gesture or something."

Ryley tilts her head. "Yeah, I figured that's why you suddenly turned into a sneaky trespasser."

Morgan looks down. "Pretty obvious, huh? I was really trying to sweep you off your feet." He rubs his neck. "Show you my daring side...which clearly needs work."

Ryley's face is hard to read. She doesn't argue with him. "I think you're cool just being yourself, " she says after a while. "You don't need all the extra stuff..."

"Right, got it." Morgan shifts. "So, should we talk about boundaries then? Rules? I don't want to mess this up if I'm getting the wrong idea."

Ryley gives a slight smile that doesn't reach her eyes. "Maybe just...cool it on the big gestures for now?" Something in her face looks hopeful and scared, but Morgan can't quite understand it. "I don't want to spend summer fishing a dead boy out of my pool." She doesn't sound as sarcastic as usual.

He forces an easy grin. "Got it, no problem..."

They drink their cocoa quietly.

"Oh, I brought you this," he says, handing her the tequila bottle.

She takes it, looking it over. "Warm liquor," she says.

"Opened...warm liquor. Thanks."

A quiet emerges, disrupted solely by the ticking of a vintage clock in the hall. Morgan's effort to think is evident.

Finally, Ryley sighs and leans into him, laying her head on his lap. She stares up at the ceiling where the scattered array of glow-in-the-dark stars adorn the ceiling–pale green pinpricks of light.

"For what it's worth, I'm glad you came over," she says softly.

"Yeah..." he murmurs. "I'm glad, too. Even if I did nearly turn into a tequila-flavored popsicle in the process."

She pulls away. "We should probably set some ground rules for our future adventures."

Morgan laughs. "Lay it on me. I bet rules 1 through 10 are all basically 'don't almost die in stupid ways,' right?"

Ryley smiles, showing her dimples. "Pretty much, yes. You're not so good at staying safe." She flicks his ear. "Let's keep Morgan Browdy alive before he ends up on the FBI's Most Wanted list, okay?"

"Yes, ma'am." Morgan ducks his head but can't help smiling. He playfully taps her fuzzy-socked foot with his.

"So that rule about when cuddling is allowed...any chance we can bend it tonight? For medical reasons, of course."

Ryley giggles. She stretches out beside him on the bed, nestling close and draping an arm across his chest. Her face hovers inches from his as she murmurs, "I guess we should keep an eye on you in case there are any lasting effects..."

A warm flush spreads across Morgan's cheeks.

Ryley adds, "This is way better than doing college apps."

"Totally agree," Morgan whispers, holding her tight. He tries not to think about college and the future, not wanting to ruin the moment. He breathes deeply, feeling her heartbeat against his chest and her waist under his hands.

A sudden, jarring noise shatters the tranquility. It starts with a low *Brrr* quickly escalating to a full-blown "BRAAAP" that ricochets around the room like a pinball of pure awkwardness.

Time freezes. Morgan's body goes stiff with horror.

"Oh my GOD!" Ryley shrieks, jumping away. "Did you seriously just fart on me?"

Morgan sits frozen in embarrassment. His whole body turns red. This perfect moment ruined.

"That's...I can't even..." Ryley fans her face, laughing. "New rule: no more of whatever you ate today!" She pinches her nose. "I think we've had enough surprises for one night."

He forces a pained laugh. "So much for sweeping you off your feet..." Morgan groans, covering his face with his hands. "Any chance we can pretend this never happened? Or maybe rewind to the part where I was just slowly freezing to death outside?"

Ryley laughs, poking him in the ribs. "No way. This is prime blackmail material. I'm thinking of having it bronzed."

"Great," Morgan mutters, peeking through his fingers at her. "I'll add that to my list of unique talents: human whoopee cushion."

8

1

Lockers bang shut with clangs while students talk and laugh. Shoes squeak on the floor as kids rush to their next class. Friends call out to each other over the crowd about their plans for the weekend. There's a loud, crazy river of noise and energy flowing between the classrooms.

Morgan rounds the corner to find Rabbit lounging by their lockers. He tries to brush past, spinning his combination lock with feigned indifference. His mind dwells on the previous night's less-than-glorious events.

"You're killing me," Rabbit whines, his mischievous grin glowing. "I've been dying to hear about the Op since first period. Spill." He angles for details about Morgan's encounter. "How many times did you...you know," he says, eyebrows dancing.

Morgan rolls his eyes, suppressing a shiver at the memory of the cold. "Oh, you mean after I was left on my own to dodge Ryley's dad like some cut-rate ninja? Yeah, thanks for that." He lowers his voice, mimicking Rabbit's earlier enthusiasm. "'Don't worry, I'll be your getaway driver.' Real smooth, man."

Rabbit's grin only widens. "Come on, it worked out, didn't it? You got your alone time with Ryley."

Heat crawls up Morgan's neck as he recalls fumbled attempts at romance derailed by an ill-timed bout of indigestion. "It had its moments," he mumbles, throat tight. He avoids Rabbit's piercing stare that cuts through his thin veneer of calm.

"That doesn't sound great–" Rabbit's eyes narrow, mind racing through possibilities. "Come on, dish! Don't leave your wingman in the dark..."

"Fine! But this stays buried forever, got it? No commentary." Rabbit wags a pinky to seal his promise.

"We went at it all night. Intense shit happening everywhere." Morgan forces a sly smirk even as his ears burn crimson.

Rabbit's childish glee turns heads in the hallway.

"Enough," Morgan hisses through clenched teeth. "I don't want anyone to know. Not into the kiss and tell bullshit."

"Oh, so 'fart-boy' is a gentleman now?" Ryley's voice cuts behind them like a knife. Her arched brow and silken hair flow past. She blows Morgan a kiss and vanishes into the sea of students.

Stunned, Morgan crumples to the floor, face buried in his hands as Rabbit gawks at Ryley's retreating figure.

"Fart boy?" He looks down at Morgan's huddled form. "You farted?"

Morgan throws his hands down. "Yes, blew the pants cannon on her. Like a damn subwoofer."

"*On* her?" Rabbit's face twists. "Wait...she's into that?"

"No, I bombed the moment," Morgan groans.

Rabbit slides down beside him in solidarity. "Holy shit..." He sits numb before a devilish grin creeps back. "That's kind of awesome!"

Morgan waves him off. "No. Absolute worst moment."

"Did you both do it at all?" Rabbit probes.

"She kept laughing every few minutes. Ruined the vibe with random giggle fits."

Rabbit winces, clasping his friend's slumped shoulder. "Rough break, fart-boy. But hey, at least you gave her a story, right? You're probably the first guy to ever do that." He offers a sympathetic grin, nudging lightly. "Could be worse...you coulda shit the bed."

2

The anxiety of tomorrow's looming game brings Morgan and JD into the crop field for a welcome distraction. The pair work at replacing worn out posts and cross-beams.

"Pass me them nails?" JD asks, hand stretched toward a box nearby. Morgan obeys while the old man fixes a new piece of pine in place, hammering it home.

Questions swirl in Morgan's mind, growing more insistent with each solid thunk of metal on wood. Finally, unable to contain himself any longer, he clears his throat.

"Were they ever happy? Mom and Dad?"

JD looks at Morgan, twirling a bent nail as he digs through memories. "You'd know more than me," he says, gesturing.

Morgan nods, a half-formed question on his lips. His fingers drum an anxious rhythm against his thigh as another thought surfaces, then another.

JD sets another board, glancing over, but Morgan just shakes his head. Unasked questions settle back into silence, buried beneath the steady thunk of hammer on wood.

"Still hung up on that girl of yours?" JD asks, wiping sweat from his brow.

"Yeah. She talks about college and leaving," Morgan says, kicking at the dirt. "Pretty sure I'll be stuck here."

JD takes a moment to watch the sunset paint the fields. "And you're scared of that?"

"I don't know," Morgan admits, tossing a piece of grass. "Can I ask you something?"

"You just did," JD quips.

"That first day we met, Coach asked you if 'it was in my blood.' What'd he mean?" He kicks at a rock. "And then that ball in the trophy case inside...were you some great old legend or something?"

JD tenses before returning to his work with the hammer. Each hit punctuates his words. "Talent fades. But heart? Heart's what matters." He taps his chest. "Anyway, I was no legend."

Morgan's brow furrows, wanting more. But before he can speak, JD sets down his hammer with a definitive clunk. He nods towards the house. "Better head in. Supper'll be ready soon."

Swallowing his unasked questions, Morgan slides off the fence. He falls in step behind JD, watching the man's steady stride as they make their way home, the moment for conversation slipping away with each step.

3

The memory of that quiet afternoon fades as Morgan's world explodes into noise and motion. The roar of the crowd drowns out any lingering questions, any doubts that might have followed him from JD's fence to this moment. Now, there's only the game, the clock, and the electric tension of a potential upset hanging in the air.

Morgan's eyes flick to the scoreboard, its bright digits searing hope into his chest. The stadium erupts as the Tigers inch toward an improbable upset over Chesapeake Heights. The scoreboard glows: Tigers 7, Mustangs 6. Minutes tick away.

One first down will cement victory for the struggling Tigers and their unexpected leader. Morgan's battered squad needs to drain the clock without catastrophe.

The Tigers huddle up, chests heaving and eyes wild with the possibility of victory. Tully is direct, low and intense. "Listen up. We're gonna bleed this clock dry." His gaze locks onto each player in turn. "I-Right, 32 Dive. Browdy, you're gonna cradle that ball like it's your firstborn and get it into Darius's hands." He slaps the halfback on the dome. "O-line, I want a wall. No heroics, just push."

All nod, swallowing hard. The weight of the moment settles.

Tully continues, "We snap on two. Every. Single. Time. Make them jump, make them sweat. But do not, I repeat, do not jump early. Understood?"

A chorus of "Yes, Coach" ripples through the huddle.

"Good. Now let's finish this. Tigers on three. One, two, three–"

"TIGERS!" The team roars, breaking the huddle.

As they line up, Morgan can see the desperation in the Mustangs' eyes. He takes a deep breath, wiping his hands on the towel hanging from his belt. The crowd's roar fades to a dull hum as he focuses on Tully's plan.

"Down!" his voice rings out. "Set!"

The tension ratchets up a notch. Morgan's muscles coil, ready to spring.

"Hut!"

Nothing moves. The defense twitches.

"HUT!"

The defense doesn't bite.

Morgan steps back, looking to the sideline. Tully motions for him to settle.

Morgan drops under center, again. "Green 18," The pin on the grenade.

"Hut!"

The line explodes into motion. Morgan receives the handoff, tucking the ball tight against his body. He pivots, slapping the ball against Darius's chest as he runs past.

The play unfolds, a brutal ballet of colliding bodies and churning turf. The star halfback, focused on the first down marker, swiftly cuts left. His cleats dig into the grass, seeking purchase as he speeds up.

In an instant, a Mustangs linebacker launches like a missile, helmet gleaming under the stadium lights. As the two players meet in a bone-jarring impact, the crowd's roar becomes a collective gasp. Darius's body twists, his left leg caught beneath him as he falls. A sickening crack echoes across the field, sending shivers down everyone's spines.

The halfback's face contorts in agony, his mouth open in a silent scream. He clutches at his ankle, fingers trembling as they trace the unnatural angle of the joint.

Nearby players recoil, some turning away, unable to look. The referee's whistle is shrill and insistent.

Trainers sprint onto the field, medical bags bouncing against their sides. They crouch by the fallen player, hands moving with practiced efficiency. One probes the injury, eliciting a sharp hiss of pain from the halfback.

Darius's eyes, wide with shock and glistening with unshed tears, dart between his leg and the scoreboard as he's loaded up and escorted off the field.

Tully's face darkens. He fixes a razor-sharp gaze on Morgan, who has jogged over to the sideline. "They're blitzing weak-side," he barks, mind racing. "Three steps, Rhythm Plan 2. Get them open!"

Ryley perches in the end-zone bleachers, apart from the frenzied crowd. Her eyes narrow on Morgan as he takes the field. She exhales, breath misting in the cold air. Her fingers tap on the metal seat.

Morgan stands tall before ten battered faces in the huddle, all pleading for a miracle. He leans closer, yelling above the swelling crowd. "Wait for my shift call. Keep them guessing until then," he instructs. Ten helmets dip in unison. No hesitation in the trenches.

A sharp clap breaks the huddle. Morgan strides to the churned line, gauging the critical distance to the final first down marker.

Crouched behind the center, he surveys the bewildered defenders shifting across New Liberty's unconventional formation.

"Down...set!" Morgan's voice surges with the electric atmosphere. "Hut! Hut!" The cadence fails to draw an early jump.

Morgan inhales. "Shift!" The Tigers slide into textbook single-back formation at his command.

His next words slice through the resonant stands: "Green 18. Green 18! Hut." The ball snaps home. Morgan drops back, three perfect strides carrying flawless timing.

The outside linebacker blitzes unimpeded. Rabbit abandons his route, blindsiding the defender and nullifying the threat.

Morgan squares up. His release sends the ball spiraling to Wheeler, already pivoting along the far sideline.

The pass hangs against the darkening sky before dropping into Wheeler's grasp. He secures it without looking, muscle memory taking over. Sensing pursuit, he sprints for the first down marker, salvation within reach. Turf explodes beneath his cleats.

A back closes in, arms spread for the tackle. At the last instant, Wheeler executes a stutter step. The defender crashes to earth, inches from Wheeler's heels. He crosses the first down, but he can get more.

4

The New Liberty sideline erupts. Tully joins the frenzy, sprinting downfield. He waves his hat like a battle flag, his voice cracking as he urges Wheeler onward.

The crowd surges to its feet. Their roar shakes the heavens as the receiver drives for the crucial yards. They pound the metal stands—a thunderous heartbeat propelling the underdogs forward.

Chesapeake's All-State safety crashes into Wheeler. The impact halts momentum, but he cannot take him down. Somehow, their tangle inches forward.

Morgan arrives, shoulder to the mass. Other Tigers converge, identities blurred into one unyielding force, shoving Wheeler forward inch by bloody inch. Through the straining bodies, his wrist extends. The ball breaks the plane. Touchdown.

The stadium quakes, its foundations long weakened by defeat now fortified anew.

The clock hits zero. A piercing buzzer sounds, heralding New Liberty's stunning upset over top-ranked Chesapeake Heights. The Tigers collide in a tangle of pads and triumph, their elation drowning the frenzied home crowd.

On his knee amid the jubilant chaos, Morgan hurls his helmet skyward. He collapses onto the grass, chest heaving with laughter as the first stars emerge above the Friday night lights.

When he rises, he spots JD in the bleachers, clapping. His shoulders stand unbowed, a rare smile creasing his aged face. The sight speaks volumes.

A blur of motion draws Morgan's gaze downfield. A woman charges onto the turf, face contorted with fury. She locks onto Wheeler. Her hands latch onto his facemask, wrenching him close. She rips off his helmet. Her fingers claw at his cheeks as stunned teammates sprint to intervene.

The celebration falters. Players converge, creating a barrier between Wheeler and the enraged woman. They guide him away, causing confusion and shock to ripple through the team's ranks.

Coach Tully pulls the team away. "Everyone off the field! Now."

As the team reluctantly shuffles towards the locker room, the crowd's cheers morph into a confused murmur. Morgan falls in line with his teammates, casting one last glance over his shoulder. He catches JD's eye, and the old man mouths: "Find a way."

5

Euphoria pulses through the locker room. Screaming faces and clanging equipment as New Liberty revels in their upset victory.

Morgan sits on the bench, his shoulder pads discarded beside him. He turns Murph's Matchbox car over in his hands, feeling every dent and scratch on its well-worn surface.

Rabbit wraps Morgan in an exuberant hug from behind. They laugh, drunk on a newfound brotherhood forged in shared triumph.

Tully's voice cuts through the locker room chatter. "Alright, settle down!" He stands at the front, command radiating from his stance. As the noise fades, his eyes lock onto Morgan. "Browdy. Front and center."

Morgan rises, confusion etched on his face. He approaches Coach, aware of every eye in the room on him. Tully reaches behind him, revealing a royal blue letterman jacket.

"You've earned this, son," he says, his gruff voice softening just a touch.

Morgan takes the jacket, surprised by its weight. It's more than just fabric and thread; it's years of tradition, expectations, and responsibility. His fingers trace the embroidered school crest–a fierce tiger, muscles coiled and ready to pounce.

As he slips it on, the jacket settles on his shoulders like a mantle. The team erupts in cheers, but Morgan barely hears them.

Across the room, Wheeler removes his pads without acknowledging the celebration and stalks toward the back bay in bitterness.

6

Morgan trails him through the locker room. Suddenly, Wheeler whirls around, his face a mask of fury. He rips off his helmet and hurls it against the lockers with a resounding crash. The sound ricochets off the concrete walls, leaving a ringing silence in its wake.

"Nash, that catch was something else." Morgan's words come tentative and unsure. He's not even certain Wheeler heard him, but it's out there now–an olive branch extended in the aftermath.

Wheeler is cold and dismissive. "Take your jacket and get bent, Browdy."

Morgan steps forward, determination in the set of his jaw. "What's your problem with me?" The words burst out, raw and demanding.

Other players drift closer, drawn by the promise of conflict. Their presence prickles against Morgan's skin.

Wheeler's back expands with a deep breath, muscles coiling beneath his jersey. When he turns, his eyes are glacial, weighing their conflicted history in a single glance. "You don't know anything," he growls.

Morgan swallows hard, knowing his next words will change everything. "I saw your mom after the game. How she treats you."

The dam breaks. Wheeler erupts, hands fisting in Morgan's jacket. He slams him against the lockers.

Air rushes from Morgan's lungs. His fingers scrabble against Wheeler's grip, instinct fighting for breath. But as he meets Wheeler's gaze, he sees beyond the anger to the raw hurt beneath. Calm washes over him, unexpected and complete.

"She hurts you," Morgan says, his voice steady despite the pressure on his chest. His palm settles on Wheeler's white-knuckled grip. "It's not your fault, Nash."

The words strike true. Wheeler's facade cracks, his eyes widening in a moment of vulnerability. A sound tears from his throat—raw and primal, fury and anguish intertwined. His fist lashes out, connecting with the locker once, twice, three times. Metal groans and buckles beneath the onslaught.

He stumbles back, chest heaving. Blood trickles from his split knuckles, dripping onto the concrete floor. For a heartbeat, he stands there, a storm of emotions playing across his face. Then, without a word, he turns and leaves. His ragged breaths and uneven footsteps echo down the corridor, fading into the shadows beyond.

In the sudden quiet, Morgan sags against the lockers, adrenaline draining from his system. The cool metal at his back grounds him as he struggles to process what just happened.

The team's stunned silence fills the room, a palpable weight pressing in from all sides.

"What the hell, you broke Wheeler," mumbles Rabbit in awe.

"Show's over," Morgan mutters, a mix of emotions churning inside him. Guilt, relief, and an unexpected sense of remorse for his former enemy. He never thought he'd feel sorry for Wheeler, but the raw pain he'd witnessed changes everything.

As the team slowly disperses, Morgan remains, staring at the dented locker. He realizes that victory comes in many forms, and sometimes it feels a lot like loss.

7

By the time Morgan buttons his father's faded Carhart over his fresh bruises, the locker bay has cleared out.

Soft steps draw down the hall. He looks up as Ryley appears, a smile playing on her lips. Her hair tumbles free, framing her eyes bright with shared pride.

"Hell of a game, new-boy," she teases, stopping before him. The old nickname rings gentle now.

Morgan's chuckle warms the sterile room. "Thought you quit calling me that," he returns, matching her tone.

Ryley shrugs, eyeing the letterman jacket on the bench. "Wow. Finally got the jock status symbol, huh?"

Morgan holds the coat between them. "Try it on," he offers.

"I've got plenty of jackets," she protests, fingers pricking the fabric like it has cooties.

Morgan pivots her to face the large mirror at the end of the bay. Standing at her back, his bruised reflection supporting hers, he drapes the coat over her frame.

"This one's mine," he says simply, smiling at her over her shoulder.

Ryley clasps the front, engulfed in wool. She arches her brows at the reflection. "You know what comes next, right?" she asks. "You have to propose."

Their laughter fills the room. Ryley hugs the jacket close, her voice light. "What's the letterman prize? Steak? Lobster?"

Morgan's arms encircle her waist, thumbing over the birthmark on her wrist, "Let's hit the diner," he suggests. "Just us."

Ryley laces her fingers through his like a half-assed game of mercy. "I'd like that," she murmurs.

Hand in hand, the quarterback and the girl leave the stadium's gate behind. They enter the night, promising dreams waiting to unfold over late pancakes and quiet conversation.

8

The parking lot lies empty, save for the GTO throttling beneath the security light's yellow glow in the deserted teacher's lot. Morgan sprints up and raps on the fogged driver's window. It descends with a shriek, unleashing a wave of country music from within.

"I'm going to stay out for a while," Morgan says, his face still warm from victory. He shifts his weight, eager to depart.

JD glimpses Ryley, wrapped in the letterman jacket, waiting by the locker room. He suppresses a smile.

"Fine, just don't be late," he mutters with feigned gruffness. "Meet me back here in an hour or two."

Morgan nods, grinning. "Yessir." He turns to leave but pauses. He takes a deep breath and pivots back as JD raises the old manual crank window.

"Can I borrow some money?" he asks, kicking at the gravel. "I'll pay you back—"

JD snorts, shaking his head. He pulls out a few worn bills from his coat and hands them over.

Grinning with gratitude, Morgan seizes the cash.

As JD's GTO drives away, Ryley turns to Morgan. "Hey," she says quietly, "I know we were thinking dinner plans...but would you hate me if I pitched something else?"

Morgan's grin falters slightly. "Like?"

"Some college crew is throwing a party. I think it's Chloe's brother or whatever."

Morgan hesitates, brow furrowing. "Who is Chloe?"

"She's in our Chem class," Ryley explains, a hint of impatience in her voice.

"I don't know, Ry–" Morgan starts, uncertainty clear in his tone.

Ryley cuts him off, enthusiasm building. "Come on, it's a lake house. *Real* booze and shit this time. Not crappy dollar store liquor. Chloe's brother is basically a full adult."

She leans in, her voice taking on a playful, challenging edge. "We've never been truly fucked up together...could be fun. Besides, we both agreed to stop letting life just happen to us, right?

Might as well make it interesting ourselves." She nudges his chest. "Unless you're scared."

Morgan frowns, visibly conflicted. He opens his mouth to protest, but Ryley presses on.

"Come on, just one night out," she says, her voice softening. "One night to be normal teenagers and leave behind our shit. Don't we deserve that?"

Morgan's resolve crumbles under the weight of her words. He sighs, relenting. "Fine. But we're not staying all night."

"Deal," Ryley says, triumphant. She pulls out her phone, already moving to the next step. "I'll text Kassidy for a ride."

As they walk towards the road, Morgan looks back, a nagging sense settling in his gut. The night seems to hold its breath, waiting.

He can't shake the feeling that they're walking into something they're not prepared for.

9

The Toyota hums down the dark road. Street lights flashing by in a rhythmic pattern. Morgan sits in the back, wedged between Ryley and some girl named Ashley. Up front, Kassidy drives while her best friend, Jenna, rides shotgun. The girls' chatter fills the car, punctuated by occasional bursts of laughter.

"So, did you hear about Misha and that guy?" Jenna asks, her voice lowered conspiratorially.

Ashley leans forward, eager for gossip. "No. Spill!"

"Apparently, she got so fucked up she couldn't even stand. Then he took her upstairs and—"

"Jesus," Kassidy interrupts, her grip tightening on the steering wheel. "That's rape. Is she okay?"

Ryley speaks up, her tone surprisingly casual. "I mean, she knew what she was getting into, right? You don't go to those parties expecting to stay sober and play fucking Monopoly."

Morgan turns to look at Ryley, startled by her callousness.

"True," Ashley nods. "Besides, I heard she's been making rounds at every party, anyway."

"So, who's that fine specimen?" Jenna drawls looking at Morgan. "You've been awfully quiet back there. Cat got your tongue... or is it Ryley?"

The girls erupt in giggles as Morgan shifts uncomfortably. Ryley rolls her eyes but can't hide her smirk. "Leave him alone," she says, but there's no real defense in her tone. "He's not used to you vultures yet."

Ashley leans across Morgan, her perfume overwhelming in the confined space. "Aw, we're just jealous, Ry. You've been hoarding this cutie all to yourself."

Morgan's face burns as the girls laugh again.

Kassidy sighs dramatically, her eyes flicking to the rearview mirror. "God, I wish we could crash that lake house party with you guys. Sounds like it's gonna be epic."

"Yeah," Jenna adds, a hint of frustration in her voice. "But we promised Jake we'd stop by his house party. His ego would be crushed if I didn't show."

"More like he'd be pissed if you didn't show up to stroke his ego," Ashley mutters.

Ryley pats Jenna's shoulder sympathetically. "Next time. We'll give you all the juicy details tomorrow."

"Oh, almost forgot! My cousin said he can hook us up with some fake IDs," Ashley says, fishing a crumpled card from her purse. "Fifty bucks each, but they'll scan at any club in the state. Hello freshman year bar crawls!"

Ryley's eyes light up. "Shit, for real? I'm in."

Catching his eye, Ryley gives Morgan a quick smile before turning back to the girls. "Hey speaking of, remember that time we snuck into that bar downtown? God, that bouncer was such a perv."

"Oh my god, yes!" Jenna exclaims. "But hey, at least we got shitfaced for free all night."

Morgan's stomach churns. He stares out the window, trying to reconcile this version of Ryley with the one he thought he knew. The trees blur by outside, and he feels a growing distance between himself and the girl beside him.

As the car rounds a bend, the lake house comes into view, pulsing with light and noise.

Kassidy parks just before the driveway. She turns to look at Morgan and Ryley in the backseat, her expression a mix of excitement and jealousy. Her warm brown eyes catch the colorful reflections from the party lights. She pulls back her curly hair into a messy bun, with a few rebellious strands framing her heart-shaped face. Her electric blue fingernails tap a nervous rhythm on the steering wheel.

Ryley asks, "Ready?"

Morgan speaks up for the first time, trying to project confidence he doesn't quite feel. "More than ready."

Ryley, craning to see the blitz of energy seeping from the cottage, says, "I'm actually kinda hyped now."

"I'll be back to pick you up in a little while, okay? Text me if you need anything before then," Kassidy confirms.

As Ryley and Morgan climb out of the car, Kassidy calls, "And hey–no glove, no love, got it?"

Ryley laughs, waving Kassidy off. The bass from the house thrums through the soles of their shoes, and for a moment, despite his reservations, Morgan can't help but feel alive, anticipating where their evening is headed.

10

The front door swings open, unleashing a wall of sound and heat. Morgan and Ryley step inside, immediately engulfed by the party's chaos. The room smells of spilled beer, sweat, and something herbal.

Multicolored lights pulse in time with the music, casting strange shadows across unfamiliar faces. Bodies press close, dancing, laughing, shouting over the din. The pair inches forward, squeezing through the crowd, their shoulders bumping against strangers offering sideways glances.

This is not like the party where he and Ryley met. Here, everything is amplified, more intense. He glances at Ryley, seeing his own uncertainty mirrored, however brief.

As they push deeper into the house, the press of bodies separates them slightly. He tugs at Ryley's sleeve, his voice barely audible over the thundering music. "Do you see Chloe anywhere?"

Ryley scans the crowded living room, searching for the familiar face. But all she sees are strangers–and not just strangers, but older strangers. The partygoers' faces hold a world-weariness that makes Morgan and Ryley's high school concerns seem suddenly childish.

"Maybe she's in the kitchen?" Morgan suggests, trying to keep the unease out of his voice. They push their way through the throng, dodging elbows and sloshing drinks.

In the kitchen, no sign of Chloe, just more of the same.

"This can't be the right place," Ryley mutters, confused. "Chloe said it would just be a few of her brother's friends."

Morgan nods, fumbling for his phone. "Maybe we should text Kassidy to come back. What's her number?"

But as he pulls out his phone, he realizes he has no service. He looks up to find Ryley has drifted away, caught in animated conversation with a man who looks old enough to be her father. The stranger's hand rests on her shoulder. Too familiar, too possessive. She throws her head back, laughing at something he says.

"Here," a rough voice stops his spiraling thoughts. "Drink up, man!" Morgan turns to face a guy whose stubble and bloodshot eyes tell of a night far gone. He extends a red plastic cup, the contents sloshing close to the rim.

Morgan hesitates but catches Ryley already accepting a cup of her own, her gaze flicking to Morgan in silent acceptance. The implication hangs between them: Don't be a buzzkill. Live a little.

With a resigned sigh, Morgan takes the cup. The ominous liquid foams, the smell alone enough to make his head swim.

Before finishing the cup, Ryley is on the move again. With surprising agility, she weaves to reach a small group on the far side of the room. Morgan follows, reluctance at every step. His free hand reaches out, trying to catch her arm, but she always remains just out of reach.

They settle onto a worn couch, springs groaning in protest beneath them. Morgan's nerves ease when he considers that at least they're together. At least he can keep an eye on her here.

But the relief is short-lived.

"Truth or dare!" someone shouts. A cheer goes up from the group, Ryley's voice among the loudest.

"Ry," he leans close, lips brushing her ear. "Maybe we should–"

"Lighten up," she interrupts, playfully shoving his shoulder. "It's just a game."

The bottle spins, neck pointing accusations around the circle. Morgan watches as inhibitions fall away with each round. Secrets spilled, boundaries pushed and broken.

When the bottle lands on Ryley, her eyes light up with dangerous excitement. "Dare," she says without hesitation.

A guy with a shark-like grin leans forward. "I dare you...to go skinny dipping in the pool out back."

The group erupts in drunken cheers. Ryley stands, swaying, a reckless grin plastered across her face. "Watch me."

"Ryley, no." Morgan grabs for her wrist, but she twists away.

"Don't be such a prude." She's already headed toward the porch, the crowd parting to let her pass.

Morgan scrambles to catch up, the world tilting beneath him. When did he finish his drink? His thoughts feel sluggish, limbs uncooperative.

"Wait!" he calls, pushing through the throng of bodies. But the press of the crowd works against him, elbows and shoulders creating an ever-shifting maze.

Finally, he grabs hold of her. "What the hell are you thinking?"

"Stop protecting me. If you want to go, just go!"

She's gone before he can reply.

11

Back at the farmhouse, Wilke's hand fumbles across his cluttered nightstand. Fingers brush past crumpled papers and empty bottles before finding purchase on the sweating cardboard of a fresh six-pack. As he drags them closer, the cans clink together, a metallic chorus in the stifling room.

With practiced ease, he pops the tab on the lukewarm Bud Light. Escaping carbonation hisses, momentarily breaking the oppressive stillness. Wilke raises the can to his lips, letting the bitter liquid numb his throat.

A sudden flood of light invades his sanctuary. Headlights slice through the darkness, casting stark shadows across the peeling wallpaper and piles of unwashed laundry. He squints against the glare, his eyes struggling to adjust after hours in the gloom.

Curiosity—or perhaps a flicker of something long-dormant—stirs within him. He plants his palms against the sagging mattress, grunting himself upright. His joints protest the movement, reminding him of time's relentless march.

He shuffles towards the window, his bare feet navigating the minefield of discarded possessions littering the floor. At the grimy pane, he presses his forehead against the cool glass and peers out.

A waiting car idles at the drive, and a lone figure gets out of the back seat.

The warped screen door groans as Wilke steps onto the porch, holding up a palm to block the headlights illuminating the house. His eyes track to the gravel drive where the taxi pulls away, leaving an unexpected visitor standing amid scattered bottles and rural decay in the yard.

Wilke's heart clenches. Even in darkness, he recognizes the curve of those shoulders: Ailea.

Like a specter returning to haunt, Ailea pauses before the rickety steps. Her gaze rises to meet Wilke's across the tangle of weeds filled with cricket songs.

Wilke's voice scrapes out, raw with disuse and something close to emotion. "Never thought I'd see your face here."

Ailea shifts her weight, arms wrapped tight around herself. "Place looks the same as I remembered it," she murmurs, eyes darting to the sagging dormers and wilted roof.

"Yeah, well..." Wilke's fingers tighten around his beer can. "The old man clearly ain't one for home improvement."

"I suppose not," she agrees.

"You cut your hair," Wilke observes, his tone flat.

Ailea's hand rises to her shortened locks. "Needed a change."

A long moment stretches. All the possibilities of what to say next play out in their minds, but the obvious can't be ignored.

"That seems to be your thing," Wilke jabs.

Ailea's eyes flash, "That's not fair, Wilke."

"Fair?" He barks out a laugh. "You want to talk about fair?"

The crickets' chorus swells as if sensing the pain between them. Ailea opens her mouth, then closes it, swallowing whatever retort she'd prepared.

A car passes on the distant highway beyond the fields, its engine fading into the night. Ailea clears her throat. "How's...how's Morgan doing?"

Wilke's jaw clenches. "It's been rough." He leaves it at that.

"Yeah," Ailea whispers, guilt etching her features. She takes a shaky breath. "Wilke, I—"

"Why are you here, Ailea?"

She flinches at his tone. Her eyes glisten in the faint porch light. "I was sixteen when we had Morgan," she says, her voice thin.

Wilke's grip on the beer can tightens, metal creaking under the pressure. "Ancient history, now."

"I know but—it's all tangled up in my head. Us. The boys. Everything." She fights back tears.

Wilke takes another swig of beer, buying time before he speaks. "Lot of water under the bridge since then."

"Too much," Ailea agrees, her voice barely above a whisper. She wraps her arms tighter around herself as if warding off a chill only she can feel. "I keep thinking about Murph's last birthday. That ridiculous cowboy theme?"

A ghost of a smile flickers across Wilke's face, there and gone. "Kid looked like a damn rodeo clown."

"But he was so happy," Ailea says, her voice catching.

Wilke's expression hardens. "Until he wasn't."

The words hang between them, heavy as storm clouds. Ailea steps forward and then stops, uncertain.

"I thought I had life figured out when Murph came..." she exhales, forcing the words. "Then God took him away, and I couldn't cope."

Grief hangs thick between them under the indifferent stars.

"I couldn't stay after," she says. "It was like the walls were closing in. Every room, every corner, all I could see was him. All I could see were reminders that I failed. I failed to do what I was put on this earth to do. To protect my baby."

Her throat catches, reliving the pain she's carried for days gone by. "What kind of joke is it? To be given such a gift and then watch it get yanked away. Like your heart gets taken in the night and everything you ever loved gets tainted beyond recognition. Your identity with it. Left behind, nameless."

Fighting his hurt, Wilke speaks. "And what about us? The ones left behind? You think it was any easier for me and Morgan?"

Ailea wipes at the tears tracking down her hollow cheeks. She meets her husband's gaze across the divide. "Since you left, I kept losing," she confesses. "Every day I would pass our old house with that FOR SALE sign out front, that home where our family once laughed."

Anguish twists her features as she searches Wilke's impassive face. "I was too broken then to say it, but I need my husband."

Wilke drags a calloused hand over his stubble, exhaling hard. He steps off the porch into the overgrown grass, crossing the distance until mere feet separate them.

"I lost him too, Lea," Wilke says, his voice firm yet gentle. "Never forget that." His eyes shine.

Ailea extends a shaking hand, her wedding band catching the moonlight. Wilke studies her hopeful face, framed by fading ghosts of past accusations. His jaw unclenches. He reaches out, his weathered hand meeting her smaller one.

"I can make some coffee if you want to come in for a bit," he soothes.

12

The bass throbs through the floorboards of the lake house, a relentless heartbeat. Morgan stands at the edge of the living room, his back pressed against floral wallpaper. The smell of sweat and cheap beer cling to his skin like a second layer. His eyes scan the sea of strangers, hoping to find the one he came with.

Ryley.

He spots her across the room, her laugh bright and brittle as it cuts through. She's perched on the arm of a tattered couch, surrounded by a group. Her cup tilts as she gestures to them, liquid sloshing over the rim.

Morgan's stomach twists. This isn't their world. They don't belong here, in this run-down house with its sagging porch and windows covered with old newspapers. Now, hours deep into the night, 'a little while' stretches before them like an endless, dark road.

He pushes off the wall, making his way over. "Ryley," he calls as he reaches the couch. She turns, her smile widening.

"Morgan!" she shouts, too loud. She hops down, swaying. "Where'd you go? You have to meet everyone!" It's like she completely forgot their fight.

Before he can protest, she's dragging him into the circle. Names blur together–Albie with the earring, Lanna with blue hair, Nate who towers over them all. They nod, expressions ranging from vague interest to glazed indifference.

"You guys go to State too?" Albie asks, words slurred.

Morgan opens his mouth, but Ryley beats him to it. "Yeah! Absolutely!"

The lie hits him like a punch to the gut. He turns to her, but she avoids his gaze, focusing on the group with an intensity that borders desperation.

"I thought I recognized you," Lanna says, tilting her head. Her hair catches the light, shimmering like an oil slick. "What's your major?"

Another lie tumbles from Ryley's lips, smooth and practiced. Morgan's chest tightens. This isn't like her. The Ryley he knows isn't brash or so inclined to lie to fit in. The Ryley he knows is thoughtful and careful with her words. But tonight, she's shedding her skin, becoming someone new and reckless. Or maybe this is her...

The conversation flows around them, a current Morgan can't quite catch. He nods at the right moments, forces laughs when others do. His eyes track Ryley's cup, watching it empty and refill with alarming speed.

"Hey," he murmurs, leaning close. "Maybe we should get some water?"

She turns to him, eyes bright but unfocused. "You're a downer! We're having fun!" Her words slur together, lost in the pounding music.

Before he can argue, Nate stands over them. "Beer Pong!" he announces. "You two in?"

Ryley bounces on her toes, nodding. Morgan's protest dies on his lips as she grabs his hand and pulls him towards the kitchen. With her fingers intertwined with his and the warmth of her touch against his skin, he can almost pretend they're somewhere else–anywhere but here.

A long table dominates the space, and someone has arranged red cups in neat triangles at either end. A small crowd has already gathered, talking and laughing as they set up the game.

"You any good?" Nate asks, tossing a ping-pong ball between his hands.

Morgan chirps up. "We've never actually–"

"We'll crush you," Ryley interrupts, her grin fierce and challenging.

Nate raises an eyebrow, a slow smile spreading across his face. "Big words, frosh. Let's see you back them up."

The game begins, and Morgan's world shrinks to the bounce of small white balls and the clinking of plastic cups. Ryley takes to it with surprising skill, her aim true despite intoxication. Morgan does his best to keep up, the pressure of watchful eyes on them.

With each successful shot, the crowd grows. Cheers erupt as Ryley sinks another ball, her triumphant whoops mixing with the thumping bass from the other room. Morgan watches her shine under the attention, transforming into someone he doesn't recognize.

The game stretches on, time losing all meaning. More cups are drained, refilled, and arranged into new patterns. Morgan's head swims, the alcohol hitting him harder than he expected as he struggles to focus on the table before him.

"Last cup!" someone shouts. "Death cup!"

Ryley steps up. Her stance is wobbly but determined. The room goes quiet, all eyes on her. She takes a deep breath, pulls back her arm, and lets the ball fly.

It arcs through the air, seeming to hang there for eternity. Morgan holds his breath.

The ball drops, hitting the rim of the cup. It spins once, twice-

And falls in with a soft 'plop.'

The kitchen erupts with voices raised in celebration. Ryley throws her arms around Morgan's neck, laughing wildly. "I'm just like you. Star quarterback making touchdowns." Her words slur, but the kiss on the cheek is real. For a brief second, he lets himself get caught up in it–the joy, the triumph, the electric energy of the crowd.

Looking at Ryley, he notices the glassy sheen of her pupils and her swaying even when still. Reality comes crashing back.

"We should go," he says, leaning close to be heard over the noise.

Ryley pulls back, her smile fading. "What? No! We just won—"

"I know, but it's late and—"

"Morgan." Her voice carries a sharp edge he's never heard before. "Stop trying to ruin this. For once in your life, just...let go."

The words sting, burrowing under his skin. He opens his mouth to argue, but Ryley's already turning away, accepting congratulations and high-fives from the crowd.

A stranger pulls her into an unwelcome embrace, his hand sliding up her shirt.

Nate appears at his elbow, clapping Morgan on the back. "Come on, I think this calls for something special."

Before Morgan can protest, they're being herded back into the living room. The party has grown, bodies packed even tighter than before. The air is thick with smoke, making his eyes water.

They end up squeezed onto the sagging couch, Ryley pressed against his side. Her skin burns hot through the thin fabric of her shirt. They pass around a bottle filled with something clear and vicious-looking. Morgan watches with growing dread as Ryley takes a long swig.

Time stretches and contracts, moments blurring together. It's like he's underwater. Sounds are muffled and distorted. He can't keep count of how many times the bottle comes around and how many cups people press into his hands.

At some point, he notices a shift in the surrounding energy. The music has changed, becoming slower and more insistent. Bodies move together in ways that make him flush and look away.

Ryley leans against him, her breath hot on his neck. "Dance with me," she murmurs, tugging at his hand.

He hesitates. "I don't think–"

Her eyes are wide, pleading. "Just one song."

They stumble to a patch of floor, Ryley's arms winding around his neck. She presses close, swaying to the beat. Morgan's hands hover awkwardly at her waist, hyper-aware of every point of contact between them. Her fingers thread through his hair, nails scraping lightly against his scalp. He shivers, heat coursing through him like an explosion of pleasure. Ryley looks up at him through lowered lashes, a question in her eyes that he's unsure how to answer.

The song changes, something faster and more aggressive. Bodies press in on them, the dance floor becoming a writhing mass. Morgan loses sight of Ryley, panic clawing at his throat.

He finds her again, but she's dancing with someone else now–a guy with tattoos snaking up his arms.

Morgan reaches for her. "I think we should—"

"There you are—" A random girl appears in front of him, blocking his path. Her makeup is smeared, dark streaks under her eyes. "Let me show you something–"

Her lips find their way to his. Her mouth tastes like cigarettes. Morgan tries to step back, but there's nowhere to go. Bodies hem him in on all sides.

He breaks the lip lock and cranes his neck, searching for Ryley. He catches glimpses–a flash of her hair, the curve of her smile. But she's always just out of reach, lost in the throng of the night.

13

The song ends, transitioning into something slower. The streaked-eyed girl sways. "I don't feel so good," she mumbles.

Morgan catches her as she stumbles. He looks around, searching for help. But everyone around them remains lost in their own world, oblivious to the unfolding drama.

With a sinking feeling, he realizes it's up to him. He half-carries and half-drags the girl toward what he hopes is a bathroom. They bump into other partiers, earning glares and muttered curses.

The hallway seems endless, doors blurring together. Morgan's arms ache from supporting this girl's weight. Thankfully, he finds a bathroom where a few people linger.

He gets her to the toilet before she retches, body heaving. Morgan turns away, his own stomach churning. He wets a washcloth, glimpsing himself in the mirror. He doesn't recognize the face staring back at him. Bloodshot eyes peer out from dark, sunken sockets. His skin is pale, almost gray, with a sheen of cold sweat.

Pressing the cloth to the back of the girl's neck, he murmurs, "You're okay," the words feeling empty.

Time loses meaning as he kneels on the cold tile floor, holding the girl's hair back as she empties her stomach. His mind races.

The girl's breathing evens out and she slumps against the wall, eyes closed. "I want to go home," she whimpers.

Morgan's heart clenches. "Let's find your friends, okay?"

It takes what feels like hours to locate the girl's roommate, a harried-looking blonde who takes one look at her friend and sighs. "Not again, Megan."

Morgan watches them leave, the roommate supporting Megan's stumbling form. He feels like an empty shell, exhaustion settling deep in his bones.

14

The party rages on, but the excitement has soured. He sees now what he missed before–the desperation in some eyes, the way laughter sometimes edges towards hysteria. This isn't freedom or fun. It's an escape and a poor one.

He needs to find Ryley.

The living room is a war zone of empty cups and discarded clothing. Morgan scans the writhing mass on the dance floor, but there's no sign of her. Panic claws at his throat as he moves from room to room, calling her name.

He's about to head upstairs when a sound catches his attention. Soft sobs, barely audible over the pounding music. He follows it to a small alcove near the back door.

Ryley sits with her face buried in her knees. Her shoulders shake with each ragged breath.

"Ry?" Morgan kneels beside her, hand hovering unsure over her back. "What happened? Are you okay?"

She turns around, her face a mess. "I'm fine," she mumbles, wiping at her cheeks. "Just...needed air."

Morgan settles beside her, their shoulders touching. The music thrums through the floor, a constant reminder of the chaos beyond their little shelter. "Let's go back to your place."

Ryley shakes her head, a strange light entering her eyes. "No," she says, her voice firming. "No, I don't want to leave."

"But—"

"I'm fine." She stands, swaying slightly. "I just need another drink. Come on."

She's pulling him to his feet, leading him back into the fray. She weaves through with surprising agility, making a beeline for the makeshift bar.

There, she grabs two cups, pressing one into his hand. "Drink," she commands, a challenge in her eyes. As she raises her cup in a mock toast, he mimics the action.

After that, time becomes fluid. Cups are refilled, emptied, and discarded. The room pulsates with energy, drawing them deeper into its rhythm. Morgan can't remember how many drinks he's had or how many songs have played. He just knows that Ryley is always there, laughing too loud and dancing too close.

But as the night wears on, the music gets louder, and the room gets hazier. The laughter around him sounds distorted, almost mocking.

Morgan thinks he sees a hand hovering over their cups, dropping something in. But the moment passes, lost in the party's anthem. It was just a trick of the light, right?

He loses Ryley and loses track of himself. The world narrows to disconnected sensations—strobe lights piercing his vision, laughter echoing in his ears, the burn of alcohol down his throat. The room spins, faces blurring into unrecognizable smears of color.

Her familiar laugh breaks his fog. He blinks hard, trying to focus, but the world shifts like a funhouse mirror. She's across the room, wedged between two guys he doesn't know. Her movements are off–too loose, too uncoordinated. Her eyes roll.

Morgan stumbles in her direction. The floor seems to tilt beneath his feet.

"Ryley," he manages, reaching for her. "We should go."

One guy steps in front of him. "She's good here, man. Why don't you find your own party–"

Morgan's fist clenches, but the room won't stop moving. He can barely stand. "Something's wrong. I can't...I can't feel my legs."

The guys guide Ryley away. Panic slices through Morgan's stupor. He tries to follow, but his system gives out. The last thing he sees is Ryley disappearing with the guys into the crowd.

Then darkness.

15

In the vacant teacher's lot, JD stretches across the vinyl bench seat of the car, scuffed boots on the dash. His calloused fingers spin a worn football. He tips back a perspiring 7-Up can as Journey's muted notes drift from the cassette player. He checks his watch for the third time in as many minutes. Morgan and Ryley should have been back forty minutes ago.

He scans the looming sports wing, fixing on a single-lit window deep within. Perhaps a janitor working late or another soul restless with regret pacing those absent halls?

"Ah, what the hell..." he kills the stereo and hauls himself from the car. Pocketing his keys, JD sets off towards the entrance.

He raps on the door marked 'Coach Edward Tully' before opening it, the knock drowned by a film projector's shutter.

The cramped space reveals the aging head coach hunched behind a battleship desk buried under game tape notes and play diagrams. Tully's face shows rare vulnerability, unmoving as JD enters. His eyes stay on the grainy footage casting spectral shapes across scarred wood panels–visions of various victories and crushing defeats on replay.

JD searches for words to match the room's deep unease. "Still at it, Coach?" he attempts. "The wife's likely holding supper for you."

Tully emits a thin scoff, his stare fixed on the projected phantoms of kids who once thought him all-knowing. He rips a sheet from a tattered playbook, crumpling the page in one fist.

"Way back when you first walked from the league, I told myself you'd lost your damn mind giving up like that," he confesses to JD's solemn profile hovering by the office door. "Turning your back on giving them kids opportunities at the next level. Some were throwing pigskins as soon as they could walk, working their whole lives for that one shot..." Tully shakes his head.

"I started coaching because I believed I could mold raw athletes into even better men through this game, and I know you used to think the same way." The projector continues to whir in the small room. Tully stabs the OFF switch, plunging his gaze into shadow. "But years went by after you quit the sidelines, Jack. And I slowly started seeing exactly why you walked away."

He gestures at the darkened screen where ghostly footage flickered. "It's the dead look that comes into those boys' eyes when living knocks their legs out from under 'em. When they get their asses kicked by bigger forces despite working themselves half to death. You watch their beliefs crumble."

His voice drops. "We try building them and their dreams up–make them think that with enough heart, they can overcome anything life throws." Tully lifts his eyes to JD's stoic gaze. "But then life intervenes as it does...rips their control away. And when they turn back bloody and begging for why, for the plan now...suddenly a coach finds he's run plumb out of answers to give."

Solitude settles between the two aging men, dwelling on duty and faith wavering in the darkness of the cement cubicle. Tully rummages to extract a hidden bottle of amber spirits from the bottom desk drawer.

With slow ceremony, he sets the whiskey atop scattered play diagrams between them. But the comfort of old vices rings futile tonight in the dreary office.

Tully speaks to the peeling linoleum. "It's finished for us this season, Jack. Final division rankings just came across the wire," he intones. "Duneland pulled off a victory in their game, so they took the Conference on total wins. Browdy's..." The name hitches in his throat. "Regardless of the outcome tomorrow, it'll be your boy's last snap as our quarterback. The season is over once that clock hits zero tomorrow night."

Reality drops under revelation's weight.

"Ed, it's his senior year..." JD huffs. "What about an appeal...is there no shot at all for the final?"

Tully shakes his head.

He reaches for two chipped cups discarded in the drawer with a slight upward twitch of one cheek. No triumphant toasts or speeches to mark fallen comrades pouring out tonight.

16

Morgan wakes up, head pounding. The house is quiet now. He blinks, trying to figure out where he is. He's lying on something hard and uncomfortable: the floor. Drenched in sweat, his hair is plastered to his forehead and his clothes stick to him. His tongue feels like sandpaper. The taste in his mouth is foul, a mixture of stale alcohol and something worse that he doesn't want to think about.

The music, once loud, is now merely a faint thump upstairs. Cigarette butts and spent CO_2 canisters are littered amongst red cups and snack wrappers, scattered everywhere.

Morgan fumbles for his phone, squinting at the bright screen. 3:47 a.m.. His stomach drops.

How long was he out? He remembers nothing after seeing Ryley with those guys across the room. That was around midnight, maybe?

Ryley. Where is she...

Panic cuts through his foggy brain. He struggles to his feet, nearly falling as the room spins, forcing him to pause and steady himself against a nearby chair. His head throbs with each movement, a dull hammer thumping behind his eyes.

As he makes his way towards the stairs, the faint music grows louder. It's coming from where the bedrooms are. The bass pulses in time with his heartbeat, growing stronger as he approaches the staircase.

Each step is a challenge, and his feet feel like they are lead, clumsy. Halfway up, he has to stop, leaning against the wall as a wave of dizziness washes over him.

The music is more clear now. He can make out words, but they're muffled by walls and closed doors. As he reaches the top of the stairs, the hallway stretches out before him, a row of closed doors on either side. The sound comes from the far end, where a sliver of light escapes beneath a door.

He tries to gather his courage, not knowing what he'll find behind those doors. But he has to look. Ryley is here somewhere. She has to be.

His hand hovers over the doorknob.

One last steadying breath, he turns it and pushes.

17

She's alone. Curled up on a mattress, covers disheveled and her clothes thrown nearby. She looks small.

"Ryley," he whispers, kneeling beside her. "Ryley, wake up."

She stirs, still asleep.

Morgan clicks off the boombox that plays on the dresser nearby, and the room falls quiet. Anger flares as he spots a man's shirt and wallet by an overturned chair, close to Ryley's tangled pants. He has to wake her. But then what? If he can barely remember what happened in the last three hours, will she? A war rages in his mind. Tell her the truth, let her live with that pain, that violation?

Or...

He makes a choice.

Morgan strips off his shirt and curls beside her on the mattress. The springs creak under his added weight. He doesn't touch her, leaving a small gap between their bodies.

Ryley's breath, still tinged with alcohol, changes rhythm. She doesn't open her eyes but tenses, aware of the new presence beside her. Morgan remains still, his own breath shallow and controlled.

Minutes pass.

The room is dim, with a sliver of street light peeking through a curtain crack. Her lashes flutter just enough to see him lying there. She scoots closer, closing the distance between them.

After another long while, one that feels like hours, she rubs her red-rimmed and puffy eyes open. She looks around as if suddenly realizing this is not her bed.

She consciously takes in Morgan, shirtless, and then realizes her own bareness. Her eyes stare at his face, trying to read his vacant, distant gaze. But he can't look at her.

"Were we good?" she asks innocently.

It's a long moment before his eyes meet hers, a mix of emotions swirling. "Last night was..." he trails off, words choking.

Finally, he nods.

She lays her head on his chest, snuggling up close. He hesitates, then rests his chin on her hair, smelling the familiar tang of her hairspray. He closes his eyes and pulls her in close, and yet the gap between them seems both infinitesimal and vast.

Protecting Ryley, yet privy to the evidence of her night, feels like the heaviest weight. It settles deep. For now, the truth he's choosing to keep settles on his shoulders like a heavy cloak.

9

1

As dawn chases the night from Main Street, casting elongated shadows in its gentle light, Morgan staggers down the deserted sidewalk, passing shuttered storefronts and dark cafes. The small town's heart lies dormant, shops closed, and streets quiet.

The neon sign of Sandy's Diner flickers off as daylight creeps in. Morgan's unsteady footsteps echo off brick facades and papered windows. A distant street sweeper hums, preparing the town for a new day.

Headlights cut through the gloom, sweeping across his back. Morgan squints, raising a hand to shield his eyes as the car slows. The rumble of a familiar engine reaches him–the GTO.

Tires crunch gravel when the car pulls alongside. JD leans out the window, face set with relief and fury. His eyes, red-rimmed from hours of searching, lock onto Morgan.

"Get in," he growls, voice hoarse.

Morgan hesitates, swaying on his feet. The car door swings open with a creak.

"Now," JD barks.

Morgan complies, sinking into the passenger seat. The leather feels incredible against his feverish skin. JD guns the engine, tires spitting as they peel away.

Silence fills the car, thick and oppressive. JD's knuckles whiten on the steering wheel. Miles of dark farmland blur past before he speaks.

"Six hours, Morgan," he says, voice low and dangerous. "No word. No call."

Morgan stares at his hands, shame burning his cheeks.

The GTO's engine growls, choking the moment. Morgan slumps against the window, the world spinning beyond the glass. JD's eyes dart between the road and his wayward charge, jaw clenched.

"What happened to dinner?" JD asks above the hum of the road.

Morgan's stomach twists. "I...I don't know. Can't remember."

"Start talking, Morgan. Now."

"There was a party," Morgan mumbles. "Wasn't supposed to go, but..." He trails off.

"But you went anyway," JD finishes, voice hard. "Throwing away commitments. Lying."

Morgan flinches. "I'm sorry, I—"

"Sorry doesn't cut it," JD snaps. "Do you know what I've been through looking for you?"

"I messed up. Things got out of hand."

"Out of hand?" JD barks with a harsh laugh. "That's putting it mildly. You're lucky I found you stumbling down that road instead of in a ditch somewhere."

Rain pats against the windshield.

JD's anger fills the suffocating car. "I trusted you," he says. "Two hours, that's what we agreed on. And you threw that away for what? For—for a party?"

Morgan's head pounds. "No, it wasn't...I don't remember much after the first hour."

JD's eyes narrow. "What do you mean you don't remember?"

"Everything's fuzzy," Morgan admits, voice barely audible. "I think...someone might have put something in my drink."

"You think someone put something in your drink?"

Morgan shrinks into his seat. "I...I'm not sure. One minute, I was fine, the next..."

"The next *what*, Morgan?" JD presses.

"Everything went sideways," Morgan mumbles. "Room spinning. Couldn't think straight."

JD's breath hisses through his teeth. "And you didn't think to call me? To get help?"

"I couldn't...I don't even know how I got out of there."

The car swerves onto the shoulder before being thrown in park. JD turns, his face filled with fury and fear. "Do you have any idea what could've happened to you?

Morgan's eyes meet JD's, haunted. "Yeah," he whispers. "I do."

JD's anger falters momentarily, replaced by a flash of concern. He grips the wheel tight. "What about that girl?" he asks, voice rough. "Wasn't she with you?"

Morgan's stomach twists. "Ryley," he manages, voice steadier than he feels. "She's...she's fine. I took care of it."

JD's eyes narrow, searching Morgan's face. "Took care of it, how?"

"I made sure she got home safe."

An empty beat fills the car. JD's grip on the wheel loosens, but suspicion lingers in his gaze. "You're certain about that?"

Morgan nods, unable to meet his grandfather's eyes. "Yeah. I'm sure."

JD exhales, his posture softening. "At least there's that," he mutters.

Morgan's reflection in the window looks alien–a stranger with different eyes and a face drawn tight with guilt.

The car rolls to a stop as JD pulls into the gravel driveway. The farmhouse looms before them, its weathered siding pale in the early morning as rain clouds open up. Chickens scatter as the car approaches, their squawks breaking the eerie quiet.

Morgan's hand trembles on the door handle. He glances at JD, stiff and tight-jawed.

"Inside," JD grunts, killing the engine.

2

Morgan trudges through the front door, exhaustion weighing heavily on his bones. The familiar creak of floorboards beneath his feet offers little comfort as he braces himself for the inevitable confrontation with his dad. His bleary eyes take a moment to adjust to the dim kitchen before him.

Wilke's voice rasps from his slump in a battered chair. "Got a visitor..." His words die unfinished.

Morgan peers through the dingy light. Beside Wilke stands a figure buried in his heart, present after months of emptiness. He sags against the door frame, stunned, lungs forgetting function. "M-mom...?" he rasps hoarsely.

The world shrinks. Ailea's face emerges—thinner, eyes shadowed, yet unmistakable. Her gaze, once familiar, now holds a strange distance.

JD's solid presence at Morgan's back falters. The old man is as blindsided as Morgan.

Wilke shifts, his chair groaning.

Morgan's mind reels. The night's horrors collide with his present. His mother, here, now, at his lowest point. After walking out on them months ago, leaving only pain.

His mouth opens, wordless. What could bridge the hurt her abandonment caused? He wants to demand reasons for her vanishing act, but his voice won't function.

Ailea steps forward, pleading. "Morgan," she whispers.

Rage flares, wrestling with confusion. Morgan's fists clench. He wants to run, to shout, to break.

"Don't I deserve a hug from my boy?" Ailea tries, her forced laugh brittle.

Wilke watches their standoff.

Morgan's eyes flick between his parents, anchored at opposite ends of the kitchen.

The lack of a reply causes Ailea to drop her gaze to the scuffed floor, twisting her hands.

"We have things to say, baby..." Her voice cracks. "Tomorrow, after your game, we want to ride back with you. Talk on the drive..."

"Ride back where?" he asks, dread pooling in his gut.

Wilke shifts, face grim in the stale room. "Your mama means we're going home."

Morgan's breath catches. His pulse races as the words land. Blood roars in his ears. "No. This is home," he spits, fists clenched white. "This is my home!" His voice breaks, making Ailea jump.

The echo mocks his desperation as the walls close in. His breath quickens. He jabs at his mother. "You think you can show up and erase everything?" Voice climbs. "You can't pretend these months didn't happen!"

Ailea recoils, hands raised. "Baby, please, I know you're upset..."

"Upset?" Morgan's laugh borders on manic. "While you checked out, we had to figure shit out!" His face twists, fury seeping through pain's cracks.

Wilke avoids his son's plea. This storm rages beyond his skill. Across the room, Ailea shakes her head. "Morgan, my sweet boy," she whispers. "What happened is no one's fault."

Her words only feed Morgan's churning rage. "No, this is the same. You want me to leave everything unfinished like you did."

With a raw cry, he slams his fists against the door. The house shutters. He bolts past JD into the morning air as rain descends.

3

Morgan's sprint carries him deep into the wheat field, each pounding step an attempt to outrun the world threatening to swallow him whole. The cold rain lashes his skin, mingling with hot tears of frustration and despair. Steam rises from his heaving form as he stumbles to a halt, surrounded by whipping stalks that seem to mock his futile escape.

His chest heaves, lungs burning as he gulps the damp air. The muffled sound of his own broken sobs startles him–a raw, wounded noise he barely recognizes as his own. The weight of it all crashes down: Ryley and the visceral fear of a world without her, his mother's unexpected return, the looming shadow of his old life threatening to erase everything he's built here. And beneath it all, Murph's absence—a constant, gnawing ache that never truly fades.

He wants to scream, to rage against the unfairness of it all. But the undulating wheat swallows his cries, leaving him more diminutive and alone than ever. He yearns to keep running, to somehow outpace the suffocating future barreling toward him. But reality sinks in, cold and unyielding as the muddy earth beneath his feet—there's nowhere left to run.

JD's tenor carries above the clamor like thunder answering the drumming rain. "Morgan...!"

Squinting through the deluge, Morgan makes out the old man's broad silhouette, plowing steadily through the grasping fingers of the cropland. He wants to turn away, to reject this connection to a world that's brought him pain. But he's rooted to the spot, trembling with a maelstrom of emotions he can't untangle.

Dragging a soaked sleeve across his ravaged face, Morgan straightens. His next words come out as a bitter challenge, his voice cracking with accumulated hurt.

"This was always going nowhere, wasn't it?" The question hangs between them as JD draws near.

The old man stops a few feet away, rain coursing through the deep crags of his weathered cheeks. His eyes, usually sharp and assessing, now carry a haunted look. Morgan notices the vulnerability in his face, something that was always there, but now apparent. Like a language he finally understands.

"Why'd you even bother with me?"

"Because your daddy never got the dignity of walking off the field one last time," JD admits, his voice somber and weighted with years of regret. "So many things I should have said to him that I'm going to tell you now."

He meets Morgan's gaze, unflinching despite the driving rain. When he speaks again, his words carry the resonant cadence of a man who's seen triumph and heartbreak in equal measure.

"You have to ask yourself who you want to be. You can give up. Spend your life wondering what could have been. Wake up every morning and look around an empty house with empty bedrooms..." JD's voice catches, and Morgan sees a flash of old pain.

"Or you can finish this game. Take a shot at making something of yourself. So far, us Browdy men never chose right. Not your father when he got your sixteen-year-old mother pregnant...threw away the game I spent my life teaching him. All American, best arm in the state." He wipes his mouth as if riding a foul taste.

"And not me when I let him walk out the door without a goodbye. Don't wait for life to deliver your fate."

The words hit Morgan like a physical blow. All the questions he wanted answered now cut through the fog of despair that's clouded his vision for so long. He sniffles, struggling to find his voice.

"Tomorrow's it...isn't it? My last time playing on that field."

"Win or lose." JD nods, his expression a mixture of determination and something softer. "But that ain't what matters."

As if responding to the moment's gravity, the wind and rain lash harder, nature seeming to sympathize with their struggle. A flash of lightning illuminates the scene–grandson and grandfather, student and mentor–two generations of Browdy men facing down their demons.

Morgan takes a shaky step forward, then another. The divide between them narrows. Not just in physical distance, but in understanding. There's still so much left unsaid, so many hurts to heal, but in this moment, Morgan finds a flicker of strength.

Turning toward the distant lights of the house, Morgan senses something long forgotten–not quite hope, but the possibility of it.

4

Game day.

Cleat studs echo through the empty tile corridor as New Liberty's players march for the locker room. The air, once crackled with pre-game jitters, is ominous. News of their dashed playoff hopes found its way to all ears.

Morgan trails yards behind the group, down the lone hall.

He hesitates...one quick pit-stop to make before the inevitable.

The fluorescent lights flicker to life in the senior hallway. Posters for pep rallies and student council elections dot the walls. He stops at a locker halfway down the bank.

With trembling fingers, Morgan spins the combination on Ryley's locker. The metal door creaks open, revealing a snapshot of a life–textbooks, crumpled papers, scribbled drawings on lined paper.

With the possibility of a winning season gone, he unfolds his letterman jacket, feeling its weight heavy in his hands. From his pocket, he retrieves a folded note with Ryley's name written on the front. He tucks the paper into the jacket's breast pocket, his fingers brushing against the fabric as if sealing a promise.

Among her belongings, he arranges the coat on the shelf. His hand lingers on the fabric like it's the last time he'll see it.

Morgan stares at his phone, thumb hovering over the keyboard. Ryley's chat, dormant since the night of the party, glares up at him. Swallowing hard, he types a brief message: *Something in your locker. Owe you an apology.*

His finger hovers over 'send' before he presses it.

Ryley's locker door closes with a soft click that sounds like finality. Morgan turns and continues down the hall. His footsteps, once in sync with the team, now fall out of rhythm. He walks towards the noise and light of the locker room, leaving behind a piece of himself in that quiet metal box.

5

The subdued locker room echoes with closing doors as the team suits up without their usual banter. Battered boys sit on wooden benches, brooding over defeat and shattered hopes. This is their last walk together onto the field.

Coach Tully enters, clipboard under his arm. It takes him a long while to find the words he wants to speak.

"Normally, I'd say hell of a season," he starts. "But fate had other plans. Still, we fought like tigers to the end. That counts for something."

Quiet follows. Tully rubs his buzz-cut and sighs. "Last game together. Let's make it count. So tell me: what kind of day is it?"

A few mumble replies.

Then Morgan stands, speaking to their bowed heads.

"I get it."

Tully looks at him.

"Dreams snatched away. Chances stolen. Feeling cheated by stuff out of our control." Morgan continues.

Their eyes lift.

Morgan straightens. "Coach is right–weird season. But we made the most of it. Went down swinging."

He looks at each teammate. "Maybe the score isn't what matters. It's about who we are walking onto that field versus walking off."

The locker room hangs in a fragile balance. Doubt and hope war on faces around him. Morgan bears the burden of the unspoken question: What now?

He swallows hard, searching for words to bridge the gap. "We've lost more than games this year," he admits, voice rough with emotion. "But look around. We're still here. Still standing."

A ripple of movement passes through the team. Backs straighten. Chins lift. Morgan presses on, his voice gaining strength.

"Every practice, every play, every bruise–that was us choosing not to give up. That's something they can't take away. Something worth more than points on the board."

His words preach possibility. Morgan's heart pounds, wondering if he's reached them or if his words will fall flat.

Rabbit looks up, his usual mischief gone. "You really think taking the field means anything at this point?"

Morgan meets his gaze. "I think it means more. Every time we showed up, we made a choice. To be part of something bigger."

A murmur ripples through the team. Nods of agreement, tentative at first, then more confident.

In the back corner, a bench creaks. Wheeler stands. The team falls silent, all eyes on the player who'd stormed off days ago. He runs a hand through his hair, a gesture betraying his nerves. "Look," he starts, voice. "I've been...difficult."

A few snorts echo around the room. Wheeler's lips twitch, almost a smile. "Okay, I've been a complete jackass." His eyes find Morgan's. "Especially to you."

He pauses, struggling with words. When he continues, his voice has an edge of rawness. "There's stuff...at home. It's not great." His jaw clenches, leaving the implication hanging. "It was easier to be angry here than..." he trails off, shaking his head. "Anyway. That's not on you guys."

He looks back at Morgan, something like respect in his eyes. "You kept showing up. Even when we...when I...made it hell for you. That's..." he struggles, then simply nods. His shoulders straighten, a decision visible in his posture. "This team. It's been something solid. Even when I didn't want it to be."

He takes a breath. "So yeah. If you're leading us out there, Browdy. I'm with you."

The silence that follows is heavy with unexpected honesty. Then, slowly, nods of agreement ripple through the team.

"So, what's the play?" Wheeler asks, no challenge in his voice now. Just an offer of unity, an acknowledgment that the field is Morgan's to command.

Morgan feels their expectations, but for once, it doesn't crush him. He straightens, looking each teammate in the eye.

"The play?" He nods toward the door. "We walk out there with our heads high. Show them what New Liberty's made of."

Rabbit grins, his old spirit returning. "Hell yeah, Captain!"

The energy in the room surges. Boys who, moments ago, looked defeated now stand tall, adjusting pads and helmets with renewed purpose.

Coach Tully steps forward, pride evident in his smile. He doesn't speak; he just nods at Morgan and gestures to the door.

Morgan faces the exit, the tunnel to the field beyond. The team falls in behind him, a united front.

"Tigers on three," he calls over his shoulder, voice steady and strong. Their answering roar shakes the lockers. As one, they move toward the tunnel, toward whatever awaits them under the Friday night lights. Win or lose, they'll face it together.

6

The kitchen of Sandy's Diner echoes with the harsh scrape of steel wool against aluminum. Ryley attacks a burnt lasagna pan with vicious swipes, as if she could scour away more than just cheese residue. Her jaw clenches in rhythm with each stroke.

Sweat beads on her forehead despite the chill seeping through the cafe's thin walls. Outside, excited chatter and distant cheers filter in. Ryley scrubs harder.

Her phone buzzes for the thousandth time. Without looking, she swats it off the counter. It clatters to the floor, the screen intact.

"Piece of crap," she mutters, dunking the pan back into soapy water with enough force to splash her shirt.

The clock above the swinging doors ticks.

Thirty minutes to kick off.

Ryley yanks the pan back out, inspecting it with narrowed eyes. It's still not clean. She reaches for the steel wool again, knuckles white around the coarse pad.

The back door bangs open so hard it bounces off the wall. Sandy waddles in, one hand on her lower back, wheezing.

"Jesus, kid. You still here?" Sandy's voice is gruff, tinged with a faded New York accent.

Ryley doesn't turn. "Place won't clean itself."

Sandy snorts. "Yeah, and the dishes'll still be here tomorrow. Unlike your social life, if you don't get your ass moving."

"Didn't ask for your opinion," Ryley mutters.

"Tough shit. You're getting it." Sandy pauses, her tone softening. "This about that college thing?"

Ryley sighs, turning to face her boss. "It's complicated."

"Always is. Try me," Sandy encourages.

Ryley hesitates before admitting, "I got in, but..." She trails off, unable to finish the thought.

"But what?" Sandy presses.

"What if I'm making a mistake? Leaving all this behind."

Sandy snorts. "All this? You mean this dump of a diner?"

A faint smile tugs at Ryley's lips. "You know what I mean."

"The boy?" Sandy asks knowingly.

Ryley shakes her head. "It's not that simple. Going means leaving behind...so much."

"That's what college is for, kid. Figuring shit out," Sandy says matter-of-factly.

"Maybe. But what if I go and realize I don't belong there either?"

"Listen, kid. You're smarter than you think. Don't let fear hold you back."

"It's not just fear. It's..." Ryley pauses, struggling for words. "Commitment. To people here."

"Good things," Sandy concedes. "But they shouldn't be anchors."

Frustration creeps into Ryley's voice. "And what if I can't do it?" "Can't do what? Live?" Sandy challenges.

"Be someone who deserves to," Ryley admits.

Sandy pulls a crumpled ticket from her pocket and slaps it on the counter. "Go to the damn game."

Ryley glares at the ticket. "Why do you care?"

"'Cause I'm tired of watching you mope around my kitchen like a wet cat." Sandy's tone softens. "And 'cause you'll regret it if you don't. Might remind you who you were before all this doubt."

Ryley's shoulders sag. "It's not that simple, Sandy."

"Never is, sweetheart. But sometimes you gotta choose yourself. Now get out of my cafe before I throw you out myself."

Ryley looks at Sandy, then at the ticket.

She grabs it with a sigh that's half frustration and half relief. "You're a pain in the ass, you know that?"

Sandy grins. "Love you too, kid. Beat it."

Ryley hesitates at the door. Sandy waves her off with a dish towel. "Get the hell outta here."

7

The Tigers pack the dark tunnel. An unusual hush blankets the air, smothering the familiar roar of past victories–rare treasures in this program's present. At the line's end, Morgan stands on an island of uncanny stillness. He lifts his mask, a ritual gesture, and locks eyes with each teammate. Their gazes reflect a newfound gravity. Wordless nods ripple through the ranks as they steel themselves for the moment that waits beyond.

The world explodes.

Cymbals crash and horns bellow, shaking the foundations beneath their feet. They burst through the gateway like tearing through the veil between two realms. Their solemn procession transforms into a surge of raw energy as they cross onto the grass.

For a heartbeat, the Tigers halt, struck by the mammoth spectacle before them. The stadium, forever half-empty, now swells with row upon row of frenzied faithful. Their hands pound and cheers call, a deafening roar for the blue and orange robbed of a postseason hope.

Morgan stops at midfield, turning full circle. The thunderous applause crashes over him like a baptism. High in the bleachers, an unexpected silhouette towers among the masses. Wilke's broad frame, out of place yet unmistakable, stands rigid against the evening sky. His presence, a shock amidst the pandemonium, freezes Morgan's breath mid-stride.

The chorus swells, a tide of loyalty voiced at last. Spine electric, Morgan thrusts his fist skyward, then runs to join the unbreakable ring of believers crushing around him.

10

1

In the stillness after the last fan leaves, empty corridors resound with Morgan's solitary steps. He walks the path between the hallowed field and the mundane reality of the school halls one final time. In the vacant corridor, game lights streak through barred windows like lost souls clinging to Friday night's salvation.

Morgan passes open classrooms, their lessons seeming childish after the field's brutal education.

A "FINISH STRONG" banner hangs limp, its purpose served.

At the wall of battered lockers, dizziness overwhelms Morgan. He steadies himself against the cool metal, dropping to his rear.

How can he leave this hard-won haven and face the ghosts waiting in his old town? He closes his eyes, fighting the decision his parents have made for him.

Fading season-end murmurs drift through the hallway, beckoning him to join his brothers behind the locker room door.

But Morgan lingers here as fading light filters through tall windows. Outside, life continues, celebrations beginning without him.

A distant door creaks, followed by slow footsteps.

Coach Tully eases down beside him, joints popping.

"Got yourself lost out here instead of soaking up the victory lap, huh, Browdy?" His gruff voice sounds oddly gentle.

Morgan meets Tully's intense stare without words to share.

"I'll let you have your moment—" Tully promises before his expression softens. "But while we're here, I have something you should have."

Tully pulls out the final game ball. He weighs it in his calloused hands, then extends it to Morgan.

Coach gestures. "That final missile you threw was one of the prettiest connections I've seen in twenty years on that field." His weathered face shows a rare warmth as he relives the moment.

"In fact, last time I saw a play like that, I gave the game ball to the young buck who threw it. All them years ago. Hell, it's probably lying around your grandfather's shed somewhere, I'd figure."

Morgan takes the ball.

"Just like your father out there those years ago, I saw a warrior overcoming ghosts tonight."

It hits Morgan, the treasured football on display at the farmhouse, encased behind glass. It was his dad's.

His eyes drift to the coach.

"Pa said my dad was good," he says. "That true?"

Tully nods. "1982 State Champion. He was better than good, kid."

Their eyes lock in a moment of proper understanding. "So are you. It's in your blood...in your heart."

Rising, the coach starts off down the hall. His footsteps scuff along the empty corridor. He pauses with one hand on the door frame and turns back to the boy.

"You ever wonder why we drill you boys to say 'it's a great day to be alive?' when you're puking your guts out on the field?"

Morgan thinks long and hard.

"It's because even when you're fighting like hell, there's still something beautiful if you look hard enough. Without life, you'd be dead. Better take it for what it is."

2

The locker room lies empty, remnants of the dead season scattered under cage lights. Jerseys spill from upended lockers, cleats and playbooks abandoned by departed players.

Morgan reaches his cubby alone under an incandescent glare. He lowers onto the oak bench, grass stains bright against the wood. He strips his jersey and pads, drops them to cold tile, and then sits drained before his gaping locker.

The metal entrance door scrapes open.

Morgan turns as footsteps approach. Rabbit emerges, clean and beaming in the locker room light.

"Oh, you're still here," Rabbit says, voice softening. "Saying goodbye?"

Morgan nods, words stuck in his throat. Gratitude swells, moved by Rabbit's presence. He grips his friend's shoulder, hoping to convey what he can't say.

Rabbit pats his back."We've been through worse. This ain't the end."

"Thanks for being here for me, man."

Rabbit's eyes glint with mischief. "Where else would I be? Someone's gotta make sure you don't trip over your own feet on the way out." He mimes Morgan, stumbling, arms flailing. "Your clumsy ass needs a spotter even off the field."

Morgan laughs, wiping his eyes.

The locker room door groans open.

Startled, Morgan turns, heart skipping as Ryley slips inside. She hovers at the threshold, eyes searching his face.

Rabbit clears his throat. "I'll, uh...go make sure no one stole my cleats." He retreats, footsteps fading.

A long while stretches between the pair.

Ryley's voice cuts through the brittle moment. "I read the note."

Morgan tenses. "Ry, I–"

"Don't." She holds up a hand. "Just...don't. Not yet."

Morgan swallows hard and nods.

Ryley inhales unsteadily. "You should have told me. That night. Not...not like this."

"I know," Morgan whispers. "I thought–"

"You thought wrong," she snaps, then flinches at her own tone. "I just...I'm angry. And hurt. And I don't know how to feel about any of it."

Morgan's throat is tight. "That's fair. I screwed up."

"Yeah. You did." Ryley's voice softens. "But so did I. I shouldn't have pressured you to go to that fucking party. I knew you didn't want to, but I pushed. Just wanted to forget everything for once." She looks away, guilt flushing across her face. "Maybe if I hadn't..." Her mind races with all the what-ifs of that night at the lake house, spiraling into what-actually-happened.

Finally, Morgan speaks. "Where do we go from here?"

Ryley shrugs, exhaustion evident in the slump of her shoulders.

Morgan reaches for her hand, hesitant. She lets him take it, but her grip is loose.

She meets his gaze, her eyes sorting conflicting emotions. "I came tonight to tell you I got accepted...to college."

Morgan swallows hard.

"But right now I need time. To process. To think." She squeezes his hand once, but then she lets go, her fingers slipping away. "About all of it."

He nods, fighting back tears. "Okay. Whatever you need."

"I know," Ryley whispers.

Losing contact feels like a chasm opening between them.

Her other palm opens, revealing Murph's battered toy car. The sight shatters Morgan's walls, and tears spill.

"It was in the jacket," she says.

As she turns to leave, Morgan calls out, voice cracking. "Ryley?"

She pauses at the door, looking back.

"I'm sorry. For all of it."

Ryley nods, her own eyes glistening. "Me, too."

The door closes behind her, leaving Morgan with what's been said, and all that remains unspoken.

3

In the empty bleachers above the field cloaked in twilight, Wilke and JD sit. Their gazes sweep the vacant expanse, minds replaying the game's moments. The scoreboard glows behind them, its verdict spelled out in red light for all to witness.

Wilke's voice is coarse. "How many times do you have to repeat a name so it doesn't go forgotten?" The question carries the pain of loss–not just of Murph, but of the years between father and son.

JD eyes Wilke from the side, seeing in him both the boy he raised and the man grappling with his own son's future. The cycles of hope and disappointment of fathers and sons play out in an endless loop. He weighs his response, aware that each word could bridge or widen their separation.

"Wilke," JD begins, his voice calm. "I won't preach about loss. Twenty years ago, maybe. But that serves no purpose now." He pauses, remembering the hot-headed young man Wilke once was and the arguments that drove them apart. "We've both lost too much to waste breath on lectures."

Wilke nods, watching distant bleachers where chalk ghosts of past glories linger. Memories of his own triumphs and failures on this very field flood back. "I reckon it won't," he agrees, his tone softer than before.

JD hesitates, then rests a weathered hand on Wilke's back–the first physical contact in years. With the other, he drains the last sip from a styrofoam cup, setting it by his boots. The distance between them, built over years of unspoken regrets, closes ever slightly.

"He's got grit," the old man remarks into the quiet between them, nodding toward the field where Morgan's invisible presence lingers. The words carry more than observation–they hold pride and a hint of redemption.

Wilke allows a brief smile to grace his lips, the first JD has seen in years. Fatherhood's weight, expectations and deferred dreams, press on his shoulders. "Does he have a chance?" he wonders aloud, vulnerability creeping into his voice. "For something more?"

The old scout's eyes track a pennant flapping across the stadium. Each wrinkle on his face tells tales of countless seasons spent under stadium lights, of young men's dreams realized and shattered. Some rising to glory, others fading into obscurity. Countless dreams, both realized and broken, occupy his thoughts. His voice emerges a whisper, laden with wisdom earned through decades of watching talent bloom and wither.

"Talent fades," he says, each word measured and heavy with truth. "But heart? The rest depends on where his heart leads him."

The words are a bridge spanning generations of shared experience and missed opportunities. JD falls silent, knowing he's said all that needs saying.

Wilke looks at the scoreboard where NEW LIBERTY WINS glows; its light is a beacon in the gathering dark. He finally meets his father's eyes after years. "Thank you for what you did, Dad."

4

In the dim living room of the farmhouse, the three Browdy men stand shoulder-to-shoulder before a mirror, dressed in formal funeral wear as daylight filters through grimy windows.

JD's aged fingers fumble with a stubborn wrinkle in his frayed necktie. Nearby, Morgan worries at a frayed cuff seam, the suit jacket inherited from some long forgotten wake hanging off his thin frame.

Wilke steps closer across worn floorboards, reaching out to straighten his son's crooked collar. His eyes grow distant as he smooths the fabric.

"That last morning before it happened, Murph was fidgety and quiet," Wilke says softly. "When I asked what bugged him, he said he was still happy." Wilke's broad hand squeezes Morgan's nape—a protective, pained gesture.

"He told me he had a tickle-feeling...butterflies...I asked him why. Said he was nervous for your big game." He imitates a lighter voice. "'Not tomorrow but the new day. Brother can throw, brother can throw.'"

In the yawning wind, only the old house creaking answers their collective grief.

"You'd hardly played a single snap back then. So I'm not sure if that boy saw the future, but he believed in you."

Murph's absence hangs heavy in the room, mingling with the dust dancing in the weak sunlight. Each man stands lost in his own memories, the shared pain binding them together more tightly than blood.

JD's hands pause on his tie, his eyes misting as he gazes at his son and grandson. The generational lines blur in this moment of shared vulnerability.

Morgan swallows hard, his Adam's apple bobbing beneath the straightened collar. His father's words sink into his chest, a bittersweet ache of love and loss.

5

Wilke knocks twice on the bedroom door. "Just me, Lea," he murmurs, stepping inside. He spots his wife through the curtained window's hazy light, lost in thought. Or perhaps dreading the sight of their little boy's gravestone after so much time.

He crosses to Ailea, zipping her black dress. The familiar act speaks volumes, a touch of normalcy in their shattered world. His hand rests between her shoulders as she leans into him, reunited after a bitter absence. The space between them is thick with unspoken words and beyond the tiny house, life marches on. Yet here, time stands still.

Wilke squeezes Ailea's shoulder, conveying what his voice cannot. She turns, burying her face in his chest. He holds her, his embrace both shield and apology.

In stillness, their heartbeats sync. Something deeper passes between them—forgiveness, maybe. And as they sit there holding each other, they heal just a little.

6

The truck shudders along the rural route, its failing shocks unable to smooth the rutted back road that stretches toward an unwanted destination. Wilke's hand rests on Ailea's knee as she stares through the window. Morgan sits behind them, shoulders pressed against the rear glass, counting the passing branches. He glances back, eyeing JD in his car trailing behind.

A weathered sign looms, stranger to their moods.

WELCOME TO THE TOWN OF BLESSING

Wilke and Ailea face the road, navigating another stretch of pain-filled miles together. A pack of local boys thunders past on dirt bikes, faces bright with laughter. Their tires spray dust across the truck's grille. The vehicle trudges on, oblivious to the joy that vanishes around the bend while sorrow weighs heavy inside.

"Remember that old tree house?" Wilke's voice breaks. "The one Murph begged us to build?"

Ailea's hand tightens in his grip, a silent acknowledgment.

"Spent weeks on that thing. Murph 'helped' mostly by losing nails in the grass." He smiles at the memory. "The day we finished, he was so excited he could hardly sleep."

The truck hits a pothole. No one flinches.

"Next morning, found him curled up there with his stuffed bear. Said he wanted to be closer to the stars."

Morgan shifts in the back, leaning closer.

"I asked if he was scared, sleeping out there alone." Wilke's voice catches. "He just grinned and said, 'I got Special Star watching me.'"

Ailea's breath hitches, a soft sound of pain.

"Funny thing is," Wilke continues, "I think I believed him. Like nothing bad could touch our boy as long as he had that blind faith."

The road stretches endlessly ahead.

"Now I wonder if he knew something we didn't. If he felt closer to...wherever he is now."

The man falls quiet. The memory fills the truck as they drive on toward a reality they are forced to finally face.

Morgan blinks against rising tears, memories of better days eclipsed by loss. He sets his jaw and shifts his gaze to the windshield. The trees of his fractured present blur outside. Beyond the pines and the truck's faded radio song, closure waits under an indifferent sky.

7

Two leaves fall from the oak above the Browdy family as they stand before the small granite headstone embossed with the name they've grieved too long. Dead grass whispers in the chilling breeze around the four figures gathered to bid farewell.

Ailea places the wreath on the mound, fingers tracing the carved letters of her baby's short life. Her touch lingers as if trying to bridge life and death. She steps back into Wilke's arm, eyes shining with unshed tears that refuse to fall. Red rose petals spiral from surrounding trees.

Morgan stands beside JD, watching his parents surrender his brother to eternity under a golden horizon. Behind his mask of stoic grief, his eyes reveal a torrent of emotions when he reads the headstone. A memory resurfaces–a poem he had come across in his English class the previous year. The words seemed distant then, academic shit. Now they echo with painful clarity:

"Nothing gold can stay," he murmurs. The line from Frost's poem takes on new meaning amidst the fading sunlight and wilting flowers. He thinks of Murph's golden curls, his infectious laughter–all of it gone too soon. The brevity of joy, the inevitability of loss–it hits in a wave of understanding that leaves him breathless.

JD removes his bowler and studies Morgan's profile. The set of the boy's jaw reminds him of the same stubborn determination Wilke had in his youth.

"I paced the hospital halls the night you were born, trying to reconcile my spite," JD voices, rough with memory. "But I missed your brother those years later..." Regret colors every word.

Morgan's brows knot. "Why's that?"

"Because what time I had with your father, it was always about the game," JD admits. "When I faced the rush, I threw it away. Kicked your father out when he said he was marrying your mother."

He blows out a misty breath. "I was afraid she'd taken him away. I let that decide everything for me. That's why I retired."

Morgan finally learns the truth.

"Never really knew your brother," JD admits. "That fact haunts me every day."

Morgan's gaze drops. "He was quiet. He loved everyone."

Birdsong frames their hushed eulogy.

"There's a small academy a day's drive west that might suit you," he remarks. "They've got a fair football program I still have ties to. Scholarship could be tough, but walk-ons make rosters if the want exists...figure you finish this school term, then take your chances come summer training," JD suggests. "Maybe stake your claim. Just an idea—"

"Yeah," Morgan interjects, a slight smirk gracing his lips.

WHILE WE'RE HERE

They stand vigil, watching gold shafts of light spear across Murph's resting place. JD ropes an arm around Morgan, rubbing the back of his head. They lean into the bracing wind that carries echoes of laughter once sweet under truer skies.

11

1

Morgan stands in Murph's room, surrounded by boyhood treasures coated in dust. Sunlight casts through the window, moving shadows over relics from happier times.

He hefts a packed bag and moves to the shelf of toy cars arranged in a pattern known only to their absent keeper. Morgan pulls the red Matchbox car from his pocket–the one that once offered hope. He caresses its dented fender before returning it to its place in the shrine.

Footsteps approach.

Morgan turns to find Ailea in the doorway, her smile strained. His hands burrow into his jacket pockets as he meets her gaze, brimming with regret. Time stretches between them, highlighting the void where a family once thrived.

Ailea runs her fingers through her tangled hair and steps inside the room. "I never said things I should have, Morgan," she starts, voice quavering. "When they told us your brother would be different, I worried what people would think. I built walls. And somewhere in that I left you out. For that, I'm sorry."

Morgan listens, accepting.

"I'm going to live with Pa." His words echo in the room, filled with tired light.

Ailea watches her son, eyes heavy.

"It's my choice. I feel I can be more...than I am now."

Through tearful eyes, her gaze holds steady, tinged with understanding. She nods once. "You will be, baby," she whispers, throat tight. Unable to say more, she guides his head into her hands, pressing her lips to his brow. As he folds into her embrace, a glimmer of forgiveness seeps between their wounded souls, binding their hearts a moment longer.

2

Under faded eaves, Wilke loads Morgan's meager belongings into the waiting GTO. The engine idles, poised for new horizons across barren fields ripe with potential. JD leans on his rumbling vehicle, ready to usher his wayward grandson into the next chapter.

Wilke lingers after stowing the last bag. JD offers a gruff farewell. "Come by when you're in town," the old scout says.

Behind Wilke, Ailea stands small but determined on the decrepit stoop, cradling the SALE sign across her lap.

Touched by this truce, Wilke musters a familiar grin, eyes glistening beneath the heavy sky as Morgan exits the home.

Wilke tosses a worn ball to Morgan's waiting hands with fluid grace—a wordless blessing from father to son.

Morgan clutches the treasured sphere, raising his free hand in a silent goodbye to his parents.

The road crunches as JD reverses the GTO away from memory's edge. Wilke and Ailea stand framed in the rearview mirror, their forms dwindling against the backdrop of the fading chapter.

Morgan holds back unbidden tears, settling into worn leather as the engine roars. They speed down the rural road, life's momentum gathering as the land passes in their wake.

3

The crossroads station stands frozen in time beside the remote highway that skirts the town. A Texaco sign with twin bells looms overhead, its red star faded and peeling, revealing the bones of lost glory–a relic of American dreams surrendered to decay.

JD leans on the rusted pump, watching gallon numbers tick upward as fuel gurgles into his car's tank. His gaze drifts to the horizon where night approaches, painting the peaceful dusk in royal hues behind distant mountains. For the first time in countless bitter seasons, his face blends ease and wisdom, the old shadows banished.

On the cracked tarmac bathed in the otherworldly violet glow of day's end, Morgan perches on the chrome bumper. He rubs Flutie's ears as the dog sniffs the crisp evening air. Morgan looks back down the road they traveled toward a past now left behind.

Miles ahead, the humble sign bids farewell to the scarred way-station hamlet, fading from memory into folk myth:

THANK YOU FOR VISITING THE TOWN OF BLESSING

Thank you for reading

WHILE WE'RE HERE

by T.A. Manchester

please leave a review
on the website of
your favorite bookseller

About the Author

T.A. MANCHESTER

T.A. Manchester is an author and filmmaker known for his evocative storytelling. In 2013, he co-founded Atlas Film Studio alongside fellow creatives from The Illinois Institute of Art-Chicago. The following year, their short film *Melancholic* gained national recognition, reaching the Top 200 Finals in HBO's Project Greenlight competition. This early success laid the groundwork for his transition into long-form storytelling.

Manchester wrote and directed his debut feature film, *The Things We've Seen,* in 2016. A gripping, character-driven drama, the film earned critical acclaim on the festival circuit, securing nine awards and four nominations. Notably, it won the Gold Remi Award at the 50th WorldFest-Houston, joining past winners like George Lucas and Steven Spielberg. His screenwriting also received distinction at the Angaelica Film Fstival in Los Angeles, further cementing his reputation as a writer with a unique voice and a keen eye for human complexity.

Beyond film, Manchester's literary work continues to explore themes of fractured relationships, redemption, and the weight of the past. His storytelling is often marked by a melancholic beauty, drawing comparisons to the work of auteurs like Kenneth Lonergan and Jeff Nichols. Whether on the page or the screen, his work resonates with those who appreciate grounded realism and deeply textured character studies.

While We're Here is his first novel.

CHECK OUT OTHER GREAT READS FROM
HENRY GRAY PUBLISHING

THE LAST STAGE by Bruce Scivally

In a small Los Angeles bungalow, with his Jewish wife, Sadie, at his side, terminally ill lawman Wyatt Earp imagines an ending more befitting a man of his reputation: returning to his mining claims in a small desert town, tying up loose ends with Sadie, and – after he strikes gold – confronting a quartet of robbers in a showdown. Meanwhile, Sadie wrestles with letting go of her long-time partner, afraid to lose the one great love that made her own life an enduring adventure.

VEIL OF SEDUCTION by Emily Dinova

1922. Lorelei Alba, a fiercely independent and ambitious woman, is determined to break into the male-dominated world of investigative journalism by doing the unimaginable – infiltrating Morning Falls Asylum, the gothic hospital to which "troublesome" women are dispatched, never to be seen again. Once there, she meets the darkly handsome and enigmatic Doctor Roman Dreugue, who claims to have found the cure for insanity. But Lorelei's instincts tell her something is terribly wrong, even as her curiosity pulls her deeper into Roman's intimate and isolated world of intrigue.

THE UNDERSTUDY by Charlie Peters

"Tell your boss that I have one of his employees." With those words a kidnapping plot begins in the middle of a high-stakes corporate merger. But the kidnappers' plans don't unfold—they unravel.

"If you're thinking of committing the perfect crime, read Charlie Peters' elegant new thriller first. Find out just how many ways perfection can go wrong." – Dan Hearn, author of *Bad August*

THE DEVIL IN THE DIAMOND by Gregory Cioffi

World War II comes to a violent close. As the Battle of Okinawa rages on, American soldiers seize Shuri Castle and find a single survivor: Yuujin Miyano. U.S. Private EugeneDurante is put in charge of watching the prisoner. Although enemies, the two men find they have a common multi-generational bond: baseball. Their grandfathers – one in Japan, one in America – bore witness to the magical birth of the game and helped shape it in the late 1800s. When the war ends, the two men return to their homes to face a postwar world filled with uncertainty, until they are called to face off again, not on a field of battle, but on the baseball diamond.

THE MAN FROM BELIZE by Steven Kobrin

Life-saving heart surgeon Dr. Kent Stirling lives in paradise, dividing his time between two medical practices in the exotic Yucatan. Deeply in love with the woman of his dreams, he has everything a man could desire... until enemies from his secret past as a government hitman convene to eliminate him, including a death-dealing assassin known as the Viper.

SHELBY'S VACATION by Nancy Beverly

Fantasy. Sex. Despair. (Hey, what are vacations for?)

Shelby sets out from L.A. on a much-needed vacation to mend her heart from her latest unrequited crush. By happenstance, she ends up at a rustic mountain resort where she meets the manager, Carol, who has her own memories of the past inhibiting her ability to create a real relationship in the present. Their casual vacation encounter turns into something more profound than either of them bargained for, as each learns what holds them back from living and loving.

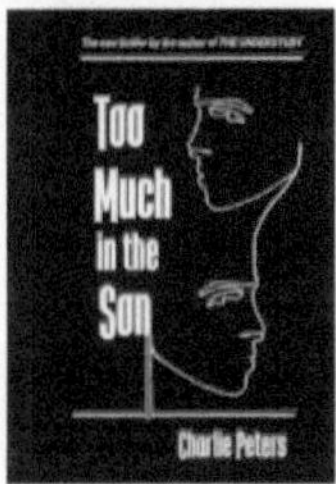

TOO MUCH IN THE SON by Charlie Peters

In Martinique, Leo Malone meets Taylor Hoffman, a young man who could be his identical twin. Whey they run afoul of a local gangster, Taylor is murdered and Leo assumes his identity to sneak safely out of the country and back to Los Angeles. But when Taylor's estranged parents meet Leo at the airport, mistaking him for their son, Leo's best-laid plans spiral out of control. Part Agatha Christie, part Elmore Leonard, with a dash of David Mamet and served with a Larry David chaser, *Too Much in the Son* examines the lies, intrigue and violence that make an unexpected family.

I CONFESS: DIARY OF AN AUSTRALIAN POPE by Melvyn Morrow

"When I became pope, almost the first word the Curia taught me was 'ricatto'—blackmail."   - *Pope John XXIV*

From acclaimed playwright Melvyn Morrow comes this engrossing tale of an Australian cardinal who has, through extraordinary circumstances, become pope. His personal diary reveals the inner workings of the Vatican and—when he begins enacting reforms and fears his tenur may be cut short—the centuries-old system in place to make sure that the status quo is maintained—at any cost.

THE ANTAGONIST by Emily Dinova

Dave Collins has a normal life - a loving wife, an angst-filled teenage stepdaughter, and a comfortable job. But one morning, he comes downstairs to find a yellow sticky-note on his refrigerator with a meticulously-drawn smiley face and the words, "You're special!"

Those two words set off a series of events that cause his entire life to implode, piece by piece, as if some unknown atagonist is purposefully ripping it apart. But who?

And more importantly — why?

A PRAYER FOR THE DAMNED by Joe Cornet

Thirteen years after the American Civil War, the desert town of Sudden, New Mexico, becomes the backdrop for a perilous quest for a lost Confederate fortune. Bounty hunter Cole arrives weary and bullet-riddled after an encounter with an unhinged man of god, the Preacher, who also seeks the fortune. Awaiting him is Mattie, his card-sharp lover, who urges him to abandon his dangerous pursuit. But Cole persists, propelling him into a deadly showdown.

REJECTED - ESSAYS IN BELONGING by Michelle Fiordaliso

In Rejected, acclaimed journalist and screenwriter Michelle Fiordaliso illuminates the kind of quiet heartbreaks and epiphanies that can punctuate a life. As a collection, these essays tell the story of a woman's decades-long journey towards wholeness and belonging. But every piece also charts a journey of its own, and often a geographic one. From Los Angeles traffic to the basement of a famous bakery in Paris, each place is an unforgettable setting for personal transformation.

HIGH - FROM CANNABIS TO CLARITY by Leonard Buschel

Vastly entertaining, brutally honest, and sharply funny, HIGH is the unflinching memoir of Leonard Lee Buschel, co-founder of Writers in Treatment and producer of the internationally acclaimed Reel Recovery Film Festivals. With a voice that is both raw and humorous, Buschel offers an eye-opening, occasionally offensive, yet deeply compelling look at addiction, recovery, and the surprising path of personal transformation that follows.

WHILE WE'RE HERE by T.A. MANCHESTER

Seventeen-year-old Morgan Browdy's world shatters in just eight seconds. After his younger brother loses his life in an accident Morgan feels responsible for, his mother's taillights disappear into the night, his father drowns in bottles of whiskey, and everything he thought was permanent unravels. Left with nowhere to turn, Morgan finds himself on the doorstep of his estranged grandfather's farmhouse—a place filled with echoes of a fractured family past.

Available at your favorite

online bookseller

For more info visit HenryGrayPublishing.com

YOU WON'T BELIEVE WHAT YOU'LL FIND WITH

PAPA ROCK'S HORROR MOVIES WORD SEARCH
by Rock Scivally and Jeffrey Breslauer

Enter, if you dare, to solve these unique puzzles for anyone who loves classic horror films from the first Frankenstein film in 1910 to the giant bug movies of the 1950s. Remember *Frankenstein? Dracula?* How about *King Kong? Godzilla? The Amazing Colossal Man? The Incredible Shrinking Man?* You can literally find them all here with 150 puzzles, each one pertaining to a specific film, where you can search for characters, actors, locations, props, and memorable lines of dialogue.

PAPA ROCK'S SON OF HORROR MOVIES WORD SEARCH
by Rock Scivally and Jeffrey Breslauer

The 1960s. The 1970s. Two decades that encapsulated a shift in screen horror. There were still films featuring Dracula, Frankenstein, werewolves, giant insects, and Godzilla, but they were now joined by Blacula, Dr. Phibes, Regan, Damien, Carrie, a killer baby, and a rat named Ben. Director Alfred Hitchcock even made us afraid to take showers—and scared of birds. All your favorite horror film favorites from 1960 to 1979 are within these pages. Grab your pen or pencil and… happy haunting…er, hunting!

PAPA ROCK'S ROMANCE MOVIES WORD SEARCH
by Rock Scivally and Jeffrey Breslauer

We'll always have word search…Between these covers, you'll find Word Search puzzles covering 150 classic Romance movies made between 1921 and 1999, from the tragedy of *Camille* to the comedy of *Notting Hill*, with stops in-between for *Gone With the Wind, Casablanca, Roman Holiday, Breakfast at Tiffany's, Love Story, The Way We Were, Somewhere in Time, An Officer and a Gentleman, When Harry Met Sally, Sleepless in Seattle, Jerry Maguire,* and *Titanic,* among many, many others.

PAPA ROCK'S WESTERN MOVIES WORD SEARCH
by Rock Scivally and Jeffrey Breslauer

Since the beginning of cinema, there have been serious Westerns, comedy Westerns, epic Westerns, and art-house Westerns. And you'll find examples of all of them in this book, so get ready to find all your favorite Western heroes — John Wayne, Gary Cooper, Randolph Scott — and classic Western movies from the 1920s to the 1990s, including *The Searchers, The Westerner, Stagecoach, My Darling Clementine, Gunfight at the O.K. Corral, Rio Bravo, The Good, the Bad, and the Ugly, Dances With Wolves, Unforgiven,* and many more.

PAPA ROCK'S WORD SEARCH *BOOKS!*

PAPA ROCK'S ANIMATED MUSICALS WORD SEARCH
by Rock Scivally and Jeffrey Breslauer

Animated movie musicals have been popular since the premiere of *Snow White and the Seven* Dwarfs in 1937. Since then, movie screens have seen musicals featuring animated animals and fantasy creatures, taking place in our own world and on imaginary words. Here you'll find 150 Word Search games with all your favorites, from Mickey Mouse to Charlie Brown to Strawberry Shortcake. Each puzzle relates to a specific film, where you can search for charaters, actors, song titles, and dialogue phrases.

PAPA ROCK'S REVENGE OF HORROR MOVIES WORD SEARCH
by Rock Scivally and Jeffrey Breslauer

All work and no wordplay makes Papa Rock a dull boy... But there's nothing dull about this collection of Word Searches, each one featuring clues from a different horror film of the 1980s and 90s. Here are all your favorites—*The Shining, Friday the 13th, A Nightmare on Elm Street, The Fog, The Evil Dead, The Howling, Night of the Demons, Scanners, Creepshow*, and many more. So grab your pen and work these puzzles until your head explodes!

PAPA ROCK'S WAR MOVIES WORD SEARCH
by Rock Scivally and Jeffrey Breslauer

Enjoy war movies? If so, then you'll enjoy this book of Word Searches where each one focuses on a particular. war film, from silents such as *The Big Parade* and *Wings* to classics like *All Quiet on the Western Front, Sergeant York, Sands of Iwo Jima, The Bridge on the River Kwai, The Great Escape, M*A*S*H, Patton, Apocalypse Now, Platoon, Saving Private Ryan*, and more!

PAPA ROCK'S SCI-FI MOVIES WORD SEARCH
by Rock Scivally and Jeffrey Breslauer

BALDLY GO WHERE NO WORD SEARCH HAS GONE BEFORE... Go back to the future with this book of Word Searches where each pages focuses on a classic science-fiction movie, from 1902's *A Trip to the Moon* to *The Day the Earth Stood Still, Invasion of the Body Snatchers*, the *Planet of the Apes* series, *2001: A Spacy Odyssey, Alien, Back to the Future*, the *Star Trek* and *Star Wars* movies, and more. Set your phasers on fun and beam aboard for hours of Word Search enjoyment!